Summer Nights and Meteorites

HANNAH REYNOLDS

G. P. PUTNAM'S SONS

G. P. PUTNAM'S SONS
An imprint of Penguin Random House LLC, New York

First published in the United States of America by G. P. Putnam's Sons,
an imprint of Penguin Random House LLC, 2024

Visit us online at PenguinRandomHouse.com.

Library of Congress Cataloging-in-Publication Data is available.

ISBN 9780593617328

1st Printing

Printed in the United States of America

LSCH

Design by Rebecca Aidlin
Text set in Maxime Pro

*To everyone who's ever had to fight
for the credit they deserve*

One

My therapist told me recently that instead of making lists about things I hated (Ethan Barbanel, Benjamin Franklin, death, entropy), I should make lists about things I loved, or even liked, or, at the very least, could appreciate in the moment.

And so: I liked the seventy-five-degree June day. I appreciated the cup of Dunkin' in my hand. I liked all the fishing boats filling the port of Hyannis.

Dad loves boats. He took me to harbor after harbor every time we visited the Cape, explaining the difference between sloops and bowriders, daydreaming out loud about the kind we'd get if we were the kind of people who could afford boats, as opposed to a widowed historian and his seventeen-year-old daughter. And while I liked looking at the small craft, I couldn't really picture myself sailing down the Charles River. Maybe because most of those people dressed a little differently from my normal all-black outfits and combat boots.

However, people underestimated the greatness of combat boots, which went on my list of things I appreciated (specifically, their arch support). I'd taken the CapeFlyer from Boston to Hyannis, and good shoes were crucial as I hauled my two suitcases from the train station to the harbor. I maneuvered my load down the sidewalk edging Hyannis's port, passing men loading giant cages onto a weathered fishing vessel next to elegant catamarans.

When I neared shouting distance of the ferry building, I dropped into one of the many Adirondack chairs lining the green. Forty minutes until my ferry left, and it hadn't arrived yet, either, though people already waited by the dock. I closed my eyes and leaned my head back, trying to let the sunshine and lapping water soothe me. How bad could this summer be? Most people would be thrilled to spend three months on Nantucket.

When I opened my eyes a few minutes later, a boy sat in the chair closest to me, eating pizza out of a box. Broad shoulders, aquiline nose, and an easy confidence in the way he took up space. Too good-looking and exactly my type. I'd dated guys with his same rangy frame and smiling eyes before, and they'd been all flirtation and flattery right up until they dumped me.

Two women walked by dressed in capris and light blouses. They paused in front of the boy. One, wearing a wide-brimmed straw hat and bedazzled sandals, made an exaggerated expression of awe.

"Is that a *salad* on your pizza?"

I glanced at the pizza. There did, in fact, appear to be a pile of arugula on top.

The boy in the chair, too, contemplated the pizza and the green leaves. "Sure seems to be."

The women both laughed. "What is that, arugula?"

"Yup."

"I love arugula on pizza," the second woman said. "Makes me feel so healthy. Where did you get it?"

I tuned out the rest because, honestly, how much could one listen to a conversation about arugula on pizza, attractive boy notwithstanding?

Yet not five minutes after the women walked on—seriously, the chair boy had probably only eaten two bites—*another* woman paused before him.

"Isn't that a good-looking pizza!"

I stared at her, astonished. I knew Hyannis was an hour and a half outside the city—a small seaside town on Cape Cod—but did people seriously talk to strangers here? About *pizza*? Not that pizza wasn't a worthy topic of conversation, but you couldn't *pay* me to talk to a stranger.

Well. Okay. I'd talk to a stranger who looked like Chair Boy.

Still, did all these women seriously consider this boy hot enough to strike up a conversation? Chair Boy was around my age. If not jailbait, close to it.

Maybe people were being friendly and I was ridiculously stand-offish.

Beyond Chair Boy, a large, multistory ferry cruised into place. My ferry. Probably my neighbor's ferry, too. I snuck another glance at him, our eyes briefly meeting before I tore mine away and focused on my phone. God, he really was my type, with an extra hint of confidence and arrogance in the way he lounged. Come to think of it, I usually *would* strike up a conversation with someone who looked like him. But I wasn't going to, not today, not anymore. It'd occurred to me recently, given the stream of guys I'd hooked up with who made me feel like shit afterward, that I was the common factor. *I* selected boys who never wanted anything to do with me long-term. My selection criteria needed to be severely recalibrated.

So I wasn't going to engage with the kind of boys I usually engaged with anymore. I wasn't going to date or hook up with anyone this summer. I *wasn't*.

I glanced over again and found him glancing at me.

And my mouth parted, and I started to say, *You're basically a walking advertisement for that pizza place, aren't you?* Only the grace of yet *another* person pausing to greet Chair Boy saved me from myself, this time an older man who apparently actually knew the guy. Not one to look a gift horse in the mouth, I headed for the ferry, checked my luggage, and got in line for the *Grey Lady IV.*

My shoulders slowly climbed toward my ears as I took in the passengers around me. I'd known the summering-on-Nantucket aesthetic would be different from mine, but I hadn't expected to feel quite so out of place. Everyone seemed to have received the same memo about their outfits: faded blues and salmon pink, men in Sperrys, and more women with blond hair than allotted by nature. No one else wore mostly black. Which, fine. Most people at school didn't, either. But I'd never felt uncomfortable dressed in black lace or fishnet tights before; I'd felt stylish. Interesting. Edgy.

It felt different wearing my clothes in a sea of beige and pearls.

I'd picked my outfit carefully this morning because I was dressing for Ethan Barbanel, who I hated, who I'd never met.

I'd wanted armor, so I chose an outfit my friends said made me look both hot and badass, and which made me feel untouchable. A black top to highlight my red-and-black tartan skirt (Alice + Olivia, thrifted for twenty dollars at the Garment District). My trusty combat boots, dangly black earrings, and cat-eye eyeliner.

A bored crew member scanned my ticket's QR code and I boarded the ship, winding my way up several staircases until I reached the top outdoor deck. Somehow I'd chosen the slowest line, but plenty of seats were still open. Including one by the rail, where Chair Boy sat, having miraculously arrived before me.

Don't do it, I told myself. *Nope. Don't. You're done with hot, bro-y boys. They're bad news bears.*

I did it. I took the seat on the other side of the aisle from him, also facing the water. But I didn't look at him as the ship pulled out from the dock, Hyannis's harbor falling away behind us. At least I had that much control.

An announcement came on about rules and regulations. To my right, women in tank tops with Greek letters poured White Claws into thermoses; boys in ACK baseball caps ate slimy-looking ham sandwiches. I noticed my shoulders had drawn up again, high and tight, and forcibly relaxed them. I wasn't being shipped off to Forks or anything, forced to handle pewter skies and brooding vampires. Plenty of people would give an arm and a leg to visit Nantucket.

Across the aisle, Chair Boy laughed.

A loud laugh. A *look at me* laugh.

I steadfastly did not look at him. I might have chosen my seat precisely to put myself in this position, but surely I had *some* willpower left? Surely I could keep myself from sliding down a slippery slope proven, time and again, to leave me feeling bad about myself.

He laughed once more.

I couldn't help it. I couldn't. I glanced over inquisitively. Our gazes collided.

He broke into a wide, contagious grin and nodded at a family standing by the rail. "They're all wearing the same socks. Even the dog."

Sure enough, the family of five wore navy socks with white anchors. Even the mini Bernedoodle.

"Isn't the whole point of dogs not to need footwear?"

"I'm not sure the *whole* point of dogs is not to need footwear," he mused. "There's gotta be something about hunting in there."

"And being our best friend."

"They do a great job there." He tilted his head. "You got a dog?"

This could be so *easy*. He wanted to talk, and I could talk an ear off an elephant.

I'd told myself this summer would be different. This summer, I wasn't getting involved with anyone. Maybe in the fall, when I started college, I could start a relationship with someone kind and smart and genuinely interested. But right now, I was going to prove I was absolutely emotionally stable, and the easiest way to do so was to avoid romantic entanglements altogether, and to focus on helping my dad.

But.

Screw it.

SUMMER NIGHTS AND METEORITES

I wasn't actually *on* Nantucket yet. The summer hadn't really begun. I still had this one short, high-speed ferry ride.

And just like that, my entire posture changed as I relaxed and smiled. "I wish. No dog, just dreams of dogs. You?"

"Two brothers, which is almost the same thing."

I laughed. "Do they shed?"

"Come to think of it, yeah. One—David—has green hair right now, so you always know when it's his fault." He nodded at me. "He'd like your outfit."

There was no judgment in his tone, no slight sneer at his brother and me, and it made me like him more, knowing he appreciated his green-haired brother with good fashion sense. "Oh?" I mirrored him, tilting my head as well. "Do *you* like it?"

His grin widened. "Definitely." He swept a hand down, indicating his own body. "What do you think of this?"

I tried to contain an appreciative smirk and instead pasted a considering look on my face. I pulled my eyes over him, lingering on his boat shoes, his salmon-pink shorts, his white cable sweater. Everything was the highest quality, but deeply worn, as though he couldn't be bothered to replace them. He had tanned skin, though the summer had barely started, like he'd spent two weeks lying on a Mediterranean shore. "I'm very impressed by all the fashion risks you've taken. Very avant-garde."

He nodded, faux-serious. "I know. Nantucket red on Nantucket? It might be too radical. I might be thrown overboard before we reach the island."

"I could tear off a little black tulle from my skirt and we could tie it around your neck. Help you fit in a little more."

"Thank god." He grinned at me. "Is this your first time on the island?"

"Yeah. What about you?" I didn't leave time for him to answer. "Let me guess—you're summer people."

"What gave me away?" he asked. "Was it the tattoo on my forehead that says *summer people*?"

I laughed. "Yes. You should probably get a hat so you can cover it up."

He patted his dark hair delicately. "It would crush my curls."

"Vain."

"I prefer to think 'reasonably aware of my positive attributes.'"

"And is the top one curls?"

"Definitely. Followed by height."

I laughed again. "It's important to know what matters."

"It's fake, actually." He pointed at his tanned, muscled calves. "These are platform boots designed to *look* like legs and feet."

"Nice." I pointed at my own boots. "I'm wearing the same thing. I'm actually a faun."

He looked startled for a moment, and I wondered if I'd been too weird for him, but then he burst into laughter. "Mr. Tumnus in the flesh. So this is what you do outside of Narnia."

"*Ms.* Tumnus to you."

He draped his arm over the back of his chair. The sun made the dark hair on his skin glow. "So, Ms. Tumnus. What brings you to Nantucket?"

"I like to ride the ferry back and forth. I never actually set foot on Nantucket. Or Hyannis. I live on the ferry."

He nodded. "I see. You're a ghost. You died on the ferry a hundred years ago and you've never left."

I *tsk*ed. "Usually it takes humans longer to figure me out. What am I doing wrong?"

"It's because you're slightly transparent. And floating a few inches off the deck."

"Ugh, and here I'd thought I had the floating under control."

The boat picked up speed, the sudden wind fluttering hats and sunglasses. The crowd of people clustered at the rail staggered inside, clutching drinks in one hand and using their others to hold seat tops as they walked. The roar of the high-speed ferry crashing through the water made it too loud to have a conversation across the aisle, but I tried. "So what's the island like?"

"What?" he yelled back.

"What's the island's deal? Anything I should know?"

"You mean, whether or not there's a Hot Topic?"

I stuck my tongue out. "What's there to do?"

"Looking for a tour guide?"

"You should be so lucky."

His smile grew. "I should." He gestured at his ear. "It's kind of loud. You mind if—" He nodded at the seat next to me.

I bit the inside of my cheek to keep from grinning too broadly. "Yeah, sure."

He grabbed his backpack and crossed the aisle. I scooted over so he could sit, and when he did, his thigh brushed mine. A familiar, intoxicating rush of anticipation filled me. For a moment, we watched the ship's spray rushing behind the boat in two long, endlessly colliding torrents. They clashed in the middle, arching and sinking into the water like a sandworm burrowing downward forever. Above, an honest-to-god rainbow formed in the spray's wake, a shimmer of red and yellow and green dancing above the white foam.

The warmth of the boy beside me was more than welcome given the wind off the sea. He was big and solid, and my heartbeat started pounding, a drum inside my chest. An electric shock of desire surged through me as he angled himself in my direction.

"What do you like to do?" he asked.

I let one shoulder rise and fall, my best Gallic shrug. "I'm really good at long walks on the beach."

"Well, have I got some good news for you . . ."

I grinned at him. He grinned at me. This was the kind of perfect, delightful flirtation I loved: the kind where you could tell you were both into each other, and you knew it would go somewhere, and the only question was how and when.

"Hey," he said. "I wanna show you something."

Ah. Now, and with a cliché. "Seriously? Does that line work for you?"

"It's not a line," he said, mock-offended. "I really *do* want to show you something."

I raised my brows to show him what I thought of that. But since I did, in fact, want to be shown, I simply said, "Okay."

"Come on." He stood with an easy grin on his face, and I returned it, my smile so wide it felt like it would break my face, like it shoved my cheeks open and crinkled up my eyes and made my teeth hurt like a sugar rush.

God, I *liked* him. He was fun and goofy and hot and I *loved* liking someone.

At first, a tiny little part of me reminded the rest. *And then they break your heart and then you're sad.*

Moot point. Nothing would happen with this guy beyond the ferry.

"Where are we going?" I asked as he pulled me down a back staircase I hadn't been aware of, open to the air but currently unused—a sterile place of metal and unexpected privacy.

"Right here." He paused on the stairs, near the bottom. He turned so he stood on the same stair as me, my back to the wall, his body right in front of me.

"Oh?" I couldn't get the grin off my face. "And what did you want to show me?"

"This," he said, and I laughed because it was *such* a line and he grinned and was kissing me.

God was he kissing me.

Normally, I wasn't into first kisses. I wasn't into tender antici-pation, into *does-he-like-me, does-he-want-to?* All the self-doubt and stomach flutters and quivering nerves: no thank you. First kisses were usually mediocre and filled with irritating, nervous uncertainty—I would rather squash all of those and move on. *Second* kisses, and third: that's where the going got good, where you didn't have to feel obnoxious feelings but could concentrate on the good stuff.

This skipped straight to the good stuff.

I twined my arms around his neck and pulled him close. Heat ran beneath my skin, a dizzy, heady fog obscuring the rest of the world so I focused on immediate sensation. His hands ran over my back and slid up my neck, and his fingers dug into the base of my skull, tugging on my hair with just enough pressure to be interesting.

Someone clattered, pointedly loud, down the stairs.

I let out an embarrassed giggle and hid my face in his shoulder, delighted to be caught, delighted to have someone to hide my face in. "I can't believe we're making out in a stairwell."

"I can." He grinned at me. "I mean, I can't believe my luck in catching your attention, but having done that all I want is *more* making out in the stairwell."

"I think we can arrange that." I pulled his face back to mine.

The next thing I knew, people were coming into the stairwell, lining up to exit the ferry, and we broke apart. I swallowed unsteady giggles. Chair Boy kept his hand on the small of my back as we joined the disembarking passengers. I hadn't even watched the island approach, which I'd meant to. Instead, my first glimpse of Nantucket came from the top of the ramp connected to the ferry's doors—a sea of busy streets bounded by shops and restaurants.

The boy stayed beside me as we shuffled down the ramp. "Want to trade numbers?"

Did I want to trade numbers?

Of course I did. Of course I wanted a steady supply of a hot, funny guy to make out with all summer.

Except I wasn't going to hook up with anyone this summer. And even if I had been, this boy was wrong for me.

When I was ready to date again, I wanted a different kind of boy. A soft boy, a cinnamon bun of a boy, warm and pliant and loving. A Peeta to smother me in cakes and to hold me when I fell apart. A boy who didn't *make* me fall apart. I didn't need a boy who I thought about for days and days as he never texted me back, who made me act like somebody I wasn't just to hold his attention.

"I'm sort of in a weird place right now," I told Chair Boy, honestly as I could. "So while this was *super* fun—"

"I get it." He stepped back, tone cooling. We'd reached the bottom of the ramp, and we moved aside as other passengers flowed off the ferry. "Just thought I'd ask."

"Sorry."

"Don't be sorry. I had a good time." He tossed me a smile— only a tad hurt pride, mostly genuine. "Have fun on Nantucket."

And he turned his back and walked away.

I almost yelled *Come back!*

Instead I stared after him for a long while. Maybe he would have been perfect. Maybe I'd messed up.

But then, I was good at that.

Two

Alone, I took in my first real view of Nantucket.

I laughed in surprise. I couldn't help myself; the wharf with its shops and crowds took me aback. I'd expected the weathered charm of the Cape, but instead everything looked new and well-kept. A red-brick pedestrian street led away from the dock, lined with wooden signs pointing toward galleries and shops.

"Hi, honey."

I turned, and there was Dad.

Emotion surged over me, so strong and powerful I almost cracked. Love and relief and resentment and happiness and anger and a deep desire to throw myself into his arms and say *Hi, Daddy* and cry.

Instead I lifted my chin. "Hey, Dad."

My father, Mr. Anthony Edelman, was a quiet, almost bashful man, the kind who thought long and hard before saying anything, then said it carefully (and then never stopped talking, if he discovered he had a willing audience). He was the smartest person I knew, and his moral compass always pointed true north.

I worried about him all the time.

"Where's your luggage?" he said, alarmed, as though I'd perhaps forgotten to pack.

"They should be bringing them out—there." We headed to the luggage racks a ferry employee pushed out. My beat-up, twenty-year-old suitcases stood out sharply in the middle of rows of designer brands. We dragged them over to a car Dad had parked in the Stop and Shop lot.

"It's like winning the lottery, getting a spot here," he said proudly, easing my bags into the trunk.

"You need more exciting lotteries. Where did the car come from?" Bringing a car onto the island cost a ridiculous amount of money, so I knew Dad got around by bike and bus.

"I borrowed it from the Barbanels for the day."

Of course he had.

I drank in the town as we drove. The buildings were taller and closer together than I'd expected. I'd imagined they'd all be rose-covered cottages with window boxes, like in the pics Dad had sent during his past three summers here. The town was large, too, multiple blocks packed with shops and restaurants. We drove down cobblestone roads, past trees incandescently green in the June sun.

When we left downtown behind, the gray-shingled cottages I'd expected flourished. Roses climbed up trellises and over doorways. I saw whale decals on walls, and pineapples, and old-timey lanterns on porches. Pink and blue hydrangea bushes grew everywhere, alongside rose hips, their bright red fruits gleaming under the sun.

"It's pretty here."

"Isn't it?" Dad sounded grateful to have a conversational gambit to latch onto. "Wait until you see Surfside. And the bluff walk out in 'Sconset, we'll have to do that."

"Cool."

"How did your trip go?" he asked, a cautious note in his voice. "The ferry was okay?"

I shrugged, pushing aside thoughts of Chair Boy. "It was fine."

"And how are Aunt Lou and Uncle Jerry?"

"They're good."

"Excited about their trip?"

"I guess."

He cleared his throat, his nervous tic. "I'm sorry I had to come over earlier than you."

"It's fine. I wanted to stay anyway, for all the graduation parties." Dad had stayed home through my high school graduation on June eighth before peacing out for Nantucket. I'd stayed for another week at my best friend Grace's house so I could attend my friends' parties.

When had it become so hard to talk to him? We used to talk about *everything*. We'd never stopped talking.

But that had been before he started preferring Nantucket to me.

I knew I wasn't being fair. Dad loved me, and we FaceTimed and texted when he was gone during the summers. But it wasn't the same. Sometimes, to be perfectly honest, it felt like he'd given up. Like he'd been presented with a choice, job or daughter, and he'd decided . . . *Eh, job.*

And I kind of got it. Teens were a lot of work. And, as my

aunt liked to tell me, every year I looked more and more like my mother. Maybe Dad didn't want the reminder. Maybe it hurt to look at me. If so—couldn't blame him for trying to find something else to look at.

But I would blame Ethan Barbanel for being the something else.

The first time I'd heard of Ethan had been my father's first summer here. I'd been fourteen years old and desperately missing my dad.

Have you heard of Mitski? Dad had texted one day. She is a singer with a folky/rock type of music I think you would enjoy.

I'd blinked at this text several times before responding. Yes Dad I've heard of Mitski. How did YOU hear of her??

I have a new research assistant, Dad had said. He played one of her songs for me.

A new research assistant with good taste in music? I'd been warily prepared for this to be a good thing—Dad could certainly use someone to organize his notes—but the more I learned about Ethan Barbanel, the less he seemed like a research assistant and more like my father's replacement child. In the last three years, my father's preference of Ethan over me had become more and more clear, as proven by the amount Ethan showed up in texts. A few excerpts:

I know you're not sure about which summer
reading book to choose—I showed Ethan the list
from your teacher and he recommends Wise Blood
or Native Son

Here is a link for an app Ethan says is great for managing time

Wasn't able to get many good pictures from the Arborids meteor shower, but here's one Ethan took

Every time Ethan Barbanel's name came up, hot jealousy flared in me, painful and tight, making heat prick behind my eyes. Sometimes I wondered where Ethan had even come from. I mean, I knew, technically. He belonged to a wealthy family on Nantucket, and he'd been introduced to Dad through a friend of his family's. But for so long, it had just been me and Dad. Two peas in a pod, living our best life, going to local maker festivals and the library and watching Star Trek marathons.

And then four summers ago, Dad had gone to Nantucket to research his book on maritime cartography and arranged for me to stay with Aunt Lou. Which had been fun, at first. Aunt Lou and Uncle Jerry were great, and their house in Medford—filled with three older cousins and located on a Boston subway line— allotted me far more freedom than my home thirty minutes deeper into the suburbs. But I'd rather have Dad.

This summer, Aunt Lou and Uncle Jerry were visiting my cousin Lauren, who was spending the year on an organic farm in Costa Rica. Since I'd be eighteen in September, I'd argued I should be allowed to stay home alone, but my case fell on un- interested ears. So now, my final summer before college, I'd been shunted off to Nantucket. Now I had Dad, but in a place that belonged to him and Ethan Barbanel, not to Dad and me.

I'd just have to reclaim my place in Dad's life, even if it was hard. Hopefully, this summer *I* could be Dad's assistant. I could help him with his research, spend time with him, and show him both that he didn't need Ethan *and* that I was totally competent and not messy at all.

As we drove up the road, the homes and grounds became more expansive and set further back from the road. Beyond them, the sea wrapped around us in an endless line, more ocean than I was used to seeing. At this hour, the line between sea and sky was distinct; the water was a deep rippling navy, the sky a yellowish parchment along the horizon before transitioning into translucent blue. A few long flat clouds lay low.

I'd refused to google the Barbanels or their house, Golden Doors, for the past few years. First out of resentment, and then sheer perversity; Dad might go into raptures about Ethan Barbanel, but I refused to give him a single extra neuron in my brain. Still, I thought I'd be prepared for Ethan Barbanel's house. I knew his family had money; his house had a name, for goodness' sake. And who but a family with a big house would be willing to take in a historian's daughter when she was foisted on him for the summer?

But I had not been prepared for this.

My jaw dropped as we pulled up to a giant mansion, with wings and a cul-de-sac lined with crushed shells and about one million windows. This was a bad idea. This was a horrible, stomach-eating, soul-shriveling idea. "I mean it, Dad," I said, a continuation of an argument we'd been having since it'd been decided I would come to Nantucket for the summer. "I can sleep on your floor."

"You'll be fine," Dad said calmly, parking to the side of the house next to several other exceedingly shiny cars. "You'll like it here."

Ha. I climbed out of the car, craning my head to take in the dormer windows and widow's walk encircling the third story. "You didn't tell me Ethan's family was *rich* rich."

Dad sounded wry. "They are the Barbanels."

"Huh?"

"Of Barbanel accounting?" Now he looked confused. "You *have* heard of Barbanel?"

Only as Ethan's last name. "Dad, why would I know anything about accounting?"

"Fair point." He pulled my bags out of the trunk. "In any case, yes, they're well-off."

No kidding. People who owned a house like this probably stuffed their mattresses with shredded Birkin bags and bathed in Jo Malone. I tugged on my skirt self-consciously, suddenly wishing I'd worn an outfit a little less attention-grabbing.

We stepped up to the door, and I noticed the mezuzah angled on the frame. It was a discreet wooden thing, not like the shiny silver one with a glittering blue letter *shin* hanging on my own family's entranceway. Dad had mentioned in passing that the Barbanels were Jewish, and I wondered now if this would stress me out or make me feel at ease: if they'd feel like family, or if I'd feel like I was failing them. Dad and I weren't very observant. We might have been, in another life, but then Mom had died.

Dad rang the doorbell.

I tightened my grip on my bags as the chime echoed through the house, shame and embarrassment washing over me. I felt like an unwanted toy, getting stashed out of sight. Wouldn't this family think it bizarre, me being tucked away with them? Their wealth made me feel even worse, like a poor relation being pawned off. My own father didn't want me.

I tried to bat the thought away. Of course Dad wanted me, he just didn't have room for me at his place. I was being melodramatic.

A woman opened the door, around Dad's age, dressed in a faded sweatshirt and jeans. Her face brightened. "Tony! We were just talking about you. Come in." She smiled at me as we stepped over the threshold. "You must be Jordan."

If I must, I almost muttered, but restrained myself and gave her a tight smile. "Hi."

Dad cleared his throat. "Stephanie, this is my daughter, Jordan. Jordan, this is Stephanie Barbanel. Ethan's mother."

Of course. "Thanks for letting me stay, Mrs. Barbanel."

"Just Stephanie," she said quickly. "There's too many of us for anyone to go by the family name. Let me get my husband, he'll want to say hi." She walked down a hall, and a moment later I heard a barely stifled "Danny, they're here!"

Dad and I waited silently in the foyer. I examined a painting of the sea, and a vase filled with roses, and the endless space dedicated solely to greeting visitors and taking off shoes. Down the hall, a giant mirror hung on the wall in a gilded frame. I'd wanted a similar one, but when I'd looked up prices, I'd choked down my desire and bought a twenty-buck Target mirror instead.

Stephanie returned with a man about her age (Danny, I presumed) and an elderly woman. "This is my husband, Dan, and my mother, Helen Barbanel," she told me, as Dan heartily greeted my dad like they were about to go fly fishing or whatever middle-aged men did to bond.

Helen Barbanel looked at me like she was calculating my worth and finding me lacking. "Do you always dress like that?"

I plucked at my tartan skirt and raised my chin defiantly. "Like what?"

"Like a Madame Alexander doll drenched in black."

Okay. Unexpected burn from the old lady. "Pretty much."

"Hm."

To my left, I could hear Dad saying, sotto voce, "Thank you *so* much for letting her stay, you have no idea how much I appreciate it." Which made my stomach sink even further. Great. Verbal evidence of how much of a burden I was.

A girl, a few years younger than me and a few decades more innocent, came down the stairs. She had dreamy eyes and wore her long, curly hair pulled back. Her headband matched her purple gingham dress.

Ethan's mom gestured her forward. "Miriam, show Jordan her room, please."

"Just Miri," she told me with a shy smile. "This way."

"Once you put your things away, I'll show you the town," Dad called after me.

Miri helped me lug my suitcases upstairs to an impeccably decorated room—*Cape chic*, Aunt Lou would call it. Airy, lots of white and blues and pale wood. A cotton rug on the hardwood floor; a low ceiling above the twin bed and slanted ceilings to the side, with windows looking out across the front lawn. Several miniature seaside landscapes hung on the white wall, and the packed bookcase had a model ship on top.

"Come on, I'll show you the bathroom," Miri said, and I followed her down the hall. "You'll share this with me, Shira, Noah, Ethan, and David. We're the oldest group of cousins. Well, and Oliver's my age, but he's in another hall."

Ethan. Of course. "How many cousins are here?"

"Right now, practically all of us—we're a dozen—but it's kind of sporadic throughout the summer."

A dozen cousins, their parents, and the occasional random guest. "How many *bathrooms* are there?"

She laughed. "Ten. Wild, right?"

Wild indeed.

Back downstairs, Dad made small talk with Ethan's parents. Or maybe not small talk: they might be new to me, but he'd known them for years at this point. Still, Dad's smile looked strained, so I expected he'd be happy to get out of here ASAP.

Dad had always been shy. I'd always thought he should date, but he never had. "I'm too busy," he'd said once, when I'd asked him why he never went out. "Maybe someday."

Fine, but someday wouldn't arrive if he never put himself out there. Dating at Dad's age wasn't like it'd been in his youth: he wasn't going to have a meet-cute in the grocery store and he didn't hang out at bars. I'd tried to hint about dating apps, but his brow had done this thing where it drew up in a triangle in the very center, lines of worry radiating outward. *I don't need to date!* he'd said, and when I'd argued he needed company, he'd countered, *I have you.*

Which, yes, he did for now. But I was going to college in a few months, and then what would he do?

"There you are." Dad looked relieved as I walked over. "Ready for the grand tour of Nantucket?"

I was ready not to be in Golden Doors, wary of running into Ethan Barbanel at any second. "Sure."

We parked on the outskirts of town before Dad led me on a very enthusiastic walking tour. Nantucket exceeded my expectations: relentlessly quaint, with flowers bursting into bloom on every corner. I loved not just the endless roses and hydrangeas, but also the window boxes with flowers I couldn't begin to name— bursts of yellows and elegant whites and madcap, multicolor arrangements set against vibrant greenery.

Dad pointed out the library—called the Atheneum—and the Whaling Museum, and the restaurants he thought I'd like. On picturesque streets, he obligingly took pictures of me whenever I asked. Which wasn't often, because I'd forgotten how bad Dad was at taking photos. "You have to take ten in a row," I said, examining the single photo he'd taken of me pretending to sniff a flower. "My eyes are half closed here."

"I like it," he protested. "You're laughing!"

Dad showed me a street lined with old-school mansions, pointing to a house painted white with tall, fluted columns. "This belonged to a whaling captain. It was built in 1846." He gestured to three brick buildings across the street. "Those belong to his brothers-in-law. See how the captain's house is much higher? On purpose! The captain wanted to *literally* be on higher ground than them!"

Thank god for people like Dad who appreciated history.

By six we'd worked up an appetite, and Dad led me to a restaurant's patio. "They have great burgers here," he said as we sat. "And the fries are really good."

I picked up the menu, fiddled with it briefly, then put it down. "Dad, staying at the Barbanels' house is going to be so uncomfortable."

He sighed. "Jordan—"

"It's weird. It's so awkward staying in some stranger's house."

"They're not strangers," he said promptly.

"They're strangers to me."

"You'll feel better once you meet Ethan," Dad said, as though I didn't hate Ethan Barbanel from my very tiptoes to the crown of my head. Dad checked his phone. "He should be here soon."

My water glass clattered against the tabletop as I set it down, hard. "He's joining us?"

Dad nodded. "I wanted you two to meet."

My jaw dropped open, but then I shut it, swallowing my anger and frustration and all the negative feelings that spurred through me. Dad wasn't *trying* to piss me off by inviting Ethan to our first dinner together. It didn't make sense to freak out about how much time Dad lavished on Ethan instead of spending it with me. That wouldn't be, as Aunt Lou put it, *productive.*

Sometimes I didn't want to be productive.

Today, though, sure. Today we were getting along. "Neat," I said, unable to keep from sounding 75 percent withering. I picked up my menu and held it in front of my face.

Huh. Some of these options *did* sound really good.

"There he is!" Dad waved. I didn't turn because I was spiteful and petty like that, instead waiting until Dad's prodigy had reached the table, until he was pulling out a chair and Dad was standing next to him, saying, "Ethan, I want you to meet my daughter, Jordan—"

And then I looked up and almost spat out my sip of water. Because Chair Boy stood at my father's right hand.

Three

In retrospect, I should have known Chair Boy would turn out to be Ethan Barbanel.

That's the way my life worked, after all. My sixteenth birthday party: a thunderstorm broke out after two traffic-filled hours driving to the beach. Prom three weeks ago: my latest fling, Austin—who'd ghosted me when I brought up trying out a relationship the month before—introduced me to his new, serious girlfriend.

If life could screw me over *and* be extra about it, it would.

Ethan Barbanel of the Chair stared at me with a kind of horrified delight. "Good to meet you," he said. "I feel like we already know each other."

Dad beamed.

"Hi." I refused to crack a smile. This was impossible. The picture I'd drawn in my mind of Ethan Barbanel was a serious, studious guy with good taste in music and pretentious taste in literature. Not a laid-back bro who liked making out with strangers.

Dad cleared his throat. "I just took Jordan by Golden Doors to drop her things off."

"Right." Ethan gave me the same laser-focused attention he'd trained on my lips just a few hours ago. A delighted realization crept over his face. "Because you're staying with us all summer."

Fuck. I'd already been horrified by the concept of staying in the same house as Ethan Barbanel. To realize I'd be staying in the same house after *making out with him* was tantamount to being told I had to room with a succubus—sexy and soul-sucking at the same time.

Ethan looked fixed on the sexy possibilities. "How'd you like Golden Doors?"

It's a house, I wanted to say bitingly, something to make it clear exactly what I thought about rich people with summer homes. But Dad looked so hopeful, wanting me to behave—wanting us all to get along. I tried not to sound too grudging. "It's nice."

Ethan's lips curved. Golden Doors vaulted so much beyond nice, the understatement sounded comical. "Sorry I wasn't there to meet you."

"Yes, Ethan, didn't you also come in on the ferry today?" Dad looked back and forth between the two of us. "You might have been on the same one!"

Ethan looked at me to see if I wanted to lob that back. My smile tightened. "Could have been."

"I'm sure I would have noticed," Ethan said. "Not too many people in all black in this heat."

My smile calcified. He hadn't been making fun of my outfit when he stuck his hand up my shirt.

"Jordan's always had her own fashion taste," Dad said blithely, as though I had single-handedly invented the dark academia trend.

We were, blissfully, interrupted by our server, who took our orders—which turned out to be nigh identical: Impossible burgers with sweet potato fries for Ethan and me, and with a side salad for Dad, who was supposed to be watching his cholesterol. I frowned. "You should have ordered the salmon. Just because it's vegetarian doesn't make the burger good for you."

"We had salmon last night," Ethan said, which made me want to punch him. Why was *he* the one hanging out with my father?

Though I guess I should be happy if he also watched Dad's cholesterol.

Dad's cell rang. When he saw the caller, his face brightened. "Sorry, I'll be right back." He picked up his phone and walked away. I watched him go, wondering why his face had lit up. A date? A crush?

When I looked back at my tablemate, Ethan Barbanel smiled at me. "So."

I scowled and plopped my chin in my hands. I had *liked* him. He had made me giddy and made me laugh and made a kaleidoscope of butterflies dart about my stomach. "So."

"You're Tony's daughter."

"And you're Ethan Barbanel."

He leaned his chair back on two legs. It'd serve him right if he fell over backward. "I don't think I would've made out with you if I knew who you were."

Hard same. Still, memories of a few hours ago rose—how very happy he'd made me, how good he'd been at kissing. I shunted them away and gave him a sharp smile. "Why not?"

"I dunno. Seems a little . . . disrespectful?"

What? "To who? I hope you don't mean because of my *dad*."

He stifled a laugh. "No. I guess I meant—it's different to hook up with a stranger than with someone you know."

I couldn't have agreed more. Strangers were devoid of complications. Ethan Barbanel came with enough complications to flatline me.

"You're not what I expected," he continued.

A full-body bristle swept through me. What did he expect? Someone smarter, someone like Dad? A kind, charming studious type, not a sarcastic mess? "Yeah, well, you're not who I was expecting Dad's assistant to be, either."

He blew out a breath, his cheeks puffing as he did so. "Don't I know it."

"What do you mean?"

He looked away. One arm dangled off the back of his chair. "I'm used to being underestimated."

"I'm not underestimating you. I'm not estimating you at all."

"Aren't you?" His gaze snapped back to mine. "You haven't been—estimating—me for years?"

Shit. Caught. "Why would I?"

He smirked. "Because I've been doing it to you. I've heard about you for ages."

"Doesn't mean you know me."

He leaned forward, the front legs of his chair landing firmly on the ground. His expression was a strange mix of satisfaction and curiosity. "I think I do."

I scoffed. "You don't know anything about me."

He gave me a look suggesting how patently false my statement had been; how we knew each other rather intimately, as of a few hours ago. "I know you're going to UMass next year and you're undecided but leaning math. You loved to run until you hurt your knee. Cilantro tastes like soap to you, and you and your best friend have worked at Lulu's Diner for three years. And—" He snapped his mouth shut.

Possibly because I was gaping with the same amount of horror as if he'd pulled his face off. I felt exposed. How could Dad tell Ethan so much about me? "And what?" I demanded.

"Nothing."

"*What?*"

He opened his mouth, shut it, then raised his chin. "I know you have a crap dating record."

I picked up my wrapped straw and lobbed it at him.

It glanced off his chest and lightly fell into his lap. He raised his brows as he placed it back on the table. "Ow."

"And you have such a good one?" Even as I said it, I realized I had no idea what his dating record was. What did I know about Ethan? He was rich, outdoorsy, and a rising sophomore at the University of Chicago. Not much else. Apparently, Dad had gossiped about me but had protected Ethan's secrets.

I really hated this boy.

Dad returned to the table, smiling brightly. "What have you two been chatting about?"

Just all the private details of my life you felt comfortable sharing, Dad. "Who was that?"

"Oh, it was, ah—it was no one."

Please let it be a date. "It wasn't no one."

Dad cleared his throat, his nervous tic. He'd never been able to lie to me. "Uh, there's some things at the house I've been meaning to get fixed. I was getting a quote from a contractor."

Oh. "Dad, we don't need a disposal or for the window to work. They're not a big deal."

"Ah, well, they'd be nice to fix."

I wanted to protest more—to tell him they weren't important enough to spend the money on—but I didn't want to admit to money struggles in front of Ethan Barbanel. I'd bring it up later. "Okay."

Our food arrived, and talk turned to what to do on the island during the summer—Dad pitched me unnecessarily hard on Nantucket, given I was already stuck here. "And there's Gibson's comet this year and the meteor shower," Dad added enticingly. "Won't that be fun? It's a big deal to see them at the same time."

Despite myself, I felt excitement flicker. Dad had instilled his love of astronomy in me. We'd spent my childhood going on late-night drives to open fields with little light pollution. Wrapped in coats and blankets, we'd stared up at the inky heavens, waiting for our eyes to adjust so we could spot shooting stars. "I suppose."

"Ethan's family is going to host a party at the end of the summer, when the comet first becomes visible," Dad said.

I chanced a glance at Ethan. "Are they super into astronomy or something?"

"I don't think you need to be super into astronomy to be excited about Gibson's comet." Ethan sounded amused. Which, fair. The comet wasn't as famous as Halley's, but Gibson's was still familiar to most people, and with a thirty-eight-year orbital period, it showed up more frequently. It was the parent body of the Arborids, one of the summer's brightest meteor showers, visible when Earth passed through the debris left from the comet's tail. "And Gibson visited Nantucket."

"Really?" I hadn't known that—didn't know anything about the origin of the comet's name, actually. I didn't even know who Gibson was. "When?"

"Early nineteen hundreds," Ethan said promptly. He shot a grin at my dad. The ease and familiarity made my stomach clench with jealousy. "He's in the book."

My gaze pinged back and forth between the two of them. My dad's first book had been about early maritime navigation and surveying; a good bulk of it had to do with Benjamin Franklin and his great-grandson Bache, who'd been the superintendent of the US Coastal Survey. I hadn't read it, but I knew it alternated between chapters where my dad tried out historical methods and chapters about the people who pioneered them. His second book would be on the same themes, but focus on other people and centuries.

"Oh?" I tried not to let my dismay show at how well Ethan fit into my father's world. "Why's he in it?"

"Gibson worked for Captain Heck, who developed wire-drag surveying." At my blank look, Ethan added, "Wire-dragging revolutionized hydrography. It was way faster than anything they'd used before."

Literally nothing he said made any sense to me. I felt a surge of panic. Was this what I should be learning if I wanted a conversation with Dad to flow? I'd thought I could spend this summer working with him, but would he even want my help when I had no idea about all the topics and people in his research?

"Ethan's helping me with Heck's chapter." Dad smiled. "He's writing an insert on Gibson's work, prior to his discovery of the comet and setting up his foundation."

Dad's proud tone hit me like a punch. When was the last time Dad had sounded proud of me? Worried, yes. Alarmed, sure. Happy, entertained, pleased—all good things. But proud?

I wasn't sure I'd ever made my father proud.

"Cool," I said softly, because I wasn't sure what else to say. Why hadn't I paid more attention to my father's work? Now I didn't speak the same language as him, and it made me feel slow and stupid and sad.

For the rest of the meal, I was silent, while Dad and Ethan talked about their research plans for the upcoming week. I toyed with the remnants of my meal, relieved when the server finally brought the check. We headed to the car, and Ethan and I both automatically went for the passenger's seat. I jolted back. My heart beat hard, disproportional to the small event. I wrapped my arms around my stomach. Ethan thought he belonged up front. Ethan probably *did* belong up front. He'd have more to talk about with my dad than I did. And this car belonged to his family.

Ethan raised his hands and stepped back. "All yours."

I nodded slowly. I almost wanted to cry.

It was past eight when we arrived at Golden Doors, but the sun was only just setting. Soft pinks and blues brushed the sky, and cotton-candy clouds drifted over the sea. I worried at the inside of my cheeks with my molars. This was it, then.

Dad parked the car, and all three of us climbed out. He shoved his hands in his pockets. "Okay," he said, dorkily as always, "you kids have fun, now!"

Ethan said goodbye and headed for the front door. I followed Dad to his bike, feeling like a little kid dropped off at kindergarten for the first time. "I'll see you tomorrow?" I said, hating the nervous note in my voice.

"We'll get dinner," Dad promised.

"Okay." I waited another moment, wanting to postpone the inevitable, wanting to suggest going to Dad's rented studio and watching a movie, or going for another walk around the island—anything to avoid being left on my own at this giant house. But we'd already fought about this over and over. "See you later, then."

Dad smiled awkwardly, clambering onto his bike. "Good night."

"Night."

Dad peddled into the darkness. With a sigh, I turned around—and found Ethan standing on the porch, staring at me.

"All right," he said, coming down the steps. "What's going on?"

Uh-oh. "What do you mean?"

"You liked me plenty on the boat, and now you don't. What happened?"

"Nothing happened. I didn't know who you were, is all."

"What's that have to do with anything?" he asked.

I looked past him, at the delicate blossoms flowering on bushes, inhaling the green, vibrant scent of summer carried by the warm breeze. "Like you said. I wouldn't have made out with you if I knew who you are."

"So is this chip on your shoulder *because* we made out? Or did you have an issue with me before?"

More than a chip, rather Chip and his siblings and Mrs. Potts herself. Yet I couldn't bring myself to admit my epic jealousy. "I don't have any issue with you. I'm sure you're great."

"Yeah, I am," he said easily, leaning against the stair's rail. "Look, I get it. You were looking for a hook-up you never had to see again. But I'm not going to make this weird."

"You're not?" I said warily.

"Course not. Especially since we're staying down the hall from each other all summer. It could get sticky." He tilted his head. "Though . . . it's a pretty good setup."

My eyes narrowed. "No."

"I had to try." He grinned, but then it fell away, and when he spoke he sounded irritatingly earnest. "I don't want to make you uncomfortable or anything. I really wouldn't have made a move if I knew you'd be living here."

"Whatever." I shoved my frizzy hair behind my ears. "It's fine. I've got to go unpack." I moved past him, up the stairs and across the porch to the front door.

"No, wait." He caught my hand, easy with the touch, and for a moment I savored the warmth of his hand, the strength of his fingers. He felt so good, and my body remembered being even closer, so close I could feel every line of his body. "You should say hi to everyone."

I pulled my hand away. I *refused* to let myself feel anything for Ethan Barbanel, no matter how good our chemistry. Besides, it was probably both impossible and bizarre to crush on someone I resented so much. "I'm tired," I said, heading inside. I unlaced my boots, placing them carefully among all the Birkenstocks and glittery sandals and practical flip-flops. "I'll meet them in the morning."

I thought I could feel Ethan's gaze on me as I climbed the grand staircase to the second story, but when I turned to look, he was already gone.

In my new room, I moved clothes from my suitcases to the empty dresser and hangers. I'd noticed a gazillion boutiques in town, and I itched to explore them, though they were probably out of my price range. Almost all of my outfits were thrifted, careful finds from the Garment District or Goodwill or Buffalo Exchange.

After showering away the day, I put on my coziest PJs and sent a few photos to my best friend, Grace Davidson: a cedar-shingled cottage covered in roses, a view of three houses sitting on the harbor, and a picture of Golden Doors itself. Wish you were here 💀

Grace responded right away:

Grace:

I wish I WAS there

Not only bc we could have a great photoshoot but bc I too would like to experience New England wealth

Me:

I googled the brand of soap in the bathroom
and its $40 a bottle

Grace:

!!!

I respect your commitment to googling strangers
belongings

Is the soap worth it

Me:

Honestly yes

It's a lavender chamomile blend

I feel like I'm in an apothecary

Like if I mixed three of these lotions together
there'd be an explosion of purple smoke and
I'd have a love spell on my hands

There's like three dozen Glossier products in
the bathroom I'm sharing

Grace:

JFC

I asked Mom for a glossier gift card for my birthday
and she blinked very slowly

I think that means the gift card will cover one half of
one lip balm

Me:

What's the goss at Camp Davidson

Grace:

No goss

My mom is driving me crazy

How am I supposed to drive Brayden to camp AND
Mackenzie to swimming lessons AND go to work I am
JUST ONE PERSON

WAIT

DID YOU MEET ETHAN

AHHHHH I ALMOST FORGOT

Me:

Uh

My phone buzzed with a video call, and laughing, I picked
up. Grace's face filled the screen, her wild hair all over the place,
like a goldendoodle had taken a nap on her head. "So?" she demanded.

"It's kind of a mess."

"I expected no less," she said. "What happened?"

I filled her in, and she responded with the appropriate amount of gasps and exclamations. "See!" she crowed at the end. "This is why you should have found pics of him before. You were being too stubborn."

"Fine, I admit in this *one instance* that would have been smart. Anyway, what are you and everyone up to?"

"Just the same old." She launched into stories of work and our friends before her tone shifted subtly. "And there's a new girl hostessing."

I straightened. Anytime anyone said "new girl" in that tone, it only meant one thing. "What's she like?"

"Uh, she's kinda quiet, but when she talks she has this super funny sense of humor . . ."

"And is she brilliant?" I teased, because Grace only went for people whose brains outshone the rest of ours.

"Maybe," Grace said, laughing slightly. "She wants to study robotics."

"Of course she does."

We killed the next two hours talking, then watched an episode of our favorite ridiculous reality dating show before falling asleep. "Good night, darlink," she said, yawning as the credits rolled. "Try not to cry too hard about being trapped in paradise for the summer."

"I'll only cry because I miss you," I promised. "Love you."

"Love you more," she said, and we signed off. I burrowed deep into my new, borrowed bed and fell asleep.

* * *

Hours later, I woke in pitch black.

I checked my phone: 2:38 a.m. Definitely not time to be awake, but I'd had trouble sleeping for years. I tried breathing deeply, tried counting sheep, tried counting backward from one thousand in Spanish. Nothing worked. In fact, I felt like I'd taken a shot of adrenaline. Eventually I caved and looked at my phone, but nothing on all the interwebs intrigued me.

By 3:40, irritated and exhausted, I got out of bed, figuring a change of scene might at least distract me. I wandered through the ancient halls of Golden Doors. Moonlight provided the only illumination, sliding in through the windows and across the floors. This house was surely haunted; how many people had lived and loved and died here? I kept wandering, no clear destination in mind. The moon kept me company through every window, half full, gleaming, bloated.

I climbed a steep, narrow staircase, my hand steadying me against the wall. At the top stood a heavy door, and I pushed it open. Cold night air rushed at me, and I looked out at a spacious deck jutting out amid the pitched gray roofs of the rest of the house, enclosed by a white fence.

Ahh. The widow's walk.

I stepped outside. The door closed behind me, and I grabbed it, struck by an instant's certainty it had locked, but it opened easily. With a deep exhale, I looked out over the rolling lawns and wooded gardens. The dark silhouette of a gazebo stood out in the distance, followed by the dunes and the crashing sea. The view was overwhelming, almost too beautiful, the kind of beauty that slipped inside and twisted and choked you, leaving no room for anything else.

I leaned my head back and breathed.

There were the stars, bright and glittering. The June sky, which my father had taught me to know and love, the constellations he'd painstakingly pointed out to pint-size me, all so much brighter here than near the city. I couldn't wait to watch the Arborids together at the end of July. Though—Dad had been watching the Arborids with Ethan for the past three summers, hadn't he? I shivered involuntarily. Ethan, my father's perfect replacement child.

Breathe.

There, the tilted summer dipper; there, past Polaris, the queen Cassiopeia, chained to her throne by a vengeful god for taking pride in her beauty. There, the Arbor, the tree of life from which it looked like the Arborids meteor shower originated each summer. And there, the Summer Triangle. The brightest star, Deneb, was two hundred thousand times brighter than our sun. The other two stars, according to Chinese folklore, were lovers separated by the Milky Way.

I breathed out and lowered my head.

And jolted. In a wing of the house curved toward me, a figure stood in a glowing window. I swallowed a scream, then peered at the figure more closely—easy to see, given the illumination of his window, the only lit window in the entire house. Ethan Barbanel.

He lifted a hand, but I ignored it and retreated quickly inside.

Four

By 8:00 a.m. I was already stressed.

I'd fallen back asleep, but it'd been broken and unsatisfying. Now the idea of going downstairs and interacting with the Barbanels made me burrow deeper in my—very luxurious—sheets. I considered myself extroverted, but maybe I was only extroverted in groups of people I already knew? I scrolled through my phone, wishing I'd brought snacks to ward off rumblings of hunger.

At ten thirty on the dot, someone knocked on my door.

Great. Hiding had made me conspicuous. "One minute!" I made sure I didn't have yesterday's underwear flung about before opening the door.

Miriam, Ethan's younger cousin, stood there, her hair in two braided pigtails. "Morning!" she chirped. "Mom wanted me to tell you there's pancakes for breakfast, if you want any."

"Thanks." I didn't move.

Miriam took pity on me. "Most people've already eaten, so you don't need to worry about a huge crowd of strangers."

"Oh. Okay." I unfroze and followed her down the hall. "Do you come here every summer?"

"Yeah."

"Must be nice."

She grinned wryly. "Bit of an understatement. My family's apartment could fit into one of the bathrooms here."

My surprise embarrassed me. I'd assumed all the Barbanels were as painfully rich as I was not. "Same."

Downstairs, Miriam showed me a room spanning the length of the house. Large windows and open French doors overlooked the rolling lawn. The soft green scent of summer wafted in, fresh-cut grass and delicate lilac notes. Inside, a few adults draped themselves over sofas, coffee at their sides. Two women with the tight dark brown curls all the Barbanels seemed to have stood in the open kitchen, chatting as they brewed tea. A four- or five-year-old played with a toddler, moving the child's limbs, and at a small table sat three identical girls, eating pancakes. I blinked.

"Iris, Lily, and Rose," Miriam said. "They're thirteen."

"How do you keep track of them?"

"We don't."

I caught the whiff of coffee and pivoted, homing in on a carafe sitting on the kitchen island. "Is it okay if I have a cup?"

"Of course!" Miriam sounded scandalized I'd bothered to ask. "You can have whatever you want."

Whatever I want. But what I wanted was to not be here; to be, instead, in my cozy house back home, with Dad there, too.

Miriam showed me the cabinet of eclectic mugs, and I poured a brimming cup into one with a Georgia O'Keeffe painting. I guess that was what counted for spicy among rich people. "Sugar or milk?" Miriam asked, a perfect tiny hostess.

"I'm good." I clutched my mug. Some days, my morning cup of coffee felt like the only good and beautiful thing in the world. What was I going to *do* here?

"What do you do?" I asked Miriam. "Do you go to camp, or have a job, or what?"

"I volunteer at the Atheneum." She nodded at the triplets across the room. "They go to theater camp—Iris wants to direct, Lily act, Rose write."

Convenient they didn't step on each other's toes. Or perhaps they'd specifically split up their interests so they wouldn't. "Organized. And is it social here? Easy to make friends?"

Miri shrugged. "I guess? We've been coming here for so long we know a lot of people already."

Made sense. Hopefully some of the older cousins could introduce me to their groups. And I bet college kids rented places for the summer and hung out at bars and at the beach. That's where I would have looked if I'd wanted to date—which I didn't. I was sick of having my heart broken, for one thing. But even more, I didn't want Dad to have any reason to worry about me. He worried too much when he should be focused on himself. He'd been so worried he'd even told Ethan Barbanel about my dating record. I had to prove I was completely and totally fine so Dad could focus on other things. With me leaving for college, I wanted him to start branching out, making friends or starting relationships, instead of spending all his time worrying if I was okay. *He* needed to have a support system so *he'd* be okay.

Still, just because I was taking a break from dating didn't

mean I wanted a break from gossip. "Does everyone usually have summer flings and stuff?"

Miri blushed furiously. "Oh, um, I wouldn't know. I've never— I'm not dating anyone. Are you?"

Cool, so I wouldn't be getting any fun stories from Miri. "Not right now." The last guy I'd been consistently hooking up with— Austin, a stoner in my AP Physics class who I didn't particularly like, but who I'd *still* developed feelings for—had ghosted me weeks ago. Before him, I'd had a brief fling with one of the regulars at Lulu's Diner. My last real relationship had ended at Thanksgiving: Louis and I had dated for seven months, since my junior year, but apparently when he went to college he lost interest. He hadn't told me until he came home in November because he wanted to do the break up in person because he "respected" me. Respect hadn't stopped him from hooking up with people at college, though. Louis! What a gem.

I wondered what kind of people Ethan usually dated.

"Hey."

Speak of the devil. Ethan strode into the room and dropped down at the kitchen island across from me. "Sorry if I freaked you out last night. I came out to the roof walk to make sure you were okay, but you were already gone."

Miriam looked back and forth between us, gaze curious.

"You didn't freak me out," I said. "I don't freak out."

"I wasn't watching you or anything. Sometimes I can't sleep. Hey, Miri."

"I knew you weren't watching me. If you had been, you would have kept your light off."

He laughed. "True. You've got your creeping figured out."

I gestured at my black shorts and tank top. "It's why I wear all black."

"Here I thought you were a professional mourner."

The corners of my mouth turned up. "Nah, for those occasions I need more fabric available to rend."

"True, any rending of current attire would be . . ." He ran his gaze over me, the smile on his lips looking as irrepressible as mine. ". . . Problematic."

"Ethan." Miriam sounded long-suffering. "Are you serious? She's staying with us for the summer."

Oh my god. How embarrassing. How had I let myself start flirting with Ethan again? Ethan was a do-not-pass-go, do-not-collect-two-hundred-dollars. There was no way any situation with him would end well. Any further banter or hooking up would be soured by my resentment and would inevitably end in anger and jealousy and probably leave me a yelling, sobbing mess.

And destroy any chance of convincing my dad I was calm and fine and he could focus on his own life.

Ethan gently bopped Miriam on her head. "Don't you worry, Miri. I'm never serious."

"I'm going to get more pancakes," she said. "I wash my hands of you."

"I'm off, too," Ethan said after Miriam had indignantly departed. "Ciao."

"Where are you going?" I asked, suddenly distressed to lose one of the few people I knew in this giant house.

"Off to see the prof," he said nonchalantly, as though he always gave this answer to this question. Then he paused. "Uh—your dad."

Ethan and my dad had plans this morning? *I* wanted to have plans with my father. I should have told Dad earlier I wanted to help him out this summer, so he wouldn't need Ethan. "Take me with you."

Ethan gave me a frankly appraising look. "Why?"

"I can help."

"With—what? Your dad's work?"

"Why not? I'm here, aren't I?"

"Yeah, but—he didn't mention you'd be helping. Did you guys plan for you to join us?"

I shrugged. I'd planned it in my head, I just hadn't really articulated it. "Does it matter?"

Ethan smiled slightly. But not the flirty, fun smile from earlier. No, now he looked like he knew something. I frowned. "What?"

"Nothing." When my frown deepened, he shoved his hands in his pockets sheepishly. "Your dad mentioned you can be impulsive sometimes."

Now I was irritated. "Are you gonna give me a ride or not?"

"Have you even had breakfast?"

I snagged two golden-brown patties off the top of the pile of pancakes. "Let's go."

Still looking skeptical, Ethan led me outside to a Jeep I had to struggle a bit to get into. Ethan turned the key, and the engine rumbled on. We started down the road, sunbaked roses and lavender sweeping over us. "Why'd you start working with my dad?" I asked. Ethan knew too much about me. I needed to level the playing field.

"You don't know?"

"I know you started three years ago when a family friend introduced you. But I don't know *why*."

"He does interesting stuff."

The title of Dad's first book was *Mapping the Atlantic: A History of American Maritime Cartography*. Which, yes, could be interesting if you were fascinated by how eighteenth- and nineteenth-century people mapped and learned to navigate the ocean's currents, floor, and coast. I just hadn't run across a ton of teenagers who were.

Ethan drove us to a strip of office buildings mid-island, a place where you couldn't even tell you were on Nantucket. He led me down a long hallway. At the end, a door had Dad's name in small white print.

"Morning, Ethan," Dad said when we walked in, then focused on me with surprise. "Jordan! What are you doing here?"

I tried not to bristle. "I thought I'd see what you were up to."

Dad looked around, as though searching for the toys he'd kept on hand to entertain me when I was a child and visited his classroom—juggling balls, non-drying clay, an action figure or two. "I'm afraid it's not very exciting—we sit here reading, most of the day—"

"I like reading."

Dad gave me a skeptical look.

Okay, I was more of a numbers girl than a book girl. "What does Ethan do?"

"Ethan's combing through old microfilms and documenting mentions of the historical figures we're interested in."

A real barrel of monkeys. "I could do that. Help you guys out."

Dad grimaced. "You don't want to do that, honey. You want to be out, exploring Nantucket, making friends—"

"I'd rather work for you."

Also, I'd be free labor for Dad. Though of course, Ethan was also free labor; he could afford an unpaid internship. He'd probably started in order to get a nice recommendation for college.

I just wanted to spend time with my dad.

"Don't you worry about us," Dad said. *Us*. I wasn't part of his "us." "You'll be happier with a job where you get to meet people! Where you don't have to hang out with your old dad."

Right. I got the message. He didn't want me here. My plan to hang out with him all summer, to remind him *I* existed, not just Ethan, and I was competent and smart and had my shit together—that was all down the drain. I really should have talked to him about this earlier; now he'd think, once more, I was being impulsive.

"Sure. Got it." I stomped toward the door, catching a flicker of some expression on Ethan's face as I left—pity?

Sweet. Really loved pity coming at me from the hot guy I'd hooked up with. Made me feel super sexy.

"Ethan can give you a ride to town—"

"It's cool," I said. "I'll walk."

"It's three miles," Ethan said.

Oof. Further than I'd expected. Unfortunately, I was too proud to back down. "I like walking."

Dad peeled several crumpled dollar bills from his wallet. "Here. You can catch the bus."

So much for my grand exit. I took the cash. "Thanks."

I caught the bus.

* * *

If I disliked anyone more than Ethan Barbanel, it was Benjamin Franklin.

But why?! one might ask. *Benjamin Franklin did a bunch of cool stuff! Unlike most of the Founding Fathers, he did eventually, belatedly, become an abolitionist.*

And yet he incurred my wrath and jealousy, for much the same reason Ethan did: because my dad devoted more time to him than to me.

Here's what, when I was a mere inkling of a girl, I used to know about Benjamin Franklin:

- *Etched onto one-hundred-dollar bills, which were occasionally referred to as "Benjamins" in media, but never real life*

- *Something about lightning?*

- *Maybe had a rivalry with Edison??*

- *People in France hated him and put him on chamber pots*

- *Balding, with long hair and spectacles; classic aging-uncle vibe*

- *Wanted turkeys to be America's national bird*
- *May or may not have been a plot point in National Treasure*

Here was what I had learned in the past three years about Benjamin Franklin, after my dad's attention-grabbing essay focused on BF himself, along with several significant chapters in the first book:

- *Benjamin Franklin's maternal grandmother belonged to a prominent Nantucket family.*

- *As postmaster general, Franklin was tasked with increasing the speed of the mail. This meant finding faster ship routes. With the help of his Nantucket relative Captain Timothy Folger, he mapped out and named the Gulf Stream, then told ships to avoid the current, and voilà, faster ships and faster mail.*

- *Franklin's great-grandson Alexander Dallas Bache headed the United States Coast Survey for two dozen years. He mapped the US coastline and instituted a lot of other real great stuff, probably, and also served as the first president of the National Academy of Sciences. (Bache got several chapters in the first book, too.)*

Did I want to know these things? Not particularly! But you can only attend so many book events before knowledge seeps in. And while I couldn't *really* blame Benjamin Franklin for my father's summers on Nantucket, I would have been much happier if Dad had been enthralled by some dude in Boston instead.

After the bus dropped me off in town, I wandered through the streets, the gentle breeze whispering of the summer to come. I was painfully aware of being on my own while everyone else my age moved in groups. Plucking up my courage, I entered a café's patio, the pancakes from earlier now a distant memory. Had I ever eaten by myself? Such a small thing, but I wasn't sure I had. I snagged a seat at a communal outdoor table, put in an online order, and tried to figure out what to do next.

If my dad didn't want my help, I'd need an actual job. I had three years of waitressing and hostessing experience, and I'd seen a few boutiques with NOW HIRING signs. Maybe if a thrift shop needed help, the employee discount would allow me to buy clothes here.

But I was more bothered than I'd expected by Dad not wanting my help. Sure, I wasn't the most academic person in the world, but I was good at math and I liked science, and while I sort of thought history was stuffy, I wasn't an *idiot*. I could be good at the kind of things Dad respected. And I wanted to prove it.

I googled *science jobs Nantucket* and winced at the results. They were almost all for an oceanographic institute back on the Cape called WHOI. Also, most of them wanted me to have a PhD. *Summer science job Nantucket* surfaced better results, including internships and fellowships at a place called the Maria Mitchell Association. Clicking through, it looked like the MMA had an aquarium and a science center. Most of the teen opportunities were volunteer work taking care of animals and directing visitors.

I glanced idly at adult opportunities. Education, development, natural sciences, astronomy.

I blinked. Astronomy?

Docent needed for Vestal Street Observatory tours, it said. Cashier needed for Open Nights at Loines Observatory.

Nantucket had an observatory? Potentially two observatories? Excitement bubbled up within me, fizzy and effervescent. I searched *Vestal Street Observatory*, which brought up another page from the Maria Mitchell Association's site with pictures of a quaint house with a dome, built in 1908. *Loines Observatory* brought up a more modern observatory with domes built in the 1960s and 1980s. I navigated to the About tab: The Maria Mitchell Association was founded in 1902 to preserve the legacy of Nantucket native astronomer, naturalist, librarian, and, above all, educator, Maria Mitchell.

The MMA's astronomy department was created over a hundred years ago, with help from Harvard. They had internships for undergrads studying astronomy and astrophysics. Past projects made my brows shoot up. Dark matter and exoplanets, star clusters and galaxy formations . . .

Maybe if I swung by the Maria Mitchell Association, I could get the inside scoop on any jobs. I finished my lunch, then plugged the address into my phone. It was a short walk; everything in town seemed to be a short walk.

Inside the small, neat building, a gray-haired woman greeted me. "How can I help you?"

Was I being ridiculous, walking into a place and asking if they had a job, as though jobs grew on trees? I cleared my throat.

"I was wondering if you had any jobs for the summer?"

The woman's patient expression didn't change. "I'm sorry, no. If you're interested in volunteering . . ."

I thought about all the money I was missing out on by not working at Lulu's Diner, about how last year, embarrassed, Dad had said the overnight school trips were too expensive. How the year before, he'd softly suggested I drop private clarinet lessons, and how I'd always known clothing came out of whatever I made at Lulu's or babysitting. If I was going to volunteer for anyone, it would have been Dad, but he didn't need a volunteer because he had Ethan.

"Um, no, thank you," I said. "I don't suppose if you know any other opportunities for astronomy on the island?" I asked, not very hopeful. I thought of my father. "Or visiting researchers who need interns?"

She looked thoughtful "It's not likely, but you can leave your name and contact info. I can ask around."

"Really?" I perked up. "That would be *great*."

* * *

At six, I met up with Dad at a pizza place he'd suggested. "How was your first full day on Nantucket?" he asked as we sat down, a little too heartily.

"Good, I guess." *Why didn't you want my help?* I wanted to ask. "I looked into jobs. And I went to one of the beaches."

"Which one?"

"Jetties, I think?" I'd walked from town to a lighthouse, passing more houses and hotels, and tall hedges and climbing flowers. The lighthouse had been short and squat, surrounded by fishermen casting their lines into the water. To the right, I could see Nantucket harbor, filled with small boats and a few massive yachts. In front of me had sailed what looked like an honest-to-god pirate ship. I'd walked along the water all the way to a public beach, filled with laughing parties and aggressive seagulls.

Dad nodded. "They have a restaurant we'll have to go to."

I tried to picture my dad at the beach bar I'd seen, with its brightly colored chairs, live music, and colorful cocktails. "Is it your local hang now?" I teased.

Dad looked embarrassed. "I haven't been. But I thought you might like it."

Guilt hit me. Right, of course Dad wasn't galivanting around restaurants. He just wanted me to have a good time here. "Yeah, okay."

Dad cleared his throat. "I thought Ethan could show you around the island a bit—so even if you haven't met anyone yet, there'll at least be someone your age—"

"Dad! You don't have to set up play dates for me, I'm not six."

His shoulders drooped again. "Right, I know," he said quietly. "I just don't want you to be lonely."

I blinked several times, my chest aching dully. "I'm not lonely," I lied in a kinder voice. "There's tons of cousins at the house." I held up the menu. "What do you think—Veggie Supreme or the Fortissimo Formaggio?"

"Definitely the Fortissimo Formaggio. Great band name."

"Wedding cover band." My role, when Dad pointed out a potential band name, was to match them with their music. "Italian ballads only. Their showstopper is 'That's Amore.'"

Dad laughed, and I felt warm and happy and like maybe this summer would be okay.

Our four-cheese pizza came, and we talked about normal, nothing topics, like the end of school and Aunt Lou's trip and what Grace and my other friends were up to for the summer. At the end, Dad picked at the food, then set his fork down decisively. "Remember how I got a call last night? About the house?"

Uh-oh. This was an alarming tone. "Yes?"

"How would you feel . . . if we lived somewhere else?"

I put down my soda. "What."

He winced. "I was thinking, after you leave for college, I'm not going to need so much room."

Was Dad planning to sell my childhood home? "But I'll be back! At Thanksgiving and winter break and the whole summer."

Dad tilted his head back and forth, as though weighing these arguments. "True, though for the last few summers, you haven't been at the house."

"Because *you* haven't been there!" I felt betrayed. "But you're not planning to come to Nantucket every summer forever, are you? How long do you need to be out here?"

"I think it might be time, Jordan."

"Why?" I asked. "I love our house. *You* love our house. Why would we leave it?"

He looked pained. "I know, honey. But if we sell, we could get a nice apartment in the city—"

I could feel my blood pressure spike. "You don't only want to sell, you want to move to *Boston*? Dad, it's where we lived with Mom."

"I know, honey," he said again, softer.

Wait. "Is this a money thing? Can we not afford it?"

"It's only partially a money thing. It's mostly a timing thing, Jordan. I think it's time."

"Well, I don't." I sat back and folded my arms. "So it's one against one."

"But I'm the dad, so I get two votes."

"That's not fair."

He grimaced. "I know. Sorry."

"If it's a money thing, if I can figure out some solution, could we stay?"

"Honey. I know this is hard. I promise it'll work out okay."

"I'm not a little kid anymore, Dad. You don't have to make me promises, especially when you don't know if you can keep them."

His lips pressed together. "Right. No, I know. You're not a little kid."

In stilted silence, we packed up our leftovers. Dad didn't have a car today, so he called me a ride, even though I insisted I could take the bus partway and walk the rest. "It'd be easier if I was staying with you," I said grumpily.

"Jordan, the Barbanels are being incredibly generous by letting you stay."

"Them being generous doesn't make me like it any more." Dad was selling our home and dumping me on strangers; could he want any less to do with me?

"Can't you try, with them?" Dad sounded tired. He pressed his hand to his forehead as the car he'd ordered rolled up beside us. "Can you please, at least, try?"

I felt like the most horrible daughter in the world: whiny and bitter and troublesome. If I wanted Dad to focus on himself, I had to give him less cause to worry about me. "Okay, Dad. Yes. I'll try."

Five

So I decided to try.

Back at Golden Doors, the windows were glowing—golden, even. A blast of music and laughter greeted me as I stepped inside. Someone was having a party, probably in the large room I'd had breakfast in earlier. I hesitated. It was only eight, which felt too early for hiding in my room, especially when normally I'd be headed out to a party or to hang with my friends. But I didn't feel comfortable walking into something I knew nothing about.

"Jordan! How are you? How was your day?"

I looked up to see Ethan's mom, Stephanie, coming down the stairs into the entryway. "Oh, hi. It was good. How are you? Are you guys having a party?"

"Just a few friends who came to the island for the week. The kids are probably hiding upstairs in the cousins' room, if you'd like to join them."

"Oh, um, okay . . . Where's that?"

"This way." She led me through a string of rooms off the foyer: a music room with a mini grand, a sitting room with ornate mirrors. We entered a hallway with a narrow staircase. "It's up there, at the end of the hall, on the right. You'll hear them."

"Thanks." I climbed the stairs, feeling somewhat fazed about crashing a roomful of cousins who'd known each other their whole lives. I might have tried to escape, but Stephanie watched, beaming, as I went up the stairs. And I wanted to try.

I took a deep breath and entered the room.

As expected, a dozen faces turned my way. They sprawled across couches and sat cross-legged on the floor, chatting and reading and playing video games. The Barbanels all had the same distinctive dark brown hair, thick and impressively curly, and liquid brown eyes with jet-black lashes. They were all very good-looking, which I—as a person best described as "striking"— found simultaneously fascinating and irritating.

Unexpectedly, every last one of them wore a spa mask plastered to their skin, holes exposing their mouths and eyes.

I picked Ethan out of the crowd right away. He sat on the floor, his back against a couch, game controller in his hands, damp white sheet massaged into his face. Something seemed very wrong about it, making him look like a monster with drooping eyes.

From her position lying prone on a couch, Miriam levered herself up. I felt lucky I could recognize her.

"Jordan! Hi."

"Hi," I said cautiously. "Am I interrupting something?"

"What? Oh!" She touched her mask. "Do you want one?"

My gaze unintentionally flicked toward Ethan, who smirked. And damned if I'd let him think I was too embarrassed to wear a face mask in front of him, especially with his own applied so badly. "Sure."

"Iris," Miriam called across the room. "Bring Jordan the basket."

"Get it yourself!" a younger girl—one of the triplets?—replied.

"Iris!"

With a put-upon sigh, the triplet fetched a basket from the far side of the room. Dozens of packets filled it, rose-oil masks and peach masks and an oyster mask. I selected a lemon-scented one.

"Shira brought them from Koreatown," Miriam told me. "Have you met Shira? Have you met everyone?"

"I don't think so."

On the other side of the couch, a girl sat up. "I'm Shira. Hi."

Even with the mask, I could tell she was exceptionally pretty, with fine-boned features and thick lashes and an easy confidence in her posture. She scooted to the middle of the couch so I had space at one end. Unfortunately, this meant I'd be sitting with Ethan at my feet.

He watched, and I imagined he expected me to cede this room to him, to storm off like I had this morning at my dad's office. But I'd ceded enough to Ethan Barbanel. I sat down, tearing my mask pouch open and attempting to plaster it to my face without a mirror.

Ethan smiled. "You look great."

"Your mask is crooked," I told him. "What did you do?"

A green-haired boy cackled. "I'm pretty sure he used the wrong holes." He gave me a nod. "I'm David."

"My brother," Ethan said. "Got another one around here somewhere, too."

"Oliver's out sketching," Shira said. Shira had oldest-girl-cousin vibes. "We're deciding what movie to watch. Any preference?"

This acted as the signal for everyone to haggle intensely until the triplets steamrolled everyone into *Lady Bird*. "We're working our way through Greta Gerwig's oeuvre," one of them told me.

With the movie on, the onus to fit in with the Barbanel clan lifted. Only one thing kept me from totally relaxing: Ethan on the floor at my feet, his shoulder and arm brushing my calf.

Don't think about it, I told myself. I didn't want to pay any attention to Ethan, to feel sparks flaring anywhere our skin brushed. He wasn't some rando to make out with anymore. He was Ethan Barbanel, my father's assistant, who I deeply resented and definitely did not lust after.

But I didn't move my leg. And he didn't move his arm.

* * *

I fell asleep more easily than usual and woke when the sun crept through my window, a little surprised I'd slept through the night. Stretching, I considered the expanse of pale, thin sky. I could see the ocean from plenty of Golden Doors' windows—surely I could find my way there. Pulling on a red bikini (an excellent clearance-rack find) and a black cover-up, I grabbed my beach towel and slipped into the quiet morning.

Birds called, soft and gentle as the light. Conical pines edged the lawn behind Golden Doors; they parted at intervals, allowing people to enter the gardens. I stepped barefoot along stone slabs, gazing at the tree branches stretching into the sky. The path forked. To the right lay wild roses and the peaked roof of a gazebo, but I went left, toward the shimmery blue line of the ocean. The path ended at a bluff, the trees and flowers and undergrowth disappearing as dunes tumbled down toward the brief shore and endless sea. A stone bench, white and worn, perched at the edge beside steep wooden steps built into the yellow-orange sand.

I gripped the handrail tightly as I breathed in the view. The town beach yesterday had been nice, but this stretch of ocean struck me deeper, jolting me hard beneath my rib cage. My lungs inflated with salt and brine. The waves hit the long, thin beach with endless white curls, and the sea went on forever. I wasn't used to islands, where the water curved around you instead of the land hugging the sea; I felt untethered. I imagined launching myself into the air to see if I could fly. My hand tightened on the rail, splinters of wood rough under my palm.

I carefully descended and stepped into the soft, deep sand. Dropping my towel and cover-up, I waded into the ocean. My whole body clenched as the cold water hit my ankles. It was so blue here, the sea paired with the cloudless sky, blue and rippling in all directions. I waded further, Aunt Lou's voice reminding me not to go swimming by myself. But I wouldn't go far, just a dip.

In one brutal, squeezing moment, I sank underwater and came up gasping, salt on my lips. I swam a few laps back and forth, failing miserably at doing the crawl in a straight line, and felt delighted anyway. Eventually, I flipped onto my back, buoyed by the salt and rocked by the waves, and let the water carry me where it would.

When I finally wore myself out, I retreated to the beach and threw myself down on my towel with abandon. This was the life: sun on my skin, cradled by sand, the lap of the water filling my head and gentling my mind. If I could get away with it, I'd peel off my bathing suit and soak in the sun everywhere. I closed my eyes and let my thoughts drift.

The sea rushed toward me and away; the sun sank through me, and I fell asleep.

* * *

"Hey."

A voice startled my eyes open. Ethan Barbanel stood ten feet from me. I pushed myself up on my elbows, wishing I could tug at my bikini bottom to make sure any stray hairs were covered and adjust my top for maximum cleavage. "Hey."

"Nice suit."

Ha, it was, wasn't it. I stretched my arms high, interlocking my fingers above my head. I felt a surge of satisfaction when his gaze fell to my chest. "You think so?"

"I do." He dropped down on my towel by my feet, his long arms draped around his bent knees. "Did you go swimming?"

He wore a boring white T-shirt and board shorts—how did he still look so casually gorgeous? "Yeah."

"You know about riptides?"

"Of course I do. I'm from Massachusetts."

He raised his hands. "Just checking. I'd hate to lose my boss's daughter."

I watched the waves dash themselves against the shore. "You don't have to take care of me."

"I would never," he said, hand over heart.

But apparently that was his instinct. Why? Because my dad had told him about my impulsive nature? Just like he'd told Ethan so much else.

"I can't believe my dad told you about my dating life." Dad could barely talk to *me* about my dating, and I was the one living it. Sure, he'd hugged me and rubbed my head whenever I got dumped, but we rarely had daylight conversations. "What did he say?"

"He didn't really," Ethan admitted. "He, uh . . . sighs a lot."

"*Excuse* me?"

"Not in a bad or judgmental way," Ethan said hurriedly. "More in a—I think the first summer he came here, you'd started dating a boy in a band?"

Oh, wow, I'd almost forgotten. I'd been fourteen at the time and the relationship had been a blip, notable only because Wyatt had been the first boy I'd gone out with who didn't go to my school. It'd been my first summer staying with Aunt Lou, Uncle Jerry, and my cousins. Lauren, the youngest, was two years older than me. She'd let me tag along to parties with her classmates, and I'd met Wyatt at one of them. "I'm not sure either *date* or *band* is technically correct."

"Yeah, well, I remember your dad talking about how excited you were, and then a month later, he was pretty stressed because the two of you had broken up. The next summer, if anyone asked if you were seeing anyone, he would sigh."

"Who even asked?" I said, affronted. Who had I been dating then? Oh, Jason from work, in a messy on-off thing that lasted about three seconds. I'd caught him making out with Lisa H. in the walk-in freezer.

Ethan shrugged. "I dunno. The aunts? I think they thought it was interesting. And they like giving advice."

How horrifying, to think the women at Golden Doors might have been keeping tabs on my dating life. "I'm pretty good at dating, I'll have you know. Not necessarily at being in a relationship, but I can always find someone to go out with."

"Is that so." Ethan grinned and shook his head. "You're a surprise."

He'd mentioned before how I hadn't been what he expected. "What did you think I was going to be like?"

"A really good, sweet girl." He gestured at his shoulders. "Pigtails. Wide eyes."

I snorted. "You're joking."

"A little. But yeah, I thought you'd feel a little younger and more—naive. Like you were swept up by these guys."

"Maybe I am swept up."

He lifted a shoulder and let it drop. "You seem pretty in control to me."

"How so?"

He slid me a glance from beneath half-lowered lids. "You seemed pretty in control on the ferry."

A silence stretched between us, hot and tight and tense, and I wanted to rip it open. I could feel the potential between us, how if one of us moved, the other would respond. I wanted to kiss him the way we had before, to close the gap between us and feel his skin on mine.

I stood abruptly. "I'm going for a swim."

"I'll come too," Ethan said, which had not been my intention.

"Fine." Then, because I was a child, "Last one in's a rotten egg."

"What—"

I ran in, plunging into the water.

"Are you crazy?" Ethan yelled when I surfaced. "It's freezing! Save that shit for September!"

I laughed, pushing my wet hair up and out of my face, spitting out salt. "You a chicken?"

"How dare you. Call me a red junglefowl or call me nothing."

"What—?"

Ethan let out a giant, ridiculous "Cock-a-doodle-do!" and charged screaming into the water. I yelped, falling down to my neck and pushing off the ocean floor, kicking away from him, unable to avoid getting splashed as he landed with what could not have been a comfortable belly flop. He emerged, shaking his hair and grinning.

"You're *so weird*," I said, both alarmed and a bit admiring. "How do you get away with being so weird?"

"It's my dashing good looks," he said. "Also, my family's loaded."

"You're a *lot*," I told him, but I couldn't keep back my snorted laughter. "What's a red junglefowl?"

"It's a chicken before they were domesticated. Basically a chicken with better plumage."

"Why do you know that?"

He gave his sopping hair another shake. The water weighed it down, straightening the curls. It felt oddly intimate to see him like this, like he'd been transformed by the water.

"I know everything."

"Okay, bro." I rolled my eyes. "If you say so."

We swam for half an hour, bobbing and floating. Our conversation was scattered and lazy and easy. I kept telling myself I didn't *like* Ethan Barbanel, but I knew if he hadn't been my father's assistant, I would have liked him a lot.

Eventually we headed back to shore and toweled ourselves dry. "Do you usually come swimming in the morning?" I asked.

"Nah, not really."

"Just feeling inspired today?" When he hesitated, I realized my earlier snark about watching out for me had been spot on. "Wait, were you checking up on me?"

"Definitely not."

"Oh my god. You and my dad. I'm completely competent, you know."

"Your dad's looking out for you."

I bristled at Ethan explaining my own father to me—as though *Ethan* could possibly understand Dad more than I did. "Thanks for the info. I understand my own dad."

"Do you?" His tone shifted. "Because your dad—he's really smart, you know."

"Dude." Didn't Ethan have his own parents? Why did he need to be my dad's favorite, too? "I know. He's *my* dad."

"Right." Ethan held up his hands. "Yeah." His phone buzzed and he glanced at it. "Oops, gotta go."

To Dad's office, probably, to spend the day bonding. I tried to keep the edge from my voice and failed spectacularly. "Spreading the word about century-old mapping techniques?"

He flashed me a grin. "Someone's got to."

"Apparently."

I burned with jealousy as I watched him go.

Then my phone rang.

* * *

A few hours later, I stood in the office of Dr. Cora Bradley, a cramped attic room on top of one of the houses downtown. She was a tall Black woman in a Cornell sweatshirt and leggings, and she studied me quizzically. "I hear you want a job."

"I'd love one. Whatever you have available." The woman who'd called me—the same one I'd talked to yesterday—had told me Dr. Bradley might have an opening and could meet with me at eleven. I'd thrown on a black skirt and shirt I often wore when hostessing at Lulu's and googled the scientist on my ride over. Her bio on Harvard's website linked to her graduate thesis and postdoc research, along with her current specialties. "Your research on classification systems sounds cool."

Dr. Bradley squinted, like she wasn't quite sure what to make of me. "You're in high school still, right? With an interest in astronomy?"

"I'm starting at UMass in the fall. But yes, I've always loved space." I felt like a kid saying this. Of course I loved space! Who didn't love space?!

"What do you know about it?"

What did I know about . . . space? Not as much as I'd like to before an interview. My lack of preparation made me feel nervous and unmoored. "I used to watch meteor showers with my dad growing up, and I know the basics of, like, the Oort cloud and string theory and which planets and moons have ice on them."

"Hm." She leaned back in her chair. According to what I'd found online, she was thirty-eight; she'd done her undergrad in Ithaca and her PhD at Princeton. Her (unlocked!) Instagram account consisted of pictures of her dog and the sunset, and her tagged photos showed her at brunch, as a bridesmaid, on beach vacays, and at conferences. "The intern I was supposed to have bailed, so I have an opening and some funding. It's not sexy work. You'd be doing a lot of data entry and QA—running tests whenever I make a change to my algorithms and comparing it to other people's, generating test results and bug reports."

"Sounds cool," I said, because while I wasn't entirely sure what everything meant, I really wanted this job. "What are all the, um, algorithms and data for?"

"Ah. Yes. I'm working on a comprehensive map of low Earth orbit space debris and the ability to calculate its location at any given moment." She rattled this off like I used to reel off people's orders at Lulu's.

My eyes widened. "Oh. Cool."

"If I can get it to work," she said wryly. "Who's to say."

"And—sorry—QA is . . . ?"

"Quality assurance. Making sure there's no bugs or inaccuracies when you roll out a change. Come look." She pulled up an image on her monitor of Earth suspended against darkness, haloed by a thick glow. Dots clustered around the planet, forming an almost solid golden aura. They became more scattered further out, like sand spread across the floor. The dots also tightened up in a distinct elliptical line around Earth.

"This is a depiction of all the space debris out there," Cora said. "You'll notice there are two distinct fields—the thick cluster in low Earth orbit, and the ring around Earth in geosynchronous Earth orbit. The Department of Defense tracks close to thirty thousand pieces, but there's a lot in low Earth orbit not being tracked. That's what I'm working on. It's smaller, but still dangerous since it moves so quickly. Fifteen thousand miles an hour—about eight hundred times faster than a speeding bullet. Plenty capable of damaging satellites or the International Space Station or space flights."

Wow, as though it wasn't bad enough we'd effed up the earth and oceans, apparently we'd managed to pollute space, too. "That seems . . . bad. How did the trash get out there?"

"It's decommissioned satellites, lost spatulas, paint flecks, all sorts of stuff."

"And if we can track it . . . you could clean it up?"

"Yeah. We'd know where pieces would be at certain times, which would help both with avoiding collisions and cleanup."

She showed me some of the programs I'd be using, and the type of data entry and reports I'd run to double-check her data and to check her predictions against those of other researchers. She didn't ask a ton of questions about my experience, but I tried to shoehorn in examples of being detail oriented and a hard worker whenever possible. After an hour, she sat back. "I could use you three times a week. The pay's not great, but depending on your school's rules we might be able to swing it for credit. I can't promise you'll get to do any original research, though."

"It sounds amazing." My words fell over each other. Was this it? She actually wanted me? "Honestly, usually I seat people at restaurants, so this would be—awesome."

"Great. I'll email you the details and some paperwork to fill out, but otherwise sounds good."

I blinked at her; she stared calmly back. "So . . . that's it, then? I'm in? I have the job?"

A laugh burst out of her. "Yeah. You have the job."

Six

"She was so cool," I babbled to Dad over dinner. We were at the Jetties Beach bar he'd mentioned yesterday, a seaside restaurant with loud music and lots of bright, frozen drinks. I'd grabbed a poke bowl and badgered my long-suffering father into a salad.

I couldn't believe I had a job. A cool job. I felt like a little kid in my excitement about space. Memories of lying on the grass, the black night spread above, suffused me. I hadn't known you could have a job in something you *liked* so much. It felt like cheating.

"I went to the library afterward—the Atheneum." The exterior of the white-columned building made it look alarmingly grand, but inside it had been lined with books and blanketed by comfortable quiet like any other library. I'd gone there for the AC and the Wi-Fi, and because I'd wanted to google Dr. Cora Bradley extensively. I'd ended up googling another woman as well. "Did you know Maria Mitchell—the woman who the science center is named after—was the first American female astronomer? And the Atheneum's first librarian?"

"I did." Dad looked delighted. "I have a whole chapter on her."

"You do?" Shouldn't I know if he had a chapter on a badass lady astronomer? "But—she's not a nautical dude."

He smothered a smile. "No, her family was more academic. Her mother ran a library in 'Sconset, and her father was a teacher and amateur astronomer. He taught all his kids mathematics, Maria especially. By twelve, she was assisting him in calculating a solar eclipse." Dad settled happily into storytelling mode. "At your age, seventeen, Maria opened her own school. She was progressive for the time—three of the first children who enrolled were Black, though local schools were still segregated. Then she became the Atheneum's librarian, which was flexible enough she kept helping her father with astronomy. And then, of course, in 1847, she discovered her comet."

"But I don't see how any of this has anything to do with your book, and the sea," I said. "It's all the sky."

Dad smiled and leaned forward. "Sometimes, they're very close to the same. Remember Bache?"

How could I not? Only this time, I was more curious than usual. "Yeah, Ben Franklin's great-grandson. Who ran the Coast Survey."

Dad nodded. "Bache hired Maria and her dad. He wanted them to establish a cardinal point for latitude and longitude for the US, to help sailors navigate. Maria was the first woman the federal government ever hired in a professional capacity. And later, she worked for the Naval Observatory's Nautical Almanac Office, calculating the orbit of Venus. We've always depended on the sky to navigate the sea. Since the very beginning."

"Celestial navigation," I recalled. Though stars stayed relative to each other, planets moved between them. If sailors knew where a planet would be at a certain time and place, they could tell their own location. When I was little, my father used to point at the sky and tell me if I could find the planets, I could find myself.

"Right. I've got a few chapters on astronomers in this one—Benjamin Banneker, the first Black American astronomer, whose 1790 almanacs charted the sun and moon and predicted weather, and whose tide tables were used by sailors. Tupaia, a Polynesian star navigator trained in immense amounts of knowledge on the cosmos and histories. He joined Captain Cook in the 1760s on the *Endeavour*."

"Like the spaceship?"

Dad smiled. "Like the space shuttle, yes. The space shuttle was named after the ship."

"Oh. Cool." I scraped a bite of quinoa out from the remnants in my bowl. "How come I didn't know you had a chapter on Maria Mitchell? Or any of these guys?"

Dad hesitated, then gave me a wry smile. "I guess we don't talk about my work too much."

Was that true? We talked about the day-to-day stuff—his agent and his editor and print runs and signing. But maybe we didn't talk about the content. "Huh."

He picked at his salad. "I never thought you were particularly interested."

I felt taken aback. Why didn't he think I was interested? Okay, maybe I didn't ask him to recite his chapters verbatim, but I wanted to hear the stories. Was my resentment of the time he spent on Nantucket clearer than I'd thought? I was proud of the books, and proud of my dad for writing them—but maybe it didn't come off that way. "I'm interested."

Dad nodded slowly. "Good to know."

Wow, I was a shitty daughter. What if, when Dad told me he didn't need my help with his research, he hadn't been pushing me away—what if he'd thought I wasn't interested and my offer to help wasn't genuine?

Dad cleared his throat. "On Friday, I thought we'd have dinner with the Barbanels."

Oh no. Abort. "We could," I said warily. "But, counter-argument—we could also not."

"Well." Dad scratched his head, right at the spot his hair began to thin. "They've invited us for Shabbat."

I stared. "Shabbat."

He looked almost embarrassed. "Sometimes when I'm here, I drop by."

Wow, wasn't this a dinner full of whiplash. Dad did Shabbat without me? I couldn't remember the last time Dad did Shabbat *with* me. This felt as bizarre and unlikely as him announcing he moonlighted as a unicycle juggler at a circus. "Shabbat," I said again, carefully. "Hm."

Dad tugged on his neckline, the way he did when flustered. "I thought you might enjoy it."

I probably would enjoy it. I liked Shabbat; I liked feeling part of something bigger than myself. But Dad rarely suggested doing anything religious. We went to Aunt Lou's for the holidays and to temple on the high holidays, but after Mom died, we'd fallen off the Shabbat bandwagon. Mom had been raised Conservative and

Dad cultural; they'd landed on Reform Judaism for our family. But Dad—on his own—disliked organized religion, so now our observances were restricted to holidays.

Which was usually fine by me. Except—every so often I wished I'd had more exposure. At Aunt Lou's, I hated how I was always a step behind everyone for each prayer and gesture. I was embarrassed how I needed to read the transliterated Hebrew, that I never knew what was kashrut or what the minor holidays were. I hated how I felt like I was bluffing my way through anything Jewish.

I'd never really talked to Dad about this because if I did, he'd feel guilty, and besides, what would be the point? We couldn't change the past, and I was basically an adult now. If I wanted to be more involved with Judaism, I could be.

I'd never expected *Dad* to be the one to suggest it.

And the idea of Shabbat with the Barbanels made me nervous. They were proper Jews, who wouldn't accidentally mix up the prayer for bread with the one for wine. I didn't even know the handwashing one. God, I was getting sweaty just thinking about this. And Ethan Barbanel would see me being a disaster. Great.

"Cool," I said, because what else could I say? I had no other plans all summer. "Why not."

After Dad brought me back to Golden Doors, I borrowed a yoga mat from Ethan's mom and took it to the widow's walk. ("The roof walk," she corrected me; maybe there were no widows on Nantucket? Maybe it was like Disney and no one could be declared dead on the property.) I spread the mat across the wooden boards, listening to the roar of the waves in the distance, taking in the glittering ocean under the darkening sky. This was the perfect place for yoga. I could watch the changing colors of the evening as I cycled through the poses, the buoyancy of the backlit clouds as they shifted from yellow to blue, the sky itself turning pink and yellow and orange.

Yoga reminded me to breathe and gave me something to think about—hips tucked, belly pulled toward the spine, head over heart. I liked poses so challenging they pushed every other thought out of my brain, so all I could think in revolved chair pose was *This hurts so much* and in crow, *Hope I don't fall.* Sometimes I didn't want to think. I wanted a blank brain and a body wrung out like a washcloth.

But tonight, no matter how hard I tried, I couldn't completely clear my mind.

Maybe it was good Dad occasionally spent Shabbat with the Barbanels. Maybe it gave him a sense of community. It clearly meant he'd healed enough from losing Mom he could do things that reminded him of her.

I was only four when my mother died of complications from open-chest surgery. I'd been told she downplayed the surgery to her friends. One year, when I was eleven or twelve, my mom's old friend Irene had come over to see my dad on the anniversary of Mom's death. She'd started crying. "I didn't know it was so serious," she'd said, over and over. "I didn't know it could be the end."

Irene, like many of my mom's friends, treated me like a delicate flower. Pain and longing filled their eyes when they stopped by. I hated it because it made me *feel* delicate, when I was in fact all steel and edges. Though that night, with Irene, I only felt fury. How *dare* she make my father comfort her, this night of all nights?

Mom's death was one of the keystones of my existence, but to my secret humiliation, I barely remembered her. Mostly, I remembered the afterward. I remembered the black velvet dress I wore to sit shiva, still folded in a tiny square in a box in my closet at home. I remembered Dad, red-eyed. I remembered how I ate Cinnamon Toast Crunch for breakfast for months when I'd never been allowed sugary cereal before. I remembered the pity.

But we'd made a good life, Dad and I. I liked our life, and I felt happy and complete and whole. And I thought Dad did, too, for the most part. I thought he'd healed enough for another relationship—but he hadn't had one. I worried he focused so much on me, he forgot to focus on himself. I worried he used me as an excuse to not try to form romantic relationships.

Three months ago, we'd been at my aunt's for dinner, and most everyone had been in the dining room eating dessert. I'd popped into the kitchen to refill my water and had come across Dad and Aunt Lou. Dad gazed out the window while Aunt Lou put away a few dishes. They hadn't seen me—the kitchen was funny shaped.

Also, I'd frozen and backed up when I heard my name.

"—anything to upset Jordan," Dad had said.

"She's seventeen," Aunt Lou had replied. "I don't think she'd be upset."

"It's been the two of us for so long. I don't want to introduce any complications . . ."

"Tony. I'm not suggesting you spring a mail-order bride on her. Just sign up for an app."

"I don't even know what apps to use."

I could practically hear Aunt Lou rolling her eyes. "It's not that hard. You want a romantic relationship, right? You've said so before. It's not going to drop into your lap. You have to be active about it."

Dad's voice had quieted. "Jordan needs me. I get nervous about her . . ."

So that had been horrifyingly alarming to hear, and it made me realize I had to get my act together, stat. No more unstable hookups, no more crying jags after bad breakups. Just nice, happy Jordan. Stable, mature Jordan. No messiness.

So I wouldn't be messy about Shabbat, either. It would be another point in favor of me being normal and healthy.

How hard could it be?

* * *

I'd almost finished my yoga video when I heard the door open. I was folded in gomukhasana, cow face pose. Knees wrapped and stacked on top of each other, torso bent. I turned my head slightly to see the intruder. Ethan.

He looked taken aback. "Hey. Sorry, didn't mean to interrupt."

In tune with the gentle, soothing voice of the YouTube instructor, I unraveled my legs and took a cat-cow. "Come to check out my moves?"

He smiled briefly. "I was sent to let you know there's an ice cream bar being set up."

An ice cream bar. Was this family for real? But also, sweet.
Literally. "I'm almost done." I stretched my legs out to either side
and bent forward, resting my forearms and head on the ground.

I heard Ethan sit beside me. He stayed there, silent, and when
I came back to a seated position I saw him with his back to the
wall, staring up at the cobalt sky, the piercing stars and wax-
ing moon. He turned. "Your dad told me you got a job about
astronomy."

A small knot released inside my chest. Dad must have thought
the internship was impressive if he'd bothered to tell Ethan about
it. "Yeah."

Ethan gave a chin nod toward the heavens. "So what've you
got?"

"What, like do I have stars in my pocket to show off?"

He laughed, then pointed to the sky. "I've got the Big Dipper.
Sometimes I say I can see the Little Dipper, too, but mostly because
people are super insistent I see it and I want them to move on."

"Ah." I smiled, reluctantly endeared to him. "You see the two
stars forming the edge of the rectangle of the Big Dipper furthest
from the tail?"

"Man, you want me to see it, too." He peered skyward. "Yeah."

"Those are the pointer stars. Dubhe and Merak. If you follow
them in a line, they lead to Polaris, which begins the handle of
the Little Dipper."

"Sure," he said dubiously. "Polaris is the North Star, right?"

"Right. Can you see it?"

"Maaaybe. Oh! Yeah!" He swiveled to look at me, grinning.
"Nice."

"Wanna know a trick? At twilight, when you can see both the North Star and the horizon, you can figure out your latitude." I held out a hand, made a fist, and then stacked my other fist atop it. Then I moved my first fist to the top, and my other hand on top of that, so I'd measured four fists between the horizon and the star. "Each fist is ten degrees."

He did the same thing as I had. "So we're at forty degrees latitude?"

"Exactly. I mean, not exactly, roughly, but yeah. It's part of celestial navigation. The fist method."

He grinned at me. "Sounds dirty."

"Ethan."

"It's not my fault, it's how I've been socialized."

I shook my head, a small smile escaping. "You said you're writing about Gibson's comet for my dad." I lifted my gaze back to the sky, as though expecting to see a ball of icy rock burning across the heavens. "You must know a little about astronomy, too, then."

"I'm actually not writing anything comet-related. I'm writing about Gibson before he discovered the comet, in the early nineteen hundreds. Your dad has a whole chapter on one of his colleagues, and since Gibson's got a Nantucket angle, we're including him. I'm writing a sidebar."

"That's really cool, you writing your own thing."

"You think so?"

"Yeah." Ethan Barbanel's existence might annoy me, but my dad's nerdiness had rubbed off: good research and hard work seemed cool.

"Thanks." He cleared his throat, and I wondered if it was a nervous habit he'd picked up from my father. "He's spent a lot of time teaching me. It's really meant a lot."

My stomach twisted, a hard, vicious yank tightening up my insides. The goodwill and friendliness I'd begun extending toward Ethan vanished.

It would have meant a lot to me, too, if Dad had bothered spending time with me. But why would he, with Ethan around? Ethan was friendly and easygoing and interested in the same things as Dad. Why wouldn't Dad pick him?

I swallowed the threatening tears and looked at the stars, fixing on the Arbor constellation. "You know what, I'm not in the mood for ice cream. But you should go back down."

In my peripheral vision, I could see confusion on Ethan's face. God, did Ethan Barbanel ever not broadcast exactly what he was feeling? How nice, to go through life in a world where you could be open about everything.

"What's wrong?" he asked. "Did I say something?"

"No."

"You're upset."

"I'm fine."

"No, you were laughing a minute ago—"

"Can you just *go*?" I bit out.

He drew back, startled. "Why are you so *prickly* all the time?"

"Why do you think?" I raked my hair out of my face, fingers digging into my scalp as though they could alleviate the pressure inside my head. "You have *two* parents. Why do you get mine as well?"

It almost hurt, the way his face softened. "I'm not trying to steal your dad."

"Well, you did, okay? You did, and now you have him, and I don't." Completely without my permission, tears slipped out. I closed my eyes, humiliated, keeping my face tipped to the stars as though that would keep the tears inside. It didn't.

I might have sat there crying silently forever if Ethan hadn't shifted next to me and wrapped his arm around my shoulder, pulling me into his side. Part of me thought I should shove him away, but a stronger part craved the contact, and I melted into him as he ran his hand in comforting strokes up and down my arm. He produced a crumpled Dunkin' napkin from his pocket. "Here."

"Thanks." I wiped my eyes and blew my nose with a long, honking noise I would've been embarrassed of at any other time. Then I leaned my head against his shoulder, drained. "I'm sorry. I'm a mess."

"It's okay." His hand continued to stroke my skin. "I didn't realize there was so much . . . emotion involved. I thought you were in a mood because you weren't back home with your friends. I didn't realize it was because . . . of me. And your dad."

I tried for a huff of laughter. "Usually I keep it tamped down better."

"You shouldn't need to."

"Really?" I lifted my head and gave him a wry look. "You think it's okay for me to yell at someone because I'm jealous he has my dad's attention?"

"More like, tell your dad how you feel."

Tell him . . . what? Tell Dad I felt awful because he spent more time with Ethan than me? Then I'd probably cry, and Dad would feel horrible and think he was a bad parent, which I never wanted him to think. I was the bad one, not him. "One hundred percent definitely not. Please. We don't talk about feelings."

"My mistake."

I leaned back and stared at the sky, at the diamond-bright stars, at the nothingness. "Usually I find better ways to cope when I'm, I don't know, feeling chaotic."

"Like what?"

I shrugged wryly. "Like hooking up with strangers to make me feel better."

His eyes snapped to mine.

And I remembered how it had felt. How his lips had sealed so perfectly against mine, how he'd tugged me close and his warmth had spread into mine. I could tell, too, how easy it would be to kiss him right now. I wanted to, more than I'd wanted anything in a long time.

But I had some pride left, and you don't throw yourself at some-one right after you've been sobbing on their shoulder. "Maybe we should make some ice cream sundaes."

He nodded and stood. "Will you do me a favor?"

"Depends on the favor."

"I'm not trying to take care of you or anything, I swear. But if you go on any more morning swims, will you knock on my door and invite me along?"

I almost snapped at him, told him he *was* trying to look out for me and I didn't need it—but actually, his offer was kind of nice.

I didn't feel like being prickly all the time. And I didn't want to die in a riptide. And I kind of liked spending time with Ethan Barbanel.

"Okay, I suppose." When he smiled at me and offered his hand, I took it and let him draw me to my feet. Together we went back into the warm glow of Golden Doors, and downstairs to eat ice cream sundaes.

Seven

I showed up at Dr. Bradley's office at 9:00 a.m. the next day.
"Jesus, you're prompt," she said, squinting at me. "Isn't
this your summer vacation? Shouldn't you be staying up until
midnight and sleeping until eleven to restore your sleep bank?"

I stared at her blankly. *Adults, man.* "I'm used to waking up at
six for school." This morning, I'd woken at six and knocked on
Ethan's door, and we'd gone down for a dip in the ocean. I'd been
surprised by how comfortable it'd felt.

"Cruel and unusual punishment," she muttered. "Thank god
I'll never have to do that again." She waved a hand at the room's
second seat, a wobbly-looking wooden chair. "You can sit . . .
there."

I sat and took in the office. A disaster, like Dad's at home,
which I found reassuring. My chair had an uneven leg; I'd need
to stuff a wad of papers under it at my first possible chance.

I waited for instructions. I was ready to do whatever grunt
work Cora wanted—data entry, scrub the windows, get a breakfast sandwich. But Cora simply stared right back at me, clutching
an exceedingly large coffee mug.

Finally, she spoke. "Okay, so, you should probably start with some background reading . . ."

"I'm reading your dissertation." I'd started at two in the morning, when I'd woken and been unable to fall back asleep.

She blinked. "You are? How did you even find it?"

"It's online."

"It should be under lock and key." She shook her head. "Okay, well. Why don't I give you an overview and set you up."

She did, and I got started on background reading. Which was, frankly, a little terrifying. Apparently space was a junkyard no one had jurisdiction over. Old satellites, rocket parts, fuel tanks, and other debris floated endlessly. Every time anything collided in space, it created more debris, which increased the chance of the International Space Station or satellites or tsunami warning systems or anything else up there getting harmed.

"Dr. Bradley?" I asked when she took a break to make more coffee.

"You can call me Cora."

Interesting proposition; I'd probably avoid calling her anything. "Okay. I have a question. People know about this, right? You know about it, I assume the government and the EPA know—why isn't more being done?"

She tilted her head, as though waiting for me to expound.

"If we know it's bad, why are billionaires allowed to send up stuff that gets turned into trash during space storms?" I hadn't even known solar storms existed until today; now I knew the sun, usually consistent, occasionally ejected solar material capable of messing with Earth's magnetic field and knocking a satellite out of orbit. "Why aren't we talking about space debris and cleaning it up or telling people they can't launch whatever they want into space?"

"Mm." She stirred some cream into her coffee. "Well, it's hard for people to look further than the immediate future, at how this could impact our ability to explore space. And there's no regulation for what people can do—no one owns space. It's like the Wild West."

"The final frontier," I murmured.

She grinned. "Exactly. And some of us are talking about how to clean it up. Giant nets, magnets, spacecraft capable of pushing deactivated satellites into the atmosphere so they burn up. Harpoons, even. But they're wildly expensive to build. Also, you need people to agree to them. Imagine if the US said it was going to send up a harpoon to take down a decommissioned satellite—other countries might be wary, because what's to stop us from taking down one of their working satellites?" She took a sip of coffee. "It becomes a huge international problem."

"So do we need a . . . space committee? Who's in charge of space?"

"There's regional programs. We have NASA, and there's the European Space Agency. Russia, China, Japan, India all have their own programs. Getting them to work together . . ." She shrugged.

"Okay, so . . ." I rubbed my forehead. "We have to figure out where all the debris is, find a way to pick it all up, fund it, and get governments all over the world to sign off."

"Great." Cora smothered a smile. "I look forward to chairing your thesis committee in ten years."

"What?"

"Bad joke," she said, still laughing to herself.

I eyed her. Sounded like the kind of joke Dad made.

"Do you want to get lunch?" Cora asked. "I thought we'd go out since it's your first day."

I brightened. "Yeah, let's."

We walked to a sandwich shop on the edge of a park. "There's walking paths and boardwalks through there." Cora nodded at the thickening woods as we took our sandwiches to a picnic table. "It used to be a pond or a bog or something."

"Cool." I took a bite of my pickle, savoring the briny flavor. "How did you end up on Nantucket? How long have you been here?"

"Nantucket has a whole history of astronomy. This is my second summer here—I've got the funding for one more, too."

"Did you always want to be an astrophysicist?" I almost tripped over the consonants.

She didn't laugh at me. "I was always interested in space. What about you? Do you know what you want to major in?"

From most people, I hated this question, but Cora seemed genuinely interested—and also, I was a bit in awe of her. "I dunno. Something with numbers." There was a beauty to equations, the way they always worked out in the end, the way they could make sense of the world. I thought if we knew enough about math, we could explain life itself, the way we'd explained the tides and the planets and the seasons.

As we walked back into town after lunch, Dr. Bradley stumbled to a halt. I glanced over to see her gazing fixedly at a man walking toward us. "Let's cross here," she said, and sped across the road despite the lack of crosswalk.

I jogged after her. "Who was that?" I asked after a block. "Bad date?"

She grimaced apologetically. "Yeah, actually. Not in the mood for awkward small talk."

"Relatable."

So Cora was dating. Cora was a smart, ambitious woman, who dated men, and she was only a few years younger than Dad. Good to know.

We returned to the office, and the afternoon hours fell away. Cora showed me how to pull reports comparing her latest location-calculating algorithms with those of colleagues making similar efforts and how to check them over. This had to be done any time she made a change in her calculations, to make sure nothing had been thrown out of whack. We mostly worked in silence, but every so often Cora came across something she thought I ought to know and called me over to explain it. Twice, other researchers stopped by to chat.

As the afternoon wound down, Dad texted to see when I wanted to be picked up before we headed to Golden Doors for Shabbat. I glanced at Cora. "What time are you heading out?"

"Five-ish today," she said. "And I know we talked about you being nine-to-five, but it's fine if you ever have to come in late or leave early. I'm here until ten some days, so don't try to keep to my schedule."

"Okay," I said. "But—today you're leaving at five?"

"Yeah, on Fridays I like to pretend I have some work-life balance."

Big goals.

It took some maneuvering to walk out at the same time as Cora, but I managed it, telling Dad I was running a few minutes late so I could wait for my boss to be ready. Outside, I pretended not to see Ethan's Jeep waiting at the curb; pretended not to feel my phone buzzing in my pocket. Instead I kept Cora chatting until Dad climbed out of the passenger seat. "Jordan!"

"Dad, hi!" My gaze ran over him, evaluating. Worn jeans, blue T-shirt—faded, but luckily unstained by laundry bleach, and with minimal holes. His hair—what little you could see of it from underneath his once blue, now gray Red Sox hat—flew out horizontally.

Not precisely the outfit I'd have suggested wearing when meeting my hot, accomplished boss for the first time, but since he'd had no idea 1) he'd be meeting her, or 2) I now had an agenda regarding them, I'd give him a pass. He looked okay, even if he was wearing socks with his sandals. Sometimes you couldn't save someone from themselves.

"This is my dad," I said to Cora, making no move toward him, so he had to cross the road to us. He did, a fleeting, almost fearful look on his face. Ha. I smiled when he reached us. "Dad, this is my boss, Dr. Bradley."

They shook hands. "I'm Cora."

"Tony."

"Cora's mapping space debris," I said. "My dad's also doing research here. He's working on a book."

"Really. What's the book about?"

"Uh—" Dad cleared his throat. "It's about, uh—Each chapter focuses on a different individual who contributed, during the sixteenth through early twentieth century, to advancing the field of maritime navigation and cartography—"

Good lord. Dad was usually much better at his elevator pitch. "He wrote an article for *The Atlantic* about Benjamin Franklin and his Nantucket family members mapping the Gulf Stream," I butted in. "It went viral."

Dad hung his head; Cora's face lit up. "I read that! You wrote it?"

"Yeah." Dad brought his hand up to the back of his head.

"That's great," Cora said. "I'm going to have to check it out again."

Dad grimaced. "Oh, uh, thanks."

Time to get out before more awkwardness commenced. "Okay," I chirped. "Thanks, Dr. Bradley, see you Monday!"

I hustled my dad toward the Jeep. Ethan twisted toward me from the front passenger seat. "How was your first day?"

"Just dandy. Except for the fact that we seem as set on polluting space as we are on polluting Earth."

Ethan looked alarmed. "That sounds bad."

"You're not wrong." I wanted to ask Dad what he'd thought of Cora, but if he thought I was trying to set him up, he'd probably never speak to her again. Instead, I had to be subtle. I had to arrange for them to be in each other's presence by seeming happenstance. Adults were very fragile. You had to make everything seem like their idea.

At Golden Doors, Dad and I were swiftly separated. The adults whisked him off, while Ethan and I were corralled into helping with dinner. Cooking fell into the teens' purview at Golden Doors; as far as I could tell, the adults never made dinner, instead treating themselves to a cocktail hour while the kids cooked everything.

"It's their greatest scam," Shira told me as we husked corn, pulling the silky strands away from yellow and white kernels. "It's why they procreated."

"I think they're playing an even longer con," Iris said from further down the counter. She and the other triplets chopped heirloom tomatoes, dark red mottled with green, each segment so juicy I struggled not to grab them all. "They say we'll be rewarded by forcing our own offspring to cook for us down the line. But really it's a psychological trick to condition us into wanting kids so they'll have grandchildren."

This caused the older teens to exchange terrified glances. It caused *me* to stare at Iris in wonder. I liked anyone who thought in terms of generational long cons.

Dinner was crusty French country bread, tomato-basil bruschetta, grilled corn gazpacho, and peach salad with goat cheese. Everyone filled their plates before heading outside to picnic tables. I found myself crammed in at a table with Ethan and the rest of the cousins his age—his brothers, green-haired David and artsy Oliver; wide-eyed Miriam; and the New York pair, Shira and Noah.

Dad sat with Ethan's parents as well as the OG Mr. and Mrs. Barbanel—ninetysomething Helen and her husband, Edward.

Helen Barbanel led the prayers. At our table, Shira offered to let me light our two white pillars, and when I declined did so herself. The rest of the prayers were familiar, even if I'd forgotten some of them. But I remembered how much Dad always liked the blessing for children, even if we hadn't done it forever.

I'd been nervous about Shabbat, but this was so normal, so easy. Dinner stretched long, the sun sinking below the horizon in a dying burst of color well past eight. Afterward, everyone idly milled about, some sipping drinks, others playing cornhole. Without the sun, the temperature dropped rapidly. It was still mid-June, not even officially summer until next week, and this close to the water the sea breeze cooled everything down.

Shira, Miriam, and I sat on lounge chairs and plucked dark red cherries from the bowl on the coffee table. "There's a party tonight," Shira said. "If you want to come."

"I absolutely want to come. I have no plans basically forever." I bit into a cherry, closing my eyes at the sweetness, then opening them to admire the deep, opaque ruby of the fruit.

"Can I come too?" Miriam asked from Shira's other side.

Shira frowned at her fifteen-year-old cousin. "I don't know . . ."

"Please," Miriam said. "I'll be so well-behaved."

"Hm."

"What time it's at?" I asked.

Shira checked her phone. "We'll probably leave in half an hour."

"Nice. Let me say bye to my dad and change into something warmer." And cooler.

I found Dad talking earnestly with Ethan's parents and grand-parents around the firepit. I perched on the edge of his Adirondack chair, listening for an opening in their conversation.

"And do you really think *Ethan* should give the talk?" Ethan's father was saying, looking incredulous. "If your funding depends on it?"

"I wouldn't say the funding *depends* on it," Dad said, laughing this off, though I gave Ethan's dad a sharp look. I wouldn't have been thrilled by my own father sounding so surprised by my capabilities—probably because he often was. "I'm the one submitting the proposal. But Ethan has been doing the research on Frederick Gibson, and it's just a little talk, part of mine—it'll be a good experience for him."

"It's very kind of you," Ethan's dad said. "But don't feel like you have to let him."

"I don't," Dad said.

"What talk?" I asked.

The adults looked at me like they hadn't noticed I was there. Classic. "The Gibson Foundation is going to be hosting a conference in August," Dad said. "Mostly it's a fundraiser—a few talks, a dinner—but they're also taking meetings for grant proposals."

Ah, *grants*, a magical word. Sing, o muse, of the ingenious hero with plentiful funding. Grants were a big deal in Dad's world. Sure, his publisher paid him for his books, but not enough to live on. He was always applying to different institutions, writing long pages about why he was worthy. The public school he taught at paid him, sure, but teachers' salaries were nothing to write home about. To afford all his re-creations of historical methods—not to mention, say, his daughter's upcoming college education—he needed an extra income stream.

I wanted to ask Dad how much the grant was for and if he thought he had a chance at it. If getting it meant we wouldn't have to sell our house. But I wouldn't embarrass Dad by bringing up money in front of the Barbanels, who probably valued grants for prestige, not financing.

"Cool," I said instead, and turned to Ethan's parents. "You must be proud of Ethan, for his talk."

They looked surprised. "Uh, yes, we are," his mom said.

Weird vibe. I turned to Dad. "I'm gonna go hang out with Shira. See you tomorrow?"

"We'll get brunch," he promised. "What are you guys up to?"

"Just hanging."

"Have fun," he said. We hugged, and I smiled and headed out to see what Nantucket parties had to offer.

Eight

I found myself crammed in a Jeep with half a dozen Barbanels, a mess of long limbs and curly dark hair and loud, demanding voices. They had no conception of personal space. It made my heart hurt a little, and I missed my cousins, and my best friend, Grace, and our other friends back home.

We parked at a beach—I had no idea which one, my tentative familiarity with the island vanquished by the darkness—and scrambled down a narrow path in the dunes to the wide expanse of sand. The ocean at night washed over me, the darkness of everything beyond the shore, the sprinkle of stars, the blaze of small fires. Anything could happen at the beach at night. The whole world could unravel.

I'd changed into black pants and a high-necked top with intricate lacework, paired with my sturdy vegan-leather jacket. Winged eyeliner and red lipstick finished the look and made me feel more like myself. I followed the Barbanels toward one of the fires, a slight unease pervading me.

I wasn't usually bad at parties.

In fact, I usually loved parties. I loved the energy, the press of people, the excitement. I loved getting ready: trying on an outfit or ten, crammed in front of one mirror with three friends. I loved trying weird styles of makeup we'd never done before, blasting the getting-ready playlist Grace and I had been curating since eighth grade, and pausing when "Stay With Me" came on so we could dramatically sing to each other.

I loved the *possibility* each party offered, even though half the time the kids were the same as always. Still, sometimes someone would sneak in alcohol and some nights it almost felt like we'd *achieved* what life was supposed to feel like. Like we'd reached the pinnacle of human experience all those movies and ads and other people's social media kept telling us existed, where we were surrounded by love and friends and excitement and possibility.

Maybe that's why I felt so uncomfortable here. Because I wasn't surrounded by any of those things.

Instead, I was an outsider. Not just an outsider, but kind of an angry one with the wrong kind of clothes. At home I wasn't weird, or it didn't matter if I was weird because all my friends were too. Sure, preppy kids existed, but they had their own parties. And I wasn't so bitter at home because I had my friends, and more to think about than how my dad didn't want to have anything to do with me and how no one wanted to date me for longer than it took to get in my pants.

Anyway. No time to spiral. Time to pay attention.

I might have stuck by Shira, but she immediately joined a very beautiful boy, the kind of gold-touched boy you often found at the center of these groups. He and Shira wandered to the edge of the party. I wasn't surprised Shira's boyfriend was as good-looking as she was: pretty people flocked together, after all. I was more surprised by a normal girl in a red romper who bounded up to the Barbanels. She gave Noah, the oldest of the cousins, a quick smack on the lips before slipping comfortably under his arm.

Great. I was surrounded by couples.

This was perhaps an unfair thing to be irritated by, given how often I was snuggled up against someone myself. But it felt different. I *felt* single. It had been ages since I'd had anything solid and real. Even Louis, my last real boyfriend, always made me feel like he was doing a favor by dating me.

The girl in the romper towed Noah over. "Hi!" The exclamation filled her body as well as her voice. "I'm Abby. You're Jordan, right? Noah says you're staying at Golden Doors."

"Hey. Yeah. Are you also here for the summer?"

"Yeah, I work at one of the bookstores. And you're Ethan's boss's daughter, right?"

"Do you know my dad?"

"No, but Ethan talks about him all the time. Here, come meet my friends."

Abby gave me girl-next-door vibes. I liked her and her friends. Her roommate, Jane, was a sharply sarcastic Black girl dressed head to toe in Madewell; their other friends consisted of Lexi—a short white girl with an undercut—and her girlfriend, Stella, an Asian American girl with a high ponytail, dark red lip, and denim overalls.

After an hour and two drinks I'd relaxed into their group, even though I'd lost sight of all Barbanels. At least forty or fifty kids spread around the blankets, and a dance pit had formed by someone's portable Sonos. "Wanna dance?" Abby asked.

"I always want to dance."

We lost ourselves in the music. I swayed back and forth, surrounded by these girls who weren't yet my friends but maybe could be, letting everything wash over me: the thrum of music, my pulsing blood, the sway of my hips. It smelled like sea brine and woodsmoke. People's arms threaded through the air, their movements loose, their hands curved around each other's hips. The trill of excited conversation and an occasional shout cut above the music. It felt familiar and easy, and for one of the first times since I'd arrived on Nantucket, I fully relaxed.

After an hour or so, I made my way to the drinks cluster and downed four cups of water in rapid succession, sitting on a closed cooler. I was desperately going to need to pee in about twenty minutes. C'est la vie.

Ethan joined me. "Having a good time?"

I considered, breathing in the night. "Yeah. Are you?"

He shrugged, then nodded.

I leaned back on my hands. "I hear you're giving a talk for my dad."

Ethan looked at me quickly, then blushed. "Oh. Uh. Yeah."

"That's pretty cool."

He ducked his head, almost shyly. "Thanks."

Shy. As though not enough people had told him it was cool. "Can I ask you a question? You don't have to answer."

He gave me a lopsided grin. "You're scaring me."

I smiled back, not wanting to come off as too judgmental of his family. "I was wondering—what's up with your parents? They sounded weird about you working for my dad. As though my dad was doing it out of pity."

"Ah. That." He stared straight ahead. For the first time since I'd met him, no merriment animated his face, and his profile was hard and unexpectedly stark without it. "They probably think he is."

"Why? My dad thinks you're brilliant."

Ethan's face swung toward mine. "Yeah?"

"Yeah. And I'm pretty sure slackers don't sign up to be historian's assistants for four summers in a row."

"They might if all they did was go out on ship excursions."

I frowned, not liking the self-recrimination in his voice, as though he didn't give himself credit for anything he did. "Sure, but I'm pretty certain you mostly do endless research."

"Yeah." His voice was lighter this time. "Weird, I guess."

I studied this boy, who I resented and who I desired, who aggravated me and who made me laugh. I'd thought I'd figured him out before I came here: a pompous rich boy. Then I'd thought I'd figured out the boy on the boat: a carefree playboy. But maybe I hadn't figured Ethan Barbanel out at all.

He turned toward the sea, looking out at the dark, rolling waves. "You asked why I was working for your dad, a few days ago. Honestly . . . he was the first person to take me seriously. My family thinks I'm a goof."

"You are a goof. You yelled 'cock-a-doodle-do' while running into the ocean. That doesn't mean you can't also be serious about things."

"Wow. How very—I don't know, adult of you."

"I spent a lot of time in therapy." I shrugged. "You know. The dead mom thing."

Ethan looked like he'd been struck. "I'm sorry. That sucks."

"I know," I said, because everyone was always sorry, and it did suck. "Thank you."

"Did, uh—did the therapy help?"

"Think about how much *more* of a mess I'd be if I hadn't gone," I said lightly. "How did you know my dad would take you seriously? I mean, what made you decide to work with him in the first place?"

Ethan sat on the cooler next to me. "Let's see. I was sixteen. My parents were on me about college and what extracurriculars I needed. I'd done an adventure camp the past couple summers— camper, then CIT. But my family said I should work at the family firm, to round out my activities." He made a face.

"Not your cup of tea?"

"I'm not really a numbers kind of guy. Everyone expected Noah to be the one involved in the company anyway, so I dragged my feet."

I couldn't tell if this meant Ethan didn't want any part of it, or if he didn't think the family wanted him. "Did you *want* to be involved in the company?"

Ethan mock shuddered. "Definitely not. Too much responsibility."

I shot him a look. "Come on."

"What?"

"I just told you I don't buy your 'I'm a carefree goof and nothing more' vibe."

Surprise flickered across his face, and he gave me a somewhat twisted smile. "Everyone else does."

"I guess everyone else doesn't see how hard my dad works you, then."

"Thanks." He paused. "Okay, maybe . . . I didn't want to disappoint anyone? I wouldn't have been good at the job, and my family would have been disappointed in me, and I—I didn't want to be a failure, you know?"

His words squeezed at my chest. "I don't think you could be a failure to your family."

"Yeah, well. I'm not driven the way they are. I can't sit still for nine hours a day and look at Excel and have it make sense." He shook his head, like he was shaking the whole thing off. The wind off the sea was strong, and we both briefly shivered in a particularly cold gust. "Your dad did stuff I like—he goes out on the water, explores, experiments—and he has so much energy, you know? I knew as soon as we talked I wanted to work with him."

I wanted to say his family should appreciate him, should understand there were different ways of being smart, but Ethan wasn't the one who needed the lecture. "My dad says you're majoring in archaeology."

Ethan brightened. "Yeah. It's all about answering questions and figuring out how people work. And it's outdoorsy and active and makes you think."

"It sounds perfect."

"It kind of is." He wrapped his arms around his knees and directed his words to them, a little quietly. "Are we good, after last night?"

I flashed back to yelling at him and crying on the roof walk, and gave him a wry smile. "I should probably be the one asking you."

"I just . . . I don't want you to think I'm trying to take your place with your dad. He clearly adores you."

I looked out at the ocean, swallowing. "Thanks."

"And . . . I want us to be friends. It's nice, talking to you. I don't feel pressure. I dunno. Maybe it's because to you, I'm your dad's assistant instead of a Barbanel? It feels like you *expect* me to be smart."

It hurt my heart a little, the way he described other people's view of him. I didn't want to let on though; I didn't think he'd respond well to pity. "Like I said, my dad thinks you're brilliant. So you must be."

He smiled, broad and honest and innocent, and for the first time, I felt like there was no pretense between us, no walls or games or angles. Just a girl and a boy, on a beach, in the night, breathing in the salty, cool air.

"Hey, Ethan." A girl stood before us, with a pointed, elven chin, wide eyes, and short dark hair. "Good to see you."

In a split second, Ethan switched his attention to the girl, focusing on her like a spotlight on a Broadway star. "Dawn. You look great."

Irritation spiked through me, which was a bad sign. I should have been relieved by the interruption. I shouldn't have wanted to throw sand at this girl's face. This was a good reminder: Ethan didn't like *me*, he liked flirting. And I didn't want to fall for someone like that this summer. Or ever again.

"Thanks." She took a step closer. "How was your semester?"

"It was good, yeah. Yours?"

"Great."

They smiled at each other, and Dawn's gaze darted to me expectantly, then back to Ethan. "Okay, well, maybe I'll see you later."

"Yeah. Totally."

She walked away, ruffling her hair, and I watched Ethan watch her go. I spoke lightly. "I think you were supposed to introduce us."

"You could have introduced yourself." He grinned. "Besides, if we did introductions, she would have stuck around longer."

I raised my brows. "You didn't want her to?"

He shrugged. In the moonlight, he looked like a statue gilded in silver. "I like my current company."

Butterflies danced within me. Oh no.

Because I knew how to respond to that, and I *wanted* to respond by flirting back. The problem with me and Ethan, I was beginning to realize, was we were too much alike. We found flirting easy and comfortable. It was our default.

I turned away, pulling my knees to my chest. It was the alcohol, and the pitch-black ocean, and the moon making me drop my guard. The moon drove people mad, they used to say. "I have a goal this summer."

"A goal," Ethan echoed.

"Yeah. You know how you mentioned my—messy dating record? I don't want to be messy anymore." I wasn't sure if I was warning him away or making a promise to the universe. "No more chaotic choices. Like hooking up with strangers."

"What about non-strangers?"

I tried not to think about our encounter on the ferry, about how much I'd liked his heat, his solidness, his hands. "No," I said firmly. "I have to take a break. I suck at dating, even casually, since I always fall for whoever I'm hooking up with. I like them more than they like me, and I get my heart broken. And I'm really tired of trying to put it back together."

He looked at me a long moment, the moonlight pouring over him. "I see."

I could hear the party around us, the thump of the music, the roar of laughter and yelling, all underscored by the ceaseless roar of the surf. His eyes were bright and steady, and I wondered what he saw, or thought he did. If he understood how hard I could fall for him if I let myself, and how I refused to do so.

He glanced away first. "Well, I'm an expert at getting my heart broken. I get it broken all the time."

"Seriously?"

"Yup." He flashed a grin. "I'm like Humpty-Dumpty with my heart."

"Are you? Because they couldn't put Humpty-Dumpty together again."

Ethan blinked. "Oh. Right. Okay, I'm Humpty-Dumpty 2.0. I get better and faster at piecing my heart back together every time it gets smashed."

SUMMER NIGHTS AND METEORITES

I would have expected Ethan to do the heartbreaking, not the other way around. "Who's broken your heart?"

"Who hasn't?" Ethan said lightly. He ticked the first off on his finger. "Sophia Cooper. Told me she wanted someone smart, not a dumb jock."

"Are you serious? She called you a dumb jock?"

"Nah, but she said I only thought about lacrosse. In my defense, it was the height of the season. Trinity Chen," he continued, unfolding another finger. "Told me I wasn't serious enough. *I* thought I was serious, but apparently not. Ashley Shields. Dumped me for Brian Campedelli. He got into MIT early decision. Maya Perez. Told me she was looking for a real relationship."

I felt insulted on Ethan's behalf. "These girls sound mean."

"Nah." He rubbed the back of his neck. "They just had their own view of things."

"Well, they sound like jerks."

He smiled briefly. "What about your broken hearts?"

"Oh, wow, let's see." I leaned back on my hands. "My last real boyfriend broke up with me at Thanksgiving. Then I had a huge crush on this boy at work, who ghosted me. After him, I had a friend-with-benefits who I ended up liking, even though he was kind of a jerk. He ghosted me, too, but he went to my school so it was harder. Then he showed up at prom with a real girlfriend, which was salt in the wound."

"Wow."

"Yeah. Before Louis—my ex—I dated two guys junior year, both of whom I thought were, like, my soulmate—but they both dumped me. The summer between sophomore and junior year

109

I was obsessed with this guy at the diner, but we spent half our time fighting. So on and so forth. Apparently I'm bad at picking people."

He was quiet a moment. "Sorry. Sounds like a lot of shitty experiences."

"That's life, isn't it?" I tried to sound less weary than I felt. I shook it off, tired of the subject, tired of being the kind of person I apparently was, a person who was easy to hook up with and easy to abandon. I expected Ethan was equally tired of being considered a goof by both his family and his girlfriends. "You should tell your parents to take you more seriously. They shouldn't dismiss how hard you work."

He smiled wryly at the stars. "You should tell your dad you want to spend more time with him."

I rolled my eyes. "Fine. We've reached a standstill. Neither of us will properly communicate with our parents."

"Sounds good to me." To my surprise, Ethan covered my hand with his own, giving it a small squeeze. I had no idea what he meant by it—a shared understanding, a flirtation, an accident— but it made my chest ache. Maybe neither of us was honest with our parents, but at least we'd been honest with each other. The wind and moonlight and sea had stripped us bare, and there were no more pretenses between me and Ethan Barbanel.

Nine

On Monday, Cora arrived at her office an hour after me, sweeping in in a whirl of raindrops and giant hair. Outside, a summer storm raged, hurling fat raindrops against the roof. I was glad it had held off through the weekend, which I'd spent lying on different beaches with the Barbanel cousins and their friends. Now a torrential downpour had decimated the sunshine, water flung about by howling wind. I liked it, the rage of the storm, especially from safe inside. I felt cozy and calm, with my browser full of tabs and my steaming mug of coffee.

I'd spent the morning working on a project Cora had sent me, though I'd also read the notes she'd made on a large whiteboard. Now I draped myself over the back of my chair in her direction. "Are you working on an article?"

She looked up. "Hm?"

I nodded at the whiteboard with its large *TO DO* list. The first item was *MAKE DECISION ON HC ARTICLE!!!* Another read *DECIDE ABOUT HC ARTICLE!!* And a third, *EMAIL DF ABOUT HC ARTICLE.* A pro/con list was tacked to the adjacent bulletin board. The pros: *1) Shiny article, 2) Will get DF off my back, 3) Might not have a choice.* Cons: *1) Ugh, 2) Tedious research, 3) No time, 4) Sentences are bad.* "I'm decent at research and stuff, if you want me to do some. That's, like, my dad's whole world."

She sipped her coffee. "That's not . . . a horrible idea."

I glowed.

"I've been asked to write a piece connecting my work to the legacy of female astronomers and their stellar classification systems. It's not the worst article," she said, damning with faint phrase, "but it's human interest, not academic. I don't love the idea of writing it, but it's for a high-profile magazine and it'd be great exposure."

"If I could help, I'd love to."

"I'll think about it."

By lunch the rain had stopped, and I met up with two of the girls who I'd met at the beach party and then again over the weekend: Abby, who was dating Noah Barbanel, and her friend Stella. We picked up sandwiches downtown and ice cream after, sitting on park benches and devouring our cones as we watched bunnies dart across green lawns still glistening with raindrops.

When I got back to the office, Cora beckoned me over. As far as I could tell, she hadn't moved from her spot, but her coffee cup was full once more.

"Your idea works," she said. "I wrote up a project doc over lunch with a bunch of the info I need—names and dates and background. You good to go over it now?"

"Yeah," I said eagerly. "Sounds great."

"Cool." She leaned forward in her chair, hands clasped. "Here's the deal. The article is about the Harvard Computers, a team of female astronomers in the late eighteen hundreds who invented ways to categorize all the stars in the sky. Hopefully, I'm also going to invent a radically helpful categorization system, so the article is about the lineage. I'm going to have you pull details about their backgrounds, accomplishments, and obstacles overcome. Sound good?"

I nodded. "I didn't know there were so many early female astronomers. Like Maria Mitchell."

"Yeah, in the eighteen hundreds lots of women studied astronomy—it was considered ladylike, done in private, in the home. After Mitchell discovered her comet, she became a massive celebrity and all these young girls got into it. She got an award from the King of Denmark, met with Frederick Douglass, Sojourner Truth, Ralph Waldo Emerson. People were psyched about her." Cora sipped her coffee. "But when astronomy became professionalized a few decades later, men swept in and women were shut out."

"That seems . . . bad."

"Yep. It's rarely been easy, being a woman in STEM. Not to mention being a woman of color. Though we've always been here." She rolled her eyes. "They used to call the Harvard Computers 'Pickering's Harem.' He was the director of Harvard's observatory and they worked for him."

My mouth fell open. "What?"

"Men always think they're cleverer than they are. Anyway, it's these women you'll be researching. There're a few really famous ones—Annie Cannon, who designed the basis of our current star-categorization system; Henrietta Leavitt, whose work helped Hubble determine the size of the universe. Cecilia Payne, she came later, in the 1920s—she discovered stars are made up of hydrogen and helium. I've noted the specifics I want, but add anything interesting you come across, too, especially anything related to Nantucket—I've also been asked to write an article on the island's astronomical heritage, so we can use this research there, too."

I dove in.

In the 1880s, an amateur astronomer named Henry Draper and his wife, Mary Anna, photographed the spectrum of stars. Their photographs, which were viewed on glass plates, translated stars into shaded bars with lines through them. On her husband's death, Mary Anna donated the plates to Edward Pickering, the director of Harvard's observatory.

Pickering realized the stunning amount of information in the photos and hired a team—half women—to photograph every star in the sky. It turned out the striations corresponded to everything from chemical blend to distance to brightness and temperature. The Harvard Computers set out to photograph the heavens and analyze and classify each star. To do so, they used two new telescopes, one donated by Mrs. Draper and one bought with money from the Bache Fund: a foundation, of course, named after Ben Franklin's great-grandson.

One of the women, Annie Jump Cannon, stood out to me. Over the course of her career, she classified over three hundred and fifty thousand stars—more than anyone else. Her classification system was still in use by the International Astronomical

Union. And best of all, she'd visited Nantucket.

When the Maria Mitchell Association was founded in 1902, they reached out to Pickering, who agreed to help launch the island's nascent astronomy program. He asked Cannon to advise them, and she became a founding member of the Maria Mitchell Association. For several summers, she spent a few weeks on Nantucket teaching astronomy courses. This was exactly what I'd been looking for.

I wasn't my father's daughter for nothing; when Google turned up little on the astronomy classes, I turned to primary sources, thinking this would be a good way to beef up background for Cora's Nantucket astronomy article. The archives on the Atheneum's website included back issues of *The Inquirer and Mirror*, Nantucket's long-running newspaper. Annie Cannon's name pulled up a handful of results, and I clicked on the oldest, an issue from 1906. It opened a digitized scan. In tightly printed letters, sandwiched between an article on the cranberry bog yield and another about a dog running off with some luggage, I found a short note:

MISS ANNIE CANNON AND ASSISTANT
MISS ANDREA DARREL VISIT NANTUCKET

Miss Cannon arrives on Nantucket from Harvard Astronomical Observatory. Joining her is Nantucket local Miss Darrel, daughter of Mr. and Mrs. John Darrel. Miss Cannon and Miss Darrel will be giving astronomy lectures for the Maria Mitchell Association, inviting local Nantucketeers to learn more about the heavens.

Since I hadn't come across an Andrea Darrel before, I plugged her into Google. Her biography was short and to the point. Andrea Darrel was born in 1873, in Nantucket, Mass., and died in 1964 in Cambridge, Mass. She attended Vassar College from 1892 to 1896. From 1896 to 1924, Darrel worked as a computer at the Harvard Observatory, under Edward Pickering and later Annie Jump Cannon.

A minor astronomer, then, not as lauded as Annie Cannon or Cecilia Payne or the others I'd been reading about. But my curiosity was piqued. Dad loved researching little-known figures and bringing their stories to light; if I wanted to *really* impress him, there'd be no better way than by showing him I could do the same. And Andrea Darrel could be interesting if I was trying to stress a Nantucket connection. She would have been ten years younger than Annie Cannon, and fifty-five years younger than Maria Mitchell. What if they'd all overlapped? While Maria Mitchell would have been teaching at Vassar in upstate New York by the time Darrel was born, I imagined the famous local had loomed large over the imagination of an island girl. Especially one who decided to go to Vassar and become an astronomer herself.

"Have you heard of Andrea Darrel?" I asked Cora during her next coffee break. "She was a Harvard Computer originally from Nantucket."

"Nope." Cora listened as I described the little I'd found. "Interesting. Sounds worth checking out."

I smiled at her, a big burst of excitement in my chest. "I'll see what I can do."

* * *

After dinner with Dad, I biked back to Golden Doors. My quads burned as I pushed uphill, though the cool breeze off the sea whisked away my sweat. After changing into my pajamas, I headed to the cousins' room. I was getting used to the soundtrack of Golden Doors: piano played properly, violin played poorly, laughter, squabbling. The triplets whispering fiercely, the littles shrieking with laughter, the adults pouring wine and talking into the early hours of the morning. The birdsong floating through the open windows.

The cousins' room was always cozy, a place where you could be surrounded by others but not have to pay much attention. Tonight, a group played video games, a few more did a puzzle, and a handful read books. If Ethan had been there, it wouldn't have been restful, but he wasn't. So I fully relaxed, a blanket draped over my lap as I nestled into a couch, Miriam at the other end. I'd spent my work hours pulling reports and crunching numbers for Cora, along with the research she'd requested on the Harvard Computers, but now I wanted to see what I could find on Andrea Darrel.

Andrea Darrel diaries led to a page at Harvard Library's Archival Discovery, but to my dismay it gave the location as a physical box in a storeroom instead of, say, a downloadable PDF. Vassar was more helpful: a page on the school's website showed scanned diaries from some of the first women to attend. One of the diaries, with cramped, rounded script (plus a digital transcript, thank god) belonged to Andrea Darrel.

The diaries started in 1892, when Andrea would have been eighteen. She'd be heading off to college, like me in a few months. I didn't usually think of nineteenth-century women going to university, but I supposed some had. Had Andrea felt the way I did— uncertain, excited, thirsty for knowledge and friendship? Probably. Time and clothing and societal expectations might change, but people probably didn't.

I started at the beginning.

September 24, 1892

I arrived in New York a few hours ago. I feel a bit like I'm in a dream; I've never been further from Nantucket than Boston, and never so far from the ocean.

Uncle Henry met me at the depot. He is very against these "newfangled women's schools" and thought it important I know this on the eve of attending one. I told him Vassar was founded thirty years ago, and its first students were women of his age. He turned ruddy and said, "What man wants an overly-educated wife?"

I said, "What woman wants a husband who doesn't respect her education?" This did not start our visit on an amiable note.

But I can think of worse things than spending my life unmarried. Miss Mitchell never wed, after all, and she was the first faculty named to Vassar, and the reason I chose to come here—the reason Vassar has higher enrollments for astronomy than Harvard or Radcliffe.

"Studying the stars is a ladylike pursuit," Aunt Lisa said,

trying to calm her husband down. Unfortunately (poor Aunt Lisa) this only upset her husband outwardly and me inwardly. Uncle Henry says women should only study the hierarchies of nature and should leave debates to men, and Miss Mitchell should never have been named to the American Academy of Arts and Sciences (alarmingly, no other woman has been admitted in the 44 years since).

Then I said I am not interested in being ladylike, I'm interested in understanding the world. Aunt Lisa closed her eyes very tightly then, looking so much like Mama I apologized and excused myself to bed. At home, I would have burned off my rage by going outside to sweep the skies, but New York has too much light, so I'm writing here instead.

September 25

I'm feeling very overwhelmed about tomorrow—am I expecting too much of college? I don't know what I expect, but it seems to be everything. I remember Miss Mitchell visiting Nantucket and letting me look through her telescope and saying, "You will make a very good astronomer; you must come study with me at Vassar."

I wish she were still alive and could see I am going to be an astronomer.

Hattie says Miss Mitchell would have said as much to any child from home who showed an interest in astronomy, especially the child of people she taught when she was a young schoolteacher. I say Hattie is jealous because I left Nantucket and she's stuck there and Mama will have no one to badger except her for the next four years.

Hattie also says I shouldn't dream too much; Miss Mitchell might have become famous around the whole world, but the chance of another island girl doing so is too much to ask.

Am I reaching too far beyond my grasp? Papa is a fisherman and Mama runs the house. It's more likely I'll wind up a fisherman's wife than a lauded academic.

Merely writing that makes my whole body shiver. I want to be inducted into the Academy of Arts and Sciences. I want my college degree. I want to change the world. I want to study the stars. I want everything.

September 26

Took the train from the city to Poughkeepsie. I've never traveled by myself before—hardly left the island—and now here I am, completely independent! I am not sure whether to laugh or cry.

I met a girl on the train also bound for Vassar, a Miss Slate. At the depot, we paid a man to take our trunks to the college and caught a streetcar right to the college gates. I have never been on a streetcar before and thought it perfectly charming. Miss Slate told me it was old and rickety and in the worst condition of any streetcar she had ever been on. Clearly Miss Slate and I lead very different lives.

For whatever reason, I thought my arrival at Vassar would be more monumental. Perhaps I pictured cheers? Instead, I was one more in a teeming crowd of young women (which was quite the sensation! I'm not used to being around so many girls my own age). There are about a hundred girls in my class, and we will all be living in a dormitory together.

October 8

First few weeks have flown by! Must try to be better at chronicling my life, otherwise future biographers will be stymied about my formative years. (Thought this an entertaining quip and shared it with Miss Blanchard down the hall, who regarded me quite blankly. Perhaps I'm not as funny as I thought.)

In the first few days, I took exams to place me in my classes. Went to the chapel to receive our schedule, as follows:

Latin

French

German

Rhetoric

Algebra

Geometry

Hygiene

I am quite miserable at everything outside of maths.

The breakfast bell wakes us at 7:45 every day, and lunch is just past noon. Supper's at six, and chapel half past. The other girls are from all over the country—Miss Gallaher is from Kansas, Miss Clayden from Albany. Everyone is brilliant. I used to consider myself decently intelligent, but now I am afraid I am exceptionally mediocre.

All the teachers are lovely, but most striking is Professor Perkins, who is dark-haired and handsome, with sad eyes. Unfortunately, yesterday at lunch with Miss Alice Brady and Miss Maria Carpenter (of Boston and New York, respectively) I was informed all the girls in our class are taken with him. Another example of my extreme ordinariness, I am afraid.

Apparently I am most of note for being from Nantucket, which I realized when I mentioned home today. Everyone asked if I'd known Miss Mitchell, and when I said yes, they clustered about my skirts like children at story time. I had little to say, even though my memories of her are so strong: kind and steady and sure of herself. Though she left the Quakers, they left a strong imprint on her from childhood. She was so unlike Mama, who worries and corrects me about everything. Miss Mitchell corrected me, too, when I didn't understand how to use the telescope or said something silly about the planets, but she was kind and patient and exactly how I want to be someday.

Andrea Darrel's diary became sparser over the next years, picking up mostly when she headed home to Nantucket for the summers, or when she was stressed about a class or a friendship or a new lecturer she hero-worshipped. (Or when she was irritated with her mother or sister Hattie, with whom she must have maintained a lively correspondence, given they always seemed to be asking if she'd met anyone eligible at nearby West Point.)

I learned the details of her life, though: she played doubles tennis with her classmates and went out on the lake and attended organ concerts. She wrote with great excitement of each new scientific discovery, from the first open-heart surgery to enthu-siastically following the discussion of canals and seas on Mars, which had once been considered a certainty but which experts became skeptical of in the mid-1890s.

As graduation approached, her journals became expansive again as she tried to capture the end of an era. In November she wrote about wearing bloomers and sweaters on a rainy after-noon for the first-ever field day; in March she wrote about the heated presidential race between two men I had never heard of, William McKinley and William Bryan (presumably one of these men won?). And by May, she was filled by nostalgia for college and hope for the future.

May 5, 1896

What a night!

The astronomy club had its annual Dome Party tonight. We were told to bring poems, and some of the girls had the nerve to write rather good ones (Miss Slate set hers to music, and it was appallingly lovely). We sat at little tables under the dome and ate and laughed and shared our mostly horrible poetry.

Then Miss Antonia Maury arrived! Miss Maury is not just an alum, she works at Harvard Observatory (funded by Miss Maury's aunt, Mrs. Draper). She has calculated orbital periods and discovered a binary star. But she made it quite clear she doesn't consider the Observatory a perfect place—Dr. Pickering, the director, received credit for her discoveries, and she only made 25¢ an hour, half the salary of her male colleagues. She quit for these reasons once before, and only returned because Dr. Pickering especially asked her.

I know this should infuriate me, and it does, but I still want to work at the Observatory. After she read her poem, I made my way over to her. We both graduated with honors in physics, astronomy, and philosophy, and so I hope that will help me the way it helped her, even if her connections are far superior to mine—her family is made up of physicians and scientists and teachers.

She rather scoffed at me when I told her I hoped to work at the Observatory. "And make little money and receive no credit? It would be easier to work elsewhere."

"I don't want to work elsewhere," I said. "I want to be an astronomer. I can fight for credit, if I have discoveries to fight for."

She cannot be more than half a dozen years older than me, but she shook her head like she was weary as Atlas. "You are so young and hungry still," she said, and I couldn't tell if she meant it as a compliment or an insult. "If you want it so badly, I'll make an introduction."

I want it so badly I would bleed out my entire heart to have it. And now I think I have it. I think I may be on my way to becoming an astronomer.

May 12, 1896

Everything is a "last" these days—our last recital, last time on the lake, last walk through the orchards. Last exam! We all promise we'll return, but it won't be the same.

We went out on the lake tonight, the senior girls, with the sun setting in a blaze and the stars shining bright. We were very loud, lit with some wild fire, singing and laughing and half dancing, and when we returned to the seniors' hall we continued to make a spectacle of ourselves, and I am sure I did not imagine the younger classes looking on with envy. We're at the peak of everything, of life itself, it feels. We have the whole world in front of us and it feels like we're about to jump off a cliff and fall forever.

Or maybe fly.

Ten

The sailboat rocked as I stepped aboard. I must not have covered my alarm well, because Dad gave me a concerned look. "You sure about this?"

"Of course." I accepted the orange and slightly grody-looking life vest from his hands and slipped it on. It felt bulky and highly unfashionable buckled around my chest, but at least I wouldn't drown.

It was Thursday, one of my days off. When I'd come downstairs I'd seen Ethan bouncing like a Labrador retriever, which struck me as highly suspicious. I'd insisted he bring me along on whatever adventure he and my dad were embarking on. I wanted Dad to see I could be as good a research assistant as Ethan. Besides, I was bored.

"What exactly are we doing?" I could feel the buoyancy of the ocean beneath us as I lowered myself onto a bench. Ethan had called the activity "throwing logs" on our drive to the harbor from Golden Doors, which meant exactly nothing to me.

"It's how sailors knew how fast their ship was going." Ethan climbed aboard after me. We were on his family's sailboat, with a white fiberglass hull and cushy-looking benches, and he navigated it with ease. "They threw a wooden board in the water and measured how fast it moved away. They attached it to the ship with a knotted line and counted the knots unreeled."

"That's where the term *knots* came from? Literal knots?"

"Right. Now a nautical knot is a very specific speed—a nautical mile, about one and a half miles, per hour—but it's how the term started."

The day was gorgeous. Clouds pastoral, sun soaking into my skin, the soft breeze like a cocoon. Dad and Ethan showed me what felt like a hundred parts of the sailboat: the mainsail, topsail, ropes called sheets and poles called booms. "Here," Dad said, handing me a rope—the sheet—attached to the boom. "We want the wind to fill the sail, so you need to continuously adjust the boom to make sure we're angled to catch it."

I tried to make sure the sail didn't totally deflate (or luff, as Dad and Ethan said, denying they'd made the word up). Keeping track of where the wind came from was difficult, even with Dad's tips to "look at the ripples on the water" and "listen to the wind and make sure it's passing by both your ears equally." Thankfully, Ethan pointed out both a weathervane and a digital tracker.

After an hour of trimming and tacking, Dad and Ethan adjusted the sails in what they called a heave-to so we could pause in actively sailing. Dad took out a tiny recorder, glanced at me quickly, then started speaking. "Seventy-eight degrees, wind from the west. The water's dark blue slanting green, sky's clear, a few streaky clouds. Ethan and Jordan here, Jordan's first time on a sailboat"—he turned away and kept muttering into the microphone.

I stared after him, trying to make out what he was saying about me. "What's he doing?"

Ethan glanced at me, surprised. "Haven't you heard your dad do this before? He's taking notes so he can set the scene in the book."

I winced. "Why on us, though? *We're* not going to be in the books."

Ethan gave me the kind of incredulous look one might give a potato that had started speaking. "You haven't read your dad's stuff?"

Self-consciousness squeezed me. I had not, in fact, read my dad's stuff. I'd read the long-form article that launched his career. I'd listened to him read excerpts. But the whole book? Nope.

I'd meant to, when it came out. I was incredibly proud of my dad's accomplishments. But I didn't make it past the dedication: *To my wife, Rebecca. I will miss you forever.* Honestly, after that I just wanted to pat the books' spines affectionately whenever I walked past them. I didn't have the emotional bandwidth to crack the cover again. "I know what they're about."

"Hm." Ethan looked skeptical. "Well, they have a personal vibe to them."

"*How* personal?" The *Atlantic* article was friendly in tone, framed by first-person narration but mostly focused on history. The chapter Dad read at readings began with him, alone on a boat, trying his hand at celestial navigation, before springing backward in time to nineteenth-century navigators. "Am I in them?"

This was the most horrifying thing I'd considered in a long time.

Ethan avoided my gaze. "Not really."

I took it back. *That* was the most horrifying thing. How could I not be in a book with a "personal vibe"? I was Dad's *daughter*. You couldn't get more personal. Was *Ethan* in them more than me?

It would be just like Ethan to have a larger presence in Dad's books than me. Great. Wonderful. Thrilling.

Dad came back to our side of the sailboat. "All set. You guys ready?"

"Sure," I said. "What do we do?"

Ethan aimed his phone at the two of us.

I glanced at him, startled. "Are you—filming?"

"Ethan takes lots of notes and videos," Dad said. "It's helpful for later on."

"And for social," Ethan said.

"I am *not* in video-ready condition," I said. Ethan smirked. "Especially not if you're posting this anywhere."

"You look beautiful," Dad said, because he was contractually obligated to do so via the Parenting Handbook.

Despite myself, I glanced at Ethan, but of course he didn't agree with my dad. I didn't *want* him to agree, didn't want to be thinking about whether Ethan found me beautiful or not. I smoothed the mess of my hair gathered on the top of my head. If this was what Dad always did, I could be cool about it. "Fine."

Dad held up a triangular piece of a wood, both for me and for the camera. A rope was tied to one point and led back to a giant spool of rope, bulky with knots. "This is called a common log, a chip log, a ship log—or just a log. We'll drop it to float in the water, and let out the rope as the current carries us away." He held up a brass hourglass. "When we start, we'll turn this hourglass. When it runs out, we'll gather the rope back and count how many knots have passed through." He lifted the hourglass in one hand, wooden plank in the other. "Who wants which?"

I took the plank of wood and Ethan, the hourglass. I was more excited than expected, like a little kid about to do the baking-soda-volcano thing. "All right," Dad said. "On the count of *one, two, three, go,* turn the glass and drop the plank."

Ethan and I exchanged anticipatory grins.

"One, two, three, *go!*" Dad cried. I dropped the plank into the water and watched the rope unspooling away from it, then glanced over at the sand crystals sifting down the hourglass. It was silly and bright and joy-inducing, and the sun on my face and salt on my lips made me want to stay out on the water forever. I could see why Ethan and Dad had so much fun doing these kinds of re-creations. It felt like playing, like a game I might have done as a child.

When the hourglass ran out, we towed the plank back in and excitedly counted all the knots, nodding firmly at each other as though the amount meant something to us. Then Dad disappeared again, back to the prow of the boat, notebook in hand.

"What's he doing now?" I asked Ethan, somewhat surprised we weren't repeating the experiment or heading home.

"He likes to write the first draft when he's doing the experiment," Ethan said. "He says he's motivated. Good atmosphere." He grinned. "And we get to spend more time on the water."

"Can't disagree there." I raised my face to the sun. It bleached the inside of my eyes and waged war against my sunscreen. I thought about how this, like Andrea Darrel's excitement about college, transcended centuries. Someone in the 1890s, or the 1500s, or a thousand years ago could have felt the same joy as I did from the sun on their face and the rocking of a boat.

By the time we made it back to the island and headed to dinner, I felt deeply content and unexpectedly tired. I wasn't used to the uninterrupted sun, the wind chafing at my skin, the rise and fall of the ocean—let alone hoisting sails or controlling the boom. But I'd liked it. I'd liked hanging out with Dad and Ethan.

Maybe this was how it could be.

"Ethan and I are getting dinner and then going back to the office," Dad said as we docked. "Want to join us for dinner?"

And just like that, my stomach seized.

Did *I* want to go with *them* to get dinner. Because they were the ones with the preexisting plans; they'd be going back to the office to keep working. I could join them or not, and it didn't really matter to Dad one way or another.

The pilot light of my jealousy flared higher. "I'll pass. I told Abby I'd meet her and her friends for dinner tonight, anyway."

"Okay," Dad said, nodding and already turning toward Ethan to talk about food choices. It made my gut twist even more. He didn't even want to try to convince me to change my mind. I stuffed my water bottle and sunscreen into my tote, trying not to let my hands shake. It was fine. So I was the extra wheel. Whatever.

I did get dinner with Abby and Stella, and Stella's girlfriend Lexi, and Abby's roommate Jane, and it was nice, and by the end

I felt stable again. I needed to let go of wanting Dad to pay more attention to me. It was probably good he didn't depend on me, right? I mean, obviously I wished he'd pick me over Ethan, but I'd be going to UMass in a few months. It was good he didn't only rely on me.

And if I didn't want him to lean on Ethan, I'd have to find someone else to occupy his time.

* * *

On Friday morning, I turned to Cora. "Any plans this weekend?"

I thought she and Dad could be a good match. I didn't know if *they'd* think so—the only thing I knew about Cora's romantic life was she'd once gone on a date with a guy she'd cross the street to avoid—but they were both nerdy, kind, driven, smart people. So I didn't mind trying my hand at yenta-ing.

Cora looked up from a notepad filled with erratic equations. "More work, I guess. Catching up on sleep, if I'm lucky."

"The Barbanels are having a party tomorrow at five," I said. Apparently they always had one for the official start of summer at the end of June. "You should come."

She looked horrified. "Oh, no, thanks."

"It'll be fun." I paused. "Or maybe it won't. Honestly, who's to say? But it'll definitely be an experience. And the Barbanels told me I should invite you, and anyone you want to bring."

"They did?"

Well, Miriam had said there'd be around a hundred people at

the party, so I was pretty sure no one would notice an additional two or three. "Yeah."

"I'll think about it."

"Cool." I slung my bag over my arm. "Hopefully I'll see you tomorrow, then."

Step 1: Seed planted. Step 2: Calling Dad before the party to make sure he dressed appropriately. "Wear one of those nice button-downs Aunt Lou bought you," I said over the phone on Saturday morning. "And steam it in the shower to get rid of the wrinkles first."

"Who's the adult here?"

"The one who was probably going to wear a college T-shirt with a bleach stain on it."

"I *do* know how to take care of myself, you know."

"I have not seen concrete proof of this."

We hung up, and I showered and blew out my hair so it looked sleek and smooth instead of like a living cloud capable of eating small children. My makeup was easy because I had exactly two looks: eye makeup with red lipstick and without.

Someone knocked. "Hey, it's me," Ethan called through the door. "Can I come in?"

"No!" I shouted, panicking and wrapping my towel tighter.

"Come on, just for a second," he wheedled. "I wanna show you something."

"Oh, I've heard *that* line before," I muttered, looking around for clothes to pull on. Though on second thought—

Securing the towel, I opened the door, batting my lashes up at Ethan. "Yes?"

His gaze fell and he blinked several times. "Oh, uh—hi."

I smiled and stepped back. Daring him. "Come on in."

He hesitated in the doorway. He held a book in his hand, a familiar one. My father's. "I wanted to show you—a few passages—maybe another time."

"Chicken," I said softly as he turned to go. My lips turned up. "Red junglefowl."

He spun around, heat in his eyes, and stepped so close I could feel his breath. "Ask me to stay, then," he said, voice just as low.

I swallowed. Heat suffused my entire body, prickling and intense, and I was suddenly very aware my towel was a single piece of fabric held up by one hand. I stepped back. "I should get ready for the party."

"I'll see you down there."

I shut the door, then leaned my forehead against it. What was I doing?

Trying to ground myself, I turned back to my closet. Downstairs, I pictured a sea of white pants and linen dresses; mint greens and lemon yellows and pale pinks. Oh well. I pulled on the vegan-leather black dress I'd worn to prom and added ruby-red glass earrings to match my toenails and lipstick. Feeling much more myself, I headed downstairs.

The lawn had been transformed. White cloths covered tables laden with cascades of grapes and pyramids of cheese. Giant vats of water had been infused with chunks of coconut and pineapple. I spied trays of watermelon and tiny fruit tartlets and skewers of juicy heirloom tomatoes and mozzarella.

I'd been right about the style: no one wore all black like me, but I felt comfortable enough at Golden Doors by now not to care. The women wore nice dresses or blouses; the men had tucked in their button-downs. Their sweaters were faded, their sandals worn. But I'd been thrifting long enough to recognize quality. I could spot 100 percent cashmere at ten paces and knew the difference in how outfits hung when they'd originally been priced at three digits.

I grabbed a plate and piled it high with cucumber salad, fresh guac, and warm pitas. Balancing it on one hand, I snagged a glass of freshly squeezed lemonade with the other and carried everything to where some of the older cousins and the triplets sat.

"Jordan will know," one of the triplets said as I joined them. "You know astrology, right, Jordan?"

"Astrology?" I met the gaze of David, Ethan's middle brother, who spread his hands, palms up. "Uh, not really."

"Really?" The triplet—Lily, maybe—widened her eyes. "But you study the stars."

Another triplet—I knew there were only three, per the term, but it seemed like there were *so many* of them—spoke. "She does *astronomy*, Lils. The real one."

"Astrology is real," Lily said with a simple elegance, as though she refused to defend facts. She focused on me again. "You understand the stars, right? You know about constellations and stuff?"

"I mean, from a technical perspective," I hedged.

"What's your sign?"

"My birthday's September twenty-seventh."

"Libra. An air sign," she said. "Interesting."

"Is that—good?" Most of what I knew of constellations had to do with finding them in the sky, and not particularly even the twelve of the zodiac.

"Leo's a fire sign," she said. "But I think that's a good match."

"Who's Leo?"

Lily looked appalled; one of the other triplets smirked, and the other—dare I say it—cackled.

"Never mind them," Shira said from across the table. "I don't understand what they're saying half the time."

"She still might know," Lily said. "We have a meteor shower *and* a comet coming up. How are those going to affect our astrological charts?"

"Um," I said. "Hopefully not at all?"

Lily looked very disappointed in me.

"It's interesting, though," I said, feeling like I needed to offer something. "Meteor showers happen when the debris from a comet's trail burns up in our atmosphere, but it's not super common to see a meteor shower and its parent comet at the same time. But the Arborids come from Gibson's comet, and we'll see them close together, so that's pretty cool."

"But is it good or bad?" Lily asked.

"Um. I guess a long time ago, people thought meteors were good signs." I recalled Dad's stories from when I was a kid. "Gods listening to mortals, peeking down on us from the heavens. But, uh, I think comets were bad. Death of kings. I think a Chinese emperor once abdicated?"

"I'm not abdicating," one of Lily's sisters said.

"You don't have a throne," the other said.

I polished off my food, keeping my eyes peeled for both Dad and Cora. I spotted my boss first and felt a surge of relief that she'd come. She stood next to another woman, both of them clutching their drinks like children clutching blankies and trading laughing whispers. I'd never seen Cora in anything besides leggings or jeans, but today she'd put on a royal-blue jumpsuit and pulled her hair up into a braided high bun.

I made my way over. "Cora! Hi! You made it."

"Hey, Jordan." She gestured to the woman next to her. "This is my friend Bao, who's visiting from Boston for the weekend."

"Oh good." Bao grinned at me. "I was beginning to think we'd gate-crashed and Cora didn't want to own up to it."

"No, no, definitely a real party. I mean, a real invite." I felt unexpectedly nervous and awkward. Both these women seemed so much cooler than everyone else. Obviously I'd thought Cora was cool before, but in a nerdy-scientist way. Seeing her all glammed up made me wonder if I'd bitten off more than I could chew with this matchmaking.

Bao asked me the usual questions adults did about college and majors, and I asked her what she'd seen on Nantucket so far. I tried to keep my eyes politely on hers instead of scanning constantly for Dad. Where *was* he?

Finally, I caught sight of him on the other side of the lawn. He'd worn one of his blue-checked shirts, which meant he was Making an Effort. He still wore socks with his sandals, though. The blight of my life.

Should I steal all his socks for the duration of the summer?

"Dad!" I waved at him, too wildly to be cool, but desperate

times. "Dad!" Two parentally aged men turned in my direction. Oy. "Tony!"

Dad's eyes focused on me, surprised, then happy. He made his way across the lawn. I studied him. His shirt wasn't too wrinkled, and he'd clearly bothered to comb his hair. "Dad, you remember Dr. Bradley? And this is her friend Bao."

"Nice to meet you," Dad said politely, and, "Nice to see you again. Are you enjoying the party?"

They made affirmative noises.

All right, launching Conversational Gambit #1. "Are *you*?" I asked Dad. "Or are you still too traumatized by last night?" To the women I said, "The Red Sox game."

Bao looked unmoved—a woman after my own heart—while Cora grimaced sympathetically. "You're doing better than we are. I'm from Minneapolis."

"A Twins fan?" Dad perked up. Sportsball! "You live in Boston, though, right? We haven't rubbed off on you yet?"

"I don't think Boston can *ever* rub off on me enough to switch sides," Cora said, and they laughed. Bao took a small sip of her drink, covering a smile.

Baseball carried them for a few minutes, and when the conversation started to run out of steam, I moved us on to Conversational Gambit #2. "Dad's always trying to get me to go to sports games," I said, playing Wry Teen Daughter to a T. "Or go running, but I can barely last a mile."

"Oh, are you a runner?" Cora asked my father. Cora, according to her Instagram, had run a 10k last month.

"A bit," Dad said.

"Dad's run four marathons," I said. "He did Boston this year."

Dad looked like he might die of mortification. God forbid I mention an accomplishment not related to the book. *"Jordan."*

"Cool," Cora said, unfazed by my father's impending demise. "I did my first half six months ago."

"Good for you," Dad said, happy again. "Where was it?"

This conversation felt more concrete. Once they were firmly ensconced in a discussion about running-shoe brands, I murmured an excuse about getting more water and slipped away. It wasn't even a lie—the day had been boiling, and even now, near eight, the late-June sun felt like a comforting blanket. I downed two glasses of water in quick succession before lingering more slowly over a lemonade. Leaning against a high-top table, I tried to decipher Dad's and Cora's body language. They both looked friendly and engaged, but no more or less so than Bao, an equally weighted part of their triangle.

A movement caught the corner of my eye. Ethan settled next to me, resting his arms next to mine on the table, our forearms brushing. "Whatcha watching?"

"None of your business." I gave him a Cheshire cat smile.

"Are you trying to set your dad and Dr. Bradley up?"

I sipped the tart lemonade. "Do you think it would work?"

"I think your dad can handle dating by himself."

I snorted. "Why?"

He paused. "Okay, fair point."

"I think they'd be a good match." I looked at Ethan expectantly. He probably knew my dad better than anyone else on the island, save me. "What do you think?"

"I think . . . I dunno?"

"Well, try to know a little harder." I ticked off points on my fingers. "They're both driven and focused. She's an academic and he writes, so they're both always working really hard and learning new things. And they both like sports and sci-fi shows." Cora had cracked three Star Trek references in my hearing already.

"Wow," Ethan said. "Have you always been this invested in your dad's love life?"

"He's never had a love life."

"Really?" Ethan looked surprised. "So he hasn't dated since— Sorry."

"Don't be sorry." It was a relief to talk about it. "Exactly. I think he uses me as an excuse to not live his own life."

"What do you mean?"

I told him about the conversation I'd overheard between my dad and aunt. "So I need to make sure he doesn't worry about me."

Ethan's brows shot up. "Ah."

"Ah what?"

"Nothing." He crumbled under my gaze. "It makes sense why you've decided, you know, no more hooking up."

"I mean, also I don't feel like getting my heart broken."

"Right. But also, your whole insistence on, I don't know, *proving* to him you're capable and smart and everything, when obviously he knows you are, and you should tell him if you want to hang out more. You don't need to change yourself."

"I don't think it's changing myself to prove I'm smart," I shot back.

He groaned. "That's not what I meant."

"Besides, I don't see you telling your family they don't take you seriously enough."

He let out a long sigh, squeezing the back of his neck. It made the muscles in his arm stand out, and I tried hard not to stare at them. "I think sometimes our parents get stuck on what we were like when we were kids. They think we're the same as when we were at five, ten, fifteen. We don't change."

"But everyone changes. They have to realize that."

"I dunno," he said skeptically. "I didn't eat tomatoes until I was sixteen, and it's been two years, and my parents *still* think I don't like tomatoes."

"You didn't . . . eat tomatoes?"

He shook his head. "I thought they were shit. Watery. Gross."

This wasn't the detour I'd expected this conversation to take, but I couldn't let it go. "What about, like, pizza?"

"Oh yeah, I ate tomato sauce and cooked tomatoes. Just never fresh ones. Then I went to Turkey and the bed and breakfast we stayed at served a platter of tomatoes and cheese and olives every morning and I was *so hungry* I was like, well, better learn to like them. Also, it turns out tomatoes in Turkey are way better than here."

I stared.

He tilted his head. "You're thinking, *Fuck that boy, not all of us can fly out to Turkey to change our minds about tomatoes.*"

I snorted because he wasn't far off. "No! Just, uh, maybe you could have tried a farm-fresh tomato first."

"True." He laughed, then sobered. "I'm just saying, your dad thinks you're great."

"Hm," I said, noncommittal.

"Your job sounds cool," Ethan said, because Ethan was sometimes a golden retriever who wanted people to feel better. "I feel like we're both . . . I dunno. Cartographers. You of the sky, me of the sea."

I laughed, though I liked the way he made it sound. "More like, I'm an assistant to a cartographer of space trash, and you're an assistant to an historiographer of cartography."

He grinned. "My version's easier to say."

"You have me there." I tilted my head back. It was too light to see the stars, though the faint white moon floated through the sky. "You know Polaris?"

"The North Star? Yeah."

"I'm learning about a group of astronomers who categorized all the stars in the sky by their brightness. They needed a scale to measure the brightness against. The director, Pickering, picked Polaris as the comparison point. Not because it was the brightest star, but because its light is unwavering. It would be the steadiest, the truest. It's least susceptible to distortion. I like that, don't you? It's a nice metaphor."

"What's the metaphor?"

"You know. You don't have to be the best or the brightest to be the true star. The starriest star, the Rudolph of the stars. You just have to be unwavering."

He stared at me, for long enough I started to feel uncomfortable. "What? Was the Rudolph metaphor too weird?"

"No. Not at all. I think—being unwavering is a great quality."

His attention switched over my shoulder, and I turned. Dad approached us—Cora nowhere in his vicinity, drat.

"Hi, honey," Dad said. "Having fun?"

"Yeah."

"I was telling Jordan about 'Sconset," Ethan said, which he patently had not been. "You guys should go."

"You haven't been yet?" Dad said in surprise, as though I'd been anywhere here he didn't know about. I shook my head. "It's very nice."

I bit my lip, glancing at Ethan. He nodded in encouragement, and I looked back at Dad. Well, why the hell not. "Maybe we could check it out tomorrow?"

Dad looked surprised. "Of course. Unless—you'd rather go with your friends?"

"No, Dad," I said, more sharply than I'd intended. I just didn't think I should have to spell out wanting to hang out with him. I softened my voice. "It'd be fun if we went."

Dad looked pleased. "Great."

When I glanced over at Ethan, he smiled so broadly back, my heart hurt.

Eleven

'Sconset was a picture-perfect village on the far side of the island, all tiny cedar-shingled cottages and pink roses climbing up trellises. A gentle haze softened the line where the cerulean water met the almost cloudless sky. Only wisps of cirrus clouds marred the blue, like an artistic afterthought.

We followed a public cliff walk along the bluff, through the backyards of mansions. Sometimes the path wound beneath brambling, shady hedges, while other times we could see sweeping vistas of bent sea trees, gray-purple flowers, and scraggly grass. Wooden staircases stretched several stories down to the shore, worn out by decades of hard weather. The day was hot but not unbearable, and the breeze off the water kept me cool.

Dad and I had always loved hikes, even if he said his creaky old bones couldn't keep up with me. (Admittedly, I often teased him about this same thing.) He loved nature and history, so historical walks were basically his favorite thing. "'Sconset started as a seventeenth-century fishing village," he told me when I asked. "It became a resort town during the whaling heyday, and later an artist colony." He gestured down the bluff. "There was a neighborhood called Codfish Park, where a lot of working-class African Americans and immigrants lived, Cape Verdeans and Irish, with their own shops and bakeries. Many of them worked as domestic help or at the old casino in the early nineteen hundreds. Oh! And 'Sconset is where the first distress call from the *Titanic* was heard."

When the path ended—erosion had cut it off, Dad said—we traipsed through a public alley between two mansions to a main road, which led to the lighthouse. SANKATY HEAD had been inscribed on a boulder at the entrance. Dad took a few pictures of me—with my head in them, thank god—and I took a selfie of both of us to send to Aunt Lou and Grandma and Grandpa.

A yellowing informational sign read SANKATY HEAD LIGHT-HOUSE, ESTABLISHED 1850, with a photo of the lighthouse next to houses that no longer existed. The first bullet point announced the beginning of the US Lighthouse Establishment under Alexander Hamilton in 1789.

"You liked *Hamilton* so much when you were little," Dad said. "I don't know if you still do, but I thought you might be interested."

"Dad, everyone liked *Hamilton*. It was a cultural phenomenon." When the concern on his face didn't lessen, I softened. "I still like it. This is very cool. Oh, look!" I pointed at another bullet. 1842–1845: NANTUCKET ASTRONOMER WILLIAM MITCHELL OBSERVES THAT NEARLY 45,000 SHIPS OF ALL DESIGNS HAVE PASSED NEAR THE NANTUCKET SHOALS. "This is Maria Mitchell's dad, right?"

"Right. Probably work they were doing for the Coast Survey. He drew a really good map of the island, too."

I laughed. Dad probably hadn't meant to be funny—it probably *had* been a really good map—but I liked that someone could be remembered for a map.

Also, I thought it was very sweet Maria and her dad worked together. "You could do another whole book on fathers and daughters who worked together."

An expression of delight crossed Dad's face. "I could! Hm . . . Monet's stepdaughter, Blanche, was also a painter. And Rashi's daughters might have taken dictation from him."

"Rashi—the scholar?" I recognized him as a Talmudic scholar but couldn't recall much more.

"Yes, from eleventh-century France. His daughters married his students, and were more involved in scholarship and rituals than women usually were at the time . . ."

We walked around the squat lighthouse, admiring the sunshine washing over the land, before returning the way we'd come. In the village center, we ordered ice cream and ate our cones at small tables out back.

"Can I see your apartment?" I asked when we'd finished. "It's on the way back to town, right? It's been a couple weeks and I still haven't seen it."

He looked abashed. "There's really nothing to see . . ."

"Dad."

So we hopped off the local bus, the Wave, halfway back to town, in what Dad said was the Tom Nevers neighborhood. The trees here were tall and dense, moss carpeting their trunks. It reminded me of the forests at home, where I'd spent countless hours wandering through oceans of ferns, clambering up pines, and balancing on fallen logs. The speckled sunlight made the forest feel magical, and fleeting nostalgia stabbed at me as we walked down a bike path.

Dad rented a room in a townhouse complex, a real suburban-development vibe—a shared pool and lots of parking. Dad pointed out a nearby Salvadoran store where he got his coffee and lunches, and where I was sure he used his schoolboy Spanish, then led me to his front door. It wasn't locked, and Dad laughed at my scandalized reaction.

At least none of his prized possessions were in the downstairs common area, which consisted of a shared galley kitchen for the four boarders. Enough space to scramble eggs, but not for involved cooking projects. Too bad—Dad loved cooking.

Dad's room was on the third floor, and he led me up carpeted stairs, past a shared bathroom and laundry room. He unlocked the door. "It's not much . . ."

The room was neat as a pin, and not much larger. It was shaped like an L; the short leg contained a bed tucked beneath the eaves, while the long side had a window overlooking the road and the woods beyond. Cozied up to the foot of the bed was a desk, piled high with books, papers, and my dad's laptop. The rest of the room had a mini-fridge, microwave, and two armchairs facing each other over a round end table.

"It's nice," I said. It felt more like an Airbnb than a place to live: not bad, but impersonal. And sharing a bathroom with strangers seemed highly unpleasant, but then again, Dad usually shared with me, and I spent a large (and unfairly maligned) amount of time on my hair in the mornings.

"Have you seen the new British movie, with the blimp?" Dad

asked. "It has that young actress you like, the redheaded one, and the man who looks like a string bean . . ."

I laughed. "He doesn't look like a string bean. He's hot."

Dad gave a mock-beleaguered sigh. "I never thought my progeny would find string beans attractive."

I shook my head, still grinning. "Do you have popcorn? And mini chocolate chips?"

"What do you take me for, a monster? Of course I do."

We made stovetop popcorn and sprinkled in chocolate chips alongside the salt, letting them melt and stick the popcorn together in delicious globs. I loved hanging out with Dad like this, laughing and joking though the movie, ordering Thai food for dinner. It felt like being home.

If Dad sold the house, would anything ever feel like home again?

"Where would you want to go if we sold our house?" I asked tentatively, after the movie ended and we'd cleaned our plates. "You mentioned Boston?"

Dad had always been easy to read; now he looked surprised, like he hadn't expected this conversation. Then he braced himself, ready to make his best effort. "I'd like to live closer to the city, yes. Though it would mean less space. It'd be nice to feel not so . . . isolated."

"We don't feel isolated," I said automatically, before realizing, you know, Dad was a different human being than me and might have different feelings.

"Jordan," he said, leaning forward. "I know this is hard. I know how much you love the house."

I shrugged and looked out the window. A bird flew by, small and dark, a splash of red on its wing. "I thought we both loved it."

"We do," he said. "I do. However, sometimes change is good."

"Yeah, but I'm already going to college in two months. Do we really need more change?"

He looked away, then back at me, determinedly. "I think it might be good to live somewhere where we can make new memories."

"What do you mean?" He meant something, and I could feel it in my stomach, in the way the bottom was trying to detach and fall away.

"I love our house. More importantly, I love you. And we will always have each other. But I think it might be time to live somewhere where not all the memories are about Mom."

Oh.

Of course the house had memories of Mom for Dad. Of course he wanted somewhere new and fresh. That was good, and healthy, and right.

Only the thing was—I didn't have my own memories of Mom.

I had the house. I had the town. I had Dad, and Aunt Lou and Uncle Jerry, and anyone else who could unearth a few memories for me. I kept them in a little box in my mind, *Stories About Mom*, and I pulled them out when I needed them. I pulled them out most easily in places where I'd seen photos of us together, or where a faint ghost of a memory lingered. The rocking chair, where she'd cuddled me. The kitchen, where she'd made mac and cheese and convinced me to eat mushy carrots. The window nook in the den, where she'd read me Spot the Dog.

Dad had real memories of Mom. They'd had a life together.

He didn't need the house to keep them safe or bring them to life.

Okay. I wanted Dad to be happy, didn't I? So time for me to grow the fuck up. "What would it be like?" I asked, staring at my plate. "An apartment? Would I have a room?"

Dad sounded horrified. "Of course you would have a room."

I blinked rapidly, relief suffusing me. "Okay."

"Jordan, you will *always* have a place, wherever we are."

"Cool," I said, trying to sound cool. "Just don't want you to turn the spare room into an office as soon as I'm off at college."

"You'll have a room," Dad said again. "Always."

I borrowed Dad's bike to get home, wind in my face as I sped along the path paralleling Milestone Road, past forests and moors. I felt itchy to do something, like the summer dusk was a drug leaving me aching for experiences. Worse, a storm was coming, clouds rolling in from across the sea, the balmy day now foreboding.

I made it back to Golden Doors around nine, as raindrops started to splash against my skin. In the cousins' room, I found several Barbanels cozied up with their partners, watching a movie, with several more cousins spread about. Too tame for how I felt, so I headed to my room and called Grace. Talking soothed some of my strange agitation, but when we hung up around ten thirty, I still felt jittery.

At eleven, the thunderstorm started in earnest.

The *pitter-patter* of rain against the roof intensified, and I tore my gaze away from my phone to look out the window. It was mostly a black square of night, beaten over and over with translucent streams of water. Then the low rumble of thunder began. Water droplets clung to the windowpanes, and bright white lightning cracked the night. The thunder grew louder, crashing booms I felt in my chest.

It got to me, the deep roaring going on and on. I sat up in bed, staring out the window. I felt odd and strange, like something had slithered under my skin and wrapped around my heart and bones—this house, this island. This storm. It made me feel like something was supposed to happen. If I'd been a little kid, if I believed in fairies and dragons and quests, I would have said it was magic sparking in the air.

Rolling out of bed, I swapped my oversized T-shirt for a tank top—the less fabric the better when it came to rain on my skin. Two minutes later, I pushed open the door to the roof walk and stepped into the downpour. In seconds, the rain soaked me through—slashing, drenching rain, plastering my shirt to my skin and my hair to my head. Water dashing over my cheeks like tears. My lashes were spiky, and a *boom* of thunder made me gasp.

And I could see a light in the east wing. A silhouette, a boy. Then the light went out.

I lifted my face to the sky, half drowning in the endless deluge. There was no moon tonight, no stars, only darkness, except for when those white lines illuminated the world—the wrecking sea, the tossing waves, the whipping trees. I drank it in, this wild world, this island that people had tried to tame. People always wanted to tame things, to bend the strongest forces to their will, make them soft and palatable. But how did you tame a feeling bottled up inside you so tightly you thought it might burst? And if you *did* tame something—if you covered an island in roads and houses and cars—didn't you regret it in the end?

"What are you doing?"

I spun, almost slipping on the soaked boards. Ethan stood in the entryway. "Come inside!" he shouted. "You're soaked."

"Come outside!" I shouted back, because why not, because here we were in this wild world. "Or are you going to tell me it's dangerous?"

I won the standoff; he stepped outside. "Be careful, okay?" he said, still yelling slightly to be heard over the rain, which soaked him as immediately as it had me.

"You be careful! I don't want to be careful." My gaze slid over him, over the cotton of his T-shirt, now molded to his arms and chest.

He took a step closer and slipped. I grabbed for him, catching his arm. His left hand landed on my shoulder with a firm grip. "Careful," I said, breathless, raising my face to his. "The larger they are, the harder they fall."

"I'm not falling." The rain poured over us, streaming down our faces, sticking our clothes to our bodies.

"Good." I wasn't falling either; I wouldn't. But I did take a last little step forward, the heat in me so strong I couldn't even consider ignoring it, so strong I half expected steam to come off our bodies. I reached my hands up and placed them on his shoulders, and when he didn't pull away, I pressed my lips to his.

I felt his intake of breath, and for a moment his hand curved around my hip and he pulled me closer—and then he paused, frowning. "Are you okay? Are you drunk?"

Offended, I pushed at him—not enough to disengage but

enough to let him know he'd annoyed me. "I'm fine. I just wanted to kiss you. Silly me. Sorry."

"Don't go." He didn't let me pull away. "I just wanted to make sure you wanted this."

"Yes," I said. "I want this."

He wrapped his arms around my waist and pulled me flush against him, and my hands slid around his neck and we were kissing. The tight, hot heat inside me finally found grip on something, on him, as I pressed myself closer and deepened the kiss. I tried to drink him in, this boy. I pulled at his shirt, trying to peel the sodden fabric away from his skin, and we were laughing, wrestling the T-shirt over his head.

The rain stopped as abruptly as it had begun.

I froze. The rain had felt like a cover, keeping everything safe and secret. Without it, my sodden clothes felt heavier and more uncomfortable, and I felt like a silly, desperate fool, throwing myself at Ethan when he clearly thought I was a mess. He'd thought I was *drunk*. "I'm sorry," I said. "I shouldn't have done that."

He reached for me, but I stepped back.

"Jordan. Are you okay?"

"Yes." I took another step toward the door, the water from my hair and clothes pooling on the deck. "I was in a mood. I should go. Shower and sleep."

"Jordan—"

"Sorry," I said again, interrupting. "I shouldn't have grabbed you like that. Um—sleep tight."

I didn't sleep at all for the rest of the night.

Twelve

As the calendar flipped into July, Dad and I explored the island in the long evening light. He showed me the national forest and boggy marshes thick with cattails. We walked along the harbor, picking out our favorite boats, and sailed around Coatue, the strip of land almost entirely blocked off as a natural reserve. Tourists invaded the island, but Dad and I still managed to find untouched beaches far from town, and I felt so happy, getting back in the habit of spending time together.

Working for Cora also made me happy. She was a mix of droll humor and impressive intensity. Sometimes she'd spend a full day studying graphs with a crease between her brows, downing endless cups of coffee and barely speaking, except for long, complicated calls with collaborators. But when she did talk to me, she was patient and thorough and kind. I learned about the people she worked with—the other astrophysicists studying debris in space, the government agencies involved, the chair of her department—DH—who was not her boss, but not *not* her boss.

"Does it ever make you mad?" I asked her once, after I heard one of her male colleagues' voices become a little too condescending.

She was silent for a minute. "Often," she finally said. "But I love the work. I'm not going to be bullied out of doing something I'm brilliant at. And I remind myself the assholes are products of their society and upbringing, and it's not about me, and I'm great at my job. And I hope my accomplishments are going to make it easier for future generations of women and people of color. So yeah, I'm mad sometimes. But it doesn't stop me."

I wasn't sure an adult had ever been so honest with me. It was alarming, but I liked it.

The only thing keeping me from being totally happy was my uncertainty regarding Ethan. Were we okay? Were we a disaster? I'd apologized to him the day after making out with him in the storm. "I'm sorry," I'd said as we'd walked through the gardens in the early morning. We'd fallen into a pattern of going down to the beach for morning swims, and I'd decided the best thing to do was to continue the pattern, to act like the night before hadn't been a big deal. "I was feeling itchy, and it was storming, and you were there—"

His mouth had twitched. "I was there," he'd echoed. "Flattering."

"I didn't mean to hurt your feelings—"

"Jordan." The sky had been bright blue, washed fresh after the storm. "I am *very* happy to make out with you whenever you want to make out. As long as you're into it."

"Oh," I said in a small voice. A shiver cascaded through me. "Okay."

We hadn't talked about it again.

I'd finished pulling all the data Cora had wanted on the Harvard Computers and astronomy on Nantucket, but I continued digging into Andrea Darrel during my off hours. I emailed Harvard to see if there was a way to get digital copies of her box of papers; they said unfortunately not, but I was welcome to submit a form and, if approved, look at the boxes filled with her papers in person.

Bummed out, I mentioned it to Grace on one of our weekly video calls.

"Why don't I go for you?" Grace said.

"What?" I'd been lying on my bed, but now I sat up. "What do you mean?"

"You said people can go in person, right? I can take the bus into the square and take pictures of the pages and send them to you."

"Oh my god, Grace. You don't have to," I said automatically, though hope flared in me. "I would *love* if you did, but you don't need to."

She rolled her eyes. "I wouldn't offer if I didn't mean it. Besides . . ." Her eyes glinted. "This is a perfect ploy to ask Sierra on a date."

Sierra was the new girl at the diner who Grace had been obsessing over for the last month. "Um, how?"

"You said there's a visiting researcher form or something? I probably can't fill it out, but Sierra is eighteen." Grace, like me, was a September baby—we'd consistently been the youngest in our grade. "I'll tell her I need her help and she'll fill it out and we can go together and it'll be an adventure!"

"Look," I said, "I don't want to be too wild or anything, but why don't you just ask her to see a movie?"

"Too wild," Grace countered promptly.

"How is this girl going to have any idea you like her if you don't suggest an actual, you know, date?"

Grace clasped a hand to her heart. "She shall be overcome with love and lust for me when she sees what a good friend I am."

I snorted a laugh. "Okay. Thank you, seriously. Tell her I insisted you guys go to some super romantic spot while you're in Cambridge if you need an excuse to check out a sunset or hot chocolate or whatever. Or that I'm treating you guys to dinner so you can take her somewhere nice. Wait, I *will* treat you guys to dinner, I'm Venmoing you now."

Despite liking the Barbanel cousins and their friends— especially Abby and her crew—I missed my friends from home as the Fourth of July approached. At home, I always spent the Fourth on the banks of the Charles, listening to the Pops play the *1812* overture as fireworks exploded. We brought card games and picnic blankets and bought fried dough and over-priced lemonade from food trucks, and snuck into MIT to use their bathrooms instead of the porta potties. I knew my friends would be there now, without me. Would we ever all be together again, or would everyone be spread out next summer?

This year, I headed downtown with the Barbanel crew. It was blazingly hot; sweat plastered my tank top to my back. I'd worn my most minuscule shorts to reduce the amount of fabric on my body, yet I still wanted to peel my skin off. In the center of Nantucket, people packed the cobblestone streets, a flurry of patriotism and primary colors.

"See you guys later," Ethan said once we got downtown.

David smirked. He, like me, was one of the few wearing not red, white, and blue, but instead a blue romper to match the new color of his hair. "You bet you will."

"Where are you going?" I looked back and forth between the brothers.

"Dunk tank," they chorused.

My mouth parted. "You're *participating*? You're going to get dunked?"

"Depends how good your throwing arm is," Ethan said. Then he grimaced. "Unfortunately, my family all have great throwing arms."

David patted Ethan on the back. "You're doomed."

So of course we went to the dunk tank as soon at Ethan's shift started. He lounged in his seat above the water, heckling players as they tried to throw their balls hard enough to trigger the mechanism to plunge him down. I wished I didn't think he looked like a prince lounging on his throne—I'd tried so hard since our stormy makeout to avoid noticing how hot I found Ethan—but he did, like a laid-back, devil-may-care lordling, ready to greet his adoring crowds. I wanted to crash him into the tank in an epic wave, then watch him burst out, spewing water and laughing.

I waited in line with all the Barbanels, cheering on the failed attempts to soak Ethan to the bone. A few girls stood before us, though only one seemed interested in playing. She stepped up, flashing a grin at Ethan. "You ready for this?"

"You know I am."

I felt like I'd been punched in the stomach. I was used to seeing Ethan's grin directed at me. I knew he was a flirt, but I rarely saw him in action.

The girl wound up her arm like an all-star pitcher. She was pretty, her blond pigtails decorated with red-white-and-blue streamers, wearing a white tank top and denim shorts. She released the ball to her friends' cheers, but missed the target completely.

Ethan laughed. "That your best shot, Thompson?"

"Not even close," she returned, winding up her arm one more time.

This time, she hit the target, but not hard enough to trigger the game. But the third time, her ball hit the center. The floor opened up beneath Ethan, and he plunged into the water.

Everyone cheered. The girl's friends clapped her on the back, and she laughed giddily.

Ethan came up sputtering. His white T-shirt was plastered to his skin, and the water weighed his hair down so it lay flat against his head. The way it did when we went swimming together early in the morning, which I considered a private, intimate look. It felt weird for so many other people to see it.

No, I was being weird. There was nothing private about our relationship. We were just—roommates. We'd hooked up, sure, but it hadn't meant anything. There was nothing between us.

This didn't stop my whole body from clenching as I watched

the girl walk up to the edge of the tank, where Ethan had made his way to the ladder.

She greeted Ethan with a giant smile. "Told you I'd knock you down a peg."

Something hot and unpleasant twisted my stomach as Ethan returned her grin, swiping wet hair out of his eyes and leaning against the tank's rail. "I didn't expect you to be so literal."

She laughed. "When are you done?"

"Got another hour."

"Want to get ice cream?"

"Why not," he said. "Love ice cream."

I hated ice cream. I hated everything, including myself, for apparently developing emotions despite strict instructions to the contrary.

"Great," the girl said, and with a flip of her pigtails, she walked away.

Ethan watched her go appreciatively before hoisting himself up the ladder and out of the pool. His gaze swept the audience as he returned to his seat, and halted on me. Or, more likely, on his family surrounding me. His grin widened. "Oh, hey."

I didn't want to be here anymore.

"Get ready to live in that dunk tank," David said.

Ethan *was* looking at me. He didn't break eye contact, either. "Ready."

"I'm actually hungry," I said, turning toward Shira. "I'm gonna go grab a bite. I'll meet you after."

Shira's gaze darted to Ethan. "Sure. Text and we'll find you."

I nodded and pivoted away.

The crowds were thick, and I didn't have a destination. I wasn't hungry; I just didn't want to stand there smiling at Ethan like this was all fun and games when I was pissed off. Which I had absolutely no right to be. But also, this was exactly why I didn't want to get involved with Ethan, why I'd *known* hooking up with him had been a mistake. If I gave Ethan an inch I'd give him a mile, and then I'd be falling head over heels and when I landed my heart would splinter like glass.

"Hey!" Ethan's voice sounded behind me. "Jordan, wait up."

I turned, astonished. His hair and T-shirt were already drying in the heat. My fingers itched to fix his unruly curls. "What are you doing here? Don't you have an hour left?"

"I traded for later. Why'd you run off?"

I'd gotten so used to having Ethan to myself. To knocking on his door early in the morning and heading down to the beach. To hanging out in the cousins' room late at night, chatting with Shira and Miriam while he played video games. Last night we'd grilled tomatoes together for dinner and my fingers still smelled like garlic from chopping so many cloves. I'd become used to his attention thoroughly focused on me.

But I had absolutely no claim on him. It'd been eight days since we'd hooked up, and I'd told him it'd been because I was itchy and he was there, nothing more. "I wanted food."

"Then let's eat."

Strange, how the simple suggestion unknotted the tension inside me, how though I hadn't been hungry, now a bite sounded nice. Except—"If you eat now, your appetite will be spoiled for ice cream," I said, more snippily than I'd intended.

Ethan grinned and wrapped me in an unexpected bear hug, lifting me off my feet. I squealed in surprise. "What are you *doing*?!"

He put me down. "I like when you're jealous."

"I'm not jealous."

"That's cute." He tweaked my nose, which I would have burned anyone else alive for doing. "Let's get lunch."

We got lunch.

We watched the fireworks from a beach, giant bursts of color splashing against the night. Afterward, I followed the Barbanel cousins to a party, squeezing into a Jeep in a pile of sticky limbs and driving to a sprawling house mid-island.

Ethan and I collapsed on a love seat while around us, people laughed and danced. "Yo, Ethan!" a guy shouted. "Come play beer pong!"

"I'm busy!" Ethan called back.

"I'm serious!" his friend said. "Stop flirting and help me out! These two are undefeated!"

"Go on," I said, amused. "You can't let them continue undefeated."

"I suck at beer pong. He'd be better off with someone else."

"Really?" I grinned. "I'm great at it."

"Of course you are." Ethan seemed flatteringly content to ignore his friends' calls and stay on the love seat with me. "So what's the plan for your dad and Cora? If you're going to play matchmaker, you need a plan, right? You can't be all willy-nilly about it."

"Willy-nilly?"

"Yeah. It's a real, important, serious phrase conveying the lack of your seriousness."

"Okay, Willy." I rolled my eyes, then stopped, realizing *willy* was slang I hadn't intended. "Uh . . ."

Ethan's brows shot up. "Excuse me, what are you calling me?"

"Nothing." I started to shake with laughter. "Nothing. Where do you think the term *willy-nilly* came from?"

"You're much cruder than I gave you credit for." Ethan shook his head solemnly. "Shouting *willy* everywhere."

"Stop it," I said, unable to contain my laughter. "You're like a twelve-year-old boy. That's not what I meant."

He gave a mock-reluctant sigh. "If you say so."

"I really *hope willy-nilly* doesn't refer to . . . I'm googling it." I pulled up Merriam-Webster on my phone. "Oh. *Will I, nill I.* That makes more sense."

"Does it? Nill I?"

"Seems—Old Englishy?"

"What was your alternate etymology?" Ethan asked with a grin.

"Use your imagination."

"Oh, I *will.*"

I gave him a gentle shove, amused and wishing I didn't feel so delighted by Ethan all the time.

"Okay," he said. "Let's game-plan this. Do we write your dad and Dr. Bradley notes and sign the other person's name?"

"You're ridiculous. No. That's a terrible idea."

"No ideas are bad ideas." He put his arm around my shoulder and tugged me to his side.

It felt good—too good—and I wanted to snuggle into his side. Which meant I should probably pull away. As a compromise, I decided to call him on it. "Oh, are you yawning?"

"Nah, I'm counting shoulders. Didn't you notice? Need me to demonstrate? Because I totally can."

"Oh my god, you *are* a twelve-year-old boy."

"Aren't we all twelve-year-old boys on the inside?" Ethan said philosophically.

"No. I'm not."

Ethan laughed. "I've always thought it's cruel kids become a bar or bat mitzvah at twelve and thirteen. It's the most awkward age in the world."

"I wouldn't know. I never did."

"Really?" He turned, his face close. "How come?"

I shrugged, embarrassed and overly warm. "I don't know. I mean, I do know. Dad and I aren't really religious, and I only went to Hebrew school for two years when I was little."

"Maybe you saved yourself a lot of awkwardness."

"Maybe," I said. "I think I might have liked to, though. Sometimes, I feel a little . . . I don't know. Not Jewish enough."

"Honestly, I think a lot of people can feel that way," Ethan said. "At least according to my mom and the aunts after a glass of wine."

I had noticed the women of Golden Doors did, in fact, thoroughly enjoy a life discussion in the evening over a glass of wine. "Really?"

"Yeah. And they, at least, don't think it's possible to not be Jewish enough, especially if you want to be. Besides, you can always have an adult bat mitzvah. Miriam's mom did that."

That made me feel a little better. I wasn't sure if I did want to, but I liked the idea of the option being available. And it made me feel better, too, to hear the women of Golden Doors didn't have standards I couldn't meet. "So was yours awkward?"

"Oh, definitely. But also great. I was the king of the dance floor."

My lips turned up. "I bet you were. Bet you have great moves."

"You sound like you doubt me." He launched to his feet. "Let me prove myself."

"Oh, wow, no, you don't need to."

Ethan rocked his hips from side to side, doing the shopping cart thing. I wrapped my arms around my knees and burst into uncontainable giggles as Ethan twirled in a circle, hands in the air.

David came by, his severe expression at odds with his romper and the lei he'd acquired. "Ethan. You're embarrassing me."

Ethan grabbed his brother's hands and started shaking them in the air, too.

David let him, but shot me a long-suffering glance as if to say, *You see what I have to put up with?*

When the song finished, Ethan returned to my side, grabbed my seltzer from my hand, and took a long swig. "Back to your dad and boss. Are you sure he even wants to date?"

"I think so." I recalled the conversation I'd overheard between Dad and Aunt Lou. "And I worry about him. He'll be alone when I'm at college." I shrugged. "Don't you have people you worry about?"

He glanced over at his brother, still dancing. "Yeah."

"See? Even though you know someone can take care of themselves—you still worry."

He chewed on his lip. "I guess, for me, it's less thinking he can't—it's thinking he won't. David can be so *angry* sometimes, I worry he won't give things a chance. I worry he'll turn up his nose instead of being happy. And our little brother, Oliver—he's artistic, which is great, but he can be so sensitive and get hurt. And *Miriam*—" He shook his head.

"What?"

"She's *so* empathetic. The other day, people were shitting on Pepsi as inferior Coke, and she got this sort of sad, worried look in her eyes. I asked her why, and she said—I kid you not—she felt bad for Pepsi because some people considered it their second choice. She felt *bad*. For a *corporation*. She said it wasn't for the corporation, it was for the people who worked there who tried really hard at their jobs and took pride in them and she didn't want their feelings to be hurt if they overheard someone speaking unkindly."

I took that in. "Wow."

"Yeah. How's she's supposed to function in the world if she's feeling so much for everyone?" He sighed. "So yes, I get worrying about people."

"And you have a lot of people to worry about, if it's all your cousins."

"Tell me about it," he said wryly.

I opened my mouth to ask who worried about him, then, but before I could, the blond girl with streamers in her pigtails from earlier approached. "Ethan Barbanel. I can't believe you blew me off earlier. I can't believe you blew *ice cream* off."

I tensed.

The girl didn't look mad; she looked flirty, hand propped on her hips, lips curved. Only her eyes looked flat. She reminded me of myself, and I didn't like it. It reminded me how I never took guys I liked to task for blowing me off, how I laughed and pretended it didn't matter. How I tried to be a Cool Girl, free whenever they were next free.

Ethan scratched his head. "Oh, hey, Kylie."

I muttered, "You at least texted her?"

"Yeah," he said, then seemed to realize introductions were in order. "Uh, this is Jordan, my boss's daughter. She's staying with us for the summer. This is Kylie."

"Hi," I said, despite the sinking feeling in my stomach at her brittle smile. This girl probably had something with Ethan. Well, what had I expected? We weren't a thing. We weren't anything. We were two people who lived in the same house and liked to make out with people, occasionally each other, for fun.

"How can I make it up to you?" Ethan asked the girl.

"You can get me a drink right now," she said.

Ethan hesitated, glancing at me. But this was good. This was the reminder I needed. Ethan and I were not a plausible match, which I knew five hundred times over. I forced a smile. "You guys go on," I said, light as a feather. Hopefully not stiff as a board.

"Jordan . . ."

"It's all good." I hopped to my feet. "I'm gonna dance with David."

And I did. David and I dance-shouted through the next several bops, screaming ourselves hoarse and jumping so enthusiastically I thought I might strain a limb or lung.

Was this . . . emotional growth? Not doing what felt good in the moment because I knew it would sour into regret? I deserved a prize.

Unfortunately, the prize I wanted was Ethan.

When I found my ability to keep from looking at Ethan and the girl decaying exponentially, I sent myself home. At Golden Doors, I found Miriam in the cousins' room, and we watched three episodes of the latest messy reality dating show. When Miriam started nodding off around one in the morning, I ushered her to bed. Since I knew I wouldn't be able to sleep, I checked my email—and found Grace had sent me photos of Andrea Darrel's Cambridge diaries.

This is just the first box, Grace had written. *Tbh your girl wrote a LOT. Sierra and I are going back next week to take pictures of the rest.* She'd included a selfie of her and a cute girl with an asymmetrical haircut posing in front of a cardboard box, each holding a journal. *Also we went to JP Licks and Felipe's on your dime!* Another photo, this one of them cheersing with burritos on a rooftop.

Smiling, I opened the first photo. In the unwavering yellow light of my screen, I enlarged the old pages filled with cramped, slanted letters and began to read.

Thirteen

June 18, 1896

*Arrived in Cambridge! I've become so used to New York
that Boston seems small and quaint, though its academic air is
unrivaled. I've been here less than a day and have already heard
a number of academic complaints, chief among them grumbling
about the city's lack of interest in implementing Dr. Pickering's
lamp screens, which would prevent light from polluting the skies.
Hopefully I have not arrived in Cambridge only to have it become
too difficult to see the stars.*

*I've taken a room in a boardinghouse filled with several other
women who work at the observatory, and today I met my new colleagues. The group is run by Mrs. Fleming, a no-nonsense Scottish
woman who has been here for over a decade. She began her career
as the Pickerings' housemaid, a job she took after being aban-
doned, while enceinte, by her husband. Mrs. Pickering noticed her
talent and recommended her to Dr. Pickering, who brought her to
work as a computer. Mrs. Fleming spoke at the Chicago World's
Fair when I was a sophomore, about hiring female assistants in
astronomy, and she discovered the Horsehead Nebula in Orion's
Belt. (Though she rarely gets credited.) She's also published a*

HANNAH REYNOLDS

catalogue of the stars based on the photos the Drapers donated (Dr. Pickering gets credited there).

Most of the other women are older than me. There are a few graduates from the women's colleges, the youngest six years my senior, Miss Henrietta Swan Leavitt. She will turn 28 on the Fourth of July, which is festive. She is very musical, and studied at Oberlin Conservatory before coming to Cambridge, though she is losing her hearing slowly. Still, she loves to sing. She is a quiet, gentle soul, which I appreciate, though I do love a rowdy one as well.

There is also Miss Annie Jump Cannon, 32, from Wellesley. She is deaf, and strikes me as a little sad—one of the other girls told me her mother died two years ago. Before starting as Dr. Pickering's assistant this year, she taught physics at Wellesley, and already knows how to handle the telescopes, of which I admit I am jealous. (Mostly only the men are allowed to handle to telescopes.) I like her immensely. I feel very lucky to be assisting her at work: she is classifying the spectra of the brightest stars in the southern section of the photographed sky.

The group of computers makes about forty, half men and half women. I am loath to report such facts to Mama in case she suggests I marry one of them, but at least if I did, there would be intelligent conversation to be had in my marriage.

January 17, 1897

Miss Maury's work, the "Spectra of Bright Stars," on the northern stars, was published in the Observatory's Annals, and for

170

the first time a woman's name was ABOVE any of the men!
It is so exciting, I fear I might burst into tears. Sometimes it feels
like we work so hard for so little credit, and for once, we have
gotten it.

Andrea wrote about using a magnifying glass to study glass plates and call out measurements, and her life, playing board games and drinking hot cocoa with friends. She documented the people she met, and the obstacles she faced (often her mother and sister). She wrote about the gardens maintained by Pickering's wife and the gatherings of astronomers held in the Pickerings' mansion. In 1898, Andrea—along with the whole astronomical community—was fascinated by the discovery of a comet. (Comets: So hot at the turn of the twentieth century.) Two separate astronomers noticed it when developing their photography plates, but since Gustav Witt of Berlin filed before Auguste Charlois of Nice, it became known as Witt's planet. *I feel some sympathy for Charlois,* Andrea wrote in August. *How must it feel to independently discover something, to feel such a rush, only to have someone else win the credit?*

November 4, 1898

A new discovery—Witt's planet first came close to Earth four years ago and no one even noticed! Chandler calculated the orbit, and now of course he wants glass plates from us to corroborate his theory.

How MADDENING we had proof of a comet and we didn't

even know! It's enough to make me want to go through all our plates and see if we have missed any.

November 12, 1898

Witt's planet is returning in 1900–01. Almost too excited to write such news! This means we'll be able to measure the distance between the earth and the sun. Of course Halley closed it down to 90 to 100 million miles in the 1700s, but now we'll be able to get a more exact measurement. It's to be a huge undertaking of the international astronomical community—observatories in Africa, Europe, and the Americas will be involved. We're the only one in the United States.

With this knowledge, we'll triangulate the distance between Earth and the sun and find the solar parallax. What an undertaking. What a discovery.

She wrote about how in 1899, forty-two-year-old Mrs. Fleming finally received a title from Harvard: Curator of Astronomical Photographs. She wrote of Pickering discovering a new moon orbiting Saturn and of traveling to Georgia in 1900 to see a total solar eclipse (it sounded like a party). In 1901, she celebrated the publication of Annie Cannon's new classification system (and mentioned, briefly, the assassination of the president; his vice president, who Andrea liked for distributing ice chips during a horrible heat wave, was sworn in—Teddy Roosevelt).

Every summer she visited her parents and her sister's growing brood on Nantucket. I knew from the first time I'd come across her name in the newspaper clipping that in 1906, Andrea Darrel and Annie Cannon would teach astronomy classes on the island. This batch of diaries didn't make it there; they ended in 1903. After I'd read the last entry, I finally fell asleep.

In the morning, it took me a moment to recover from dreams of blazing comets and telescopes and women traipsing across Boston in long dresses. Then yesterday came back: the dunk tank and fireworks and *not* kissing Ethan Barbanel but coming home instead.

The sky outside showed a perfect square of blue, so I rolled out of bed and resolved to act like normal, as though I couldn't care less how Ethan's night had gone with pigtailed Kylie. Still, a devilish part of me decided it was time to try out a scandalously cut white bikini I'd brought, which should be perfect against my new golden tan.

I knocked on Ethan's door. "Good morning!" I chirped when he answered, then winced, because I never chirped.

Ethan grinned, a slow unrolling of a smile, his towel already slung over his shoulder. "Morning."

Don't ask him about last night, I told myself as we left the house. I was far too proud to let on how bothered I was by the idea of him hooking up with someone else. "I've been reading these old diaries about a woman from Nantucket," I said. "They triangulated the distance between the sun and the earth, did you know that? I didn't really realize how much science people did a hundred years ago. Or how many women were involved."

"That's cool," Ethan said. "This is for your job?"

"Kind of. I'm also curious now. And, I don't know—you're doing a speech on the Gibson comet guy, right? I feel like she might have potential for something like that. How's the speech going, by the way? You said it's about his non-comet stuff? What'd he do?"

We picked our way through the gardens, passing tall pines speckled with sunlight, roses and junipers, their perfume thick in the air. It was the kind of summer day out of a dream, the sun hot on our skin, air moist. "Your dad has a chapter on this guy, Nicholas Heck, right?" Ethan said. "He was a geophysicist for the US Coast Survey, and he perfected wire-dragging, which Gibson helped him on a bit."

"Wire-dragging?"

"It mapped rocks and wrecks beneath the ocean's surface—to make sure your own boat didn't crash into them. They'd string a wire between two ships and weigh it down to a certain depth, and when the wire encountered an obstruction, they could use the wires to map its location." He grinned at me. "More triangulation. Anyway, Gibson did some wire-dragging here on local shipwrecks, along with some other hydrography work for the Coast Survey."

We reached the staircase to the beach, falling silent as we descended, the wind whipping away any words we attempted. On the beach, I let my cover-up fall off my shoulders and puddle at my feet. I glanced over and saw Ethan's eyes widen as he took in the white bikini.

"New bathing suit?" he asked casually.

"Like it?"

His gaze flicked up to mine, and a smile spread, as blindingly bright as the sun across the water. "Yes, Jordan," he said. "Yes, I like it."

I had to turn away to hide the strength of my smile.

With the sun blazing today, the water felt cold against our baked skin, and I shivered at each sensitive point. Usually, I made it in before Ethan, but this time he ran before me, submerging in a clean, quick dive. He stayed low, only his head above the water. "Scared?" he asked.

I took another step forward, the sea level rising against my rib cage. "I'll get in when I get in."

"Red junglefowl," he taunted. "Infant human being."

I sluiced my arm along the top of the water, sending a wave in his direction.

He dove under and grabbed my legs, pulling me off balance.

"Noo!" My cry ended quickly as I dropped beneath the waves. I sputtered to the surface, wiping salt water out of my eyes. "Ethan!"

He grinned. "Wanted to make sure you were awake."

If he wanted war, I'd give him war. I tried to kick him, but the water slowed me, so I settled for throwing my body at his, tackling him underwater. I sank too, but it was worth it.

We were a tangle of wet limbs and false innocence, as though the act of wrestling absolved us from agency, as though it wasn't our intention for our slick arms to rub against each other, for our hands to glance off each other's waists and legs.

"Uncle," I finally cried, "Mercy," but more because I didn't think I could keep myself from grabbing his face and pulling it to mine if we went on like this. We caught our breath, floating under the morning sun, the water lapping in my ears and muffling the world into a cocoon of sky and sea and thoughts of Ethan Barbanel.

We unfurled our towels and dropped onto them. I traced a circle in the sand with my forefinger, and then the question burst out of me, much as I tried to suppress it. "How was the rest of the party?"

"Good."

"Did you stay long?"

He gave me an amused look. "Not very."

Great, I'd showed my hand. "Hmph," I said, lying down on my towel. I could see him smiling out of the corner of my eye.

He let it go, thank god. "What's next in Operation Get Your Dad and Your Boss to Fall in Love?"

"That's a terrible name," I said. "The acronym would be like . . ."

We slowly worked it out: OGYDYBFL, which I pronounced "oh-*guy*-dye-biffle." "I can't even say it."

"O-gy-dy-*bi*-fel," Ethan said carefully, and then we were saying it, stumbling over the syllables and laughing.

"I was thinking," I said, "isn't your grandmother doing one of those garden tours?"

Nantucket had a garden festival, which sounded like it dropped out of a quaint village on a British TV show. One weekend every July, the island celebrated its gardens and gardeners. Talks were given by horticulturalists, and—more importantly, in my mind— tours were given of gardens, including the one at Golden Doors.

"Oh, yeah." Ethan looked surprised, like I'd surfaced something previously buried in his brain. "You gonna invite them both?"

"Seems like a good next step. Right now I'm not trying to create a romantic vibe or anything, I just want them in the same space so they can see if they like each other. I read this article about how friendships are most easily formed by repeated, unplanned occurrences, and I figure romance is the same."

His lips twitched. "But this isn't unplanned."

"But they think it is."

"Manipulative."

"Everyone's manipulative. At least I'm honest about it."

"With *me*."

I arched my brows. "Yeah, well, you can't have everything."

"Hm."

For a moment we lay on our towels, listening to the surf. I heard the opening of a cap, the distinctive squeeze of a bottle, then Ethan: "Sunscreen my back?"

My eyes whipped open. "Are you kidding me? Speak of manipulative!"

He gave me an innocent look. "My hands don't reach."

"You've managed okay so far."

He pulled a sad moue. "I got burned the other day, and the sun's really bright right now."

"Then put your shirt back on."

He held out the yellow bottle pleadingly. "Skin cancer is serious business."

"Again! Shirt back on!" My gaze dropped to the gleaming expanse of his golden skin, as though I'd ever not been excruciatingly aware of it, before managing to focus on the glittering ocean.

He spoke in a falsely sympathetic tone. "What's wrong?"

He was baiting me, and it worked. Glaring, I grabbed the sunscreen from his hand and squirted the lotion into mine. "Turn around."

"Aye, aye, Captain."

I smoothed the lotion onto his back, moving my hands in slow circles across his shoulder blades and down the length of his spine. "You're a menace."

"You love it," he teased. He craned his neck to see me. "What about you? You probably washed away your first round."

"I actually didn't put on a first round."

"Then you *definitely* need more." He pivoted so he faced me.

"Sounds like you're looking for an excuse."

"For what?" he asked, eyes wide. "I just want to help you, too, escape skin cancer."

"Hmph," I said, but I turned, because I also rather desperately wanted an excuse for his hands to be on my body.

He massaged the sunscreen into my back. My head dropped forward.

He stopped.

"Wait, no," I cried. "You can't start a massage and then stop."

He laughed, low in his throat. "I thought I was putting sunscreen on you. Not giving you a massage."

"Pleeease." Sometimes I had strength of mind, but not when

massages were involved. I wiggled my shoulders and looked back hopefully.

"Fine." He sounded more amused than anything else. "Since you asked so nicely."

I dropped my chin down to my chest. Victory. Luxury. "Thank you."

His hands roamed over my back, pressing deep in the small of it, thumbs drawing along my spine. One hand came up to massage the knots at the base of my neck, and I let out an involuntary groan.

"Lie down," he said softly, and I knew it was a bad idea, a very bad idea. But the responsible corner of my brain was far away and not very loud and so I ignored it and lay on my stomach. Ethan's knees settled on either side of me, and he leaned into the massage. I felt like I was melting into the sand.

And I knew it was just a massage. It was supposed to relax me. But the longer it went, the less relaxed I was. Instead, a hunger grew deep inside, a craving I was unable to ignore.

I twisted over onto my back.

Ethan hovered above me for a moment before I took hold of his shoulder and tugged him down. Then there was no space between us, just his lips on mine and sun-warmed skin on skin, with barely any clothing between us, only the thin strips of my bikini and the fabric of his swim trunks. It was easy to get lost in him, lost in sensation and warmth and touch. And I wanted to be lost because it felt so wonderfully good. It was intoxicating. I didn't want it to end.

Which meant it wouldn't end, if one of us didn't do something. I put my hands on his shoulders. "Wait."

He stilled. "Okay."

Easy to say wait; harder to mean it when my body very much wanted to keep going. But I knew what happened afterward, I knew I felt shitty and sad and small. "We should stop."

Ethan inhaled deeply, then rolled off me. He sat up, draping his arms over his knees. "Okay."

I was afraid if we kept staring at each other with heavy-lidded eyes, I'd jump him again. "I'm gonna go for another swim."

"Good idea."

We both ran toward the water and plunged ourselves almost desperately in, Ethan screaming like a small child at the cold. The cold was probably good, distracting and draining us of our heat and energy. By the time we returned to the beach, I felt almost normal again.

Almost.

As we gathered our things, we glanced at each other once or twice, and I could feel the unspoken words bubbling between us. *What are we doing? Should we talk about this?*

But neither of us said anything.

Instead, we climbed the steep, treacherous stairs to the top of the bluff. "So that was fun," Ethan said as we wound our way through the garden. From the leafy tree branches, a choir of songbirds serenaded us, while sunlight wicked the remaining water from our skin.

"Yeah," I said. "It was fun."

We reached the house and climbed in silence to our hall. "See you later," Ethan said from his doorway.

"See you," I said from mine. I watched him shut his door.

In the bathroom, I sank into the tub, the showerhead raining hot water down. What the hell was I doing? I'd been so proud of myself the night before for choosing the right thing, for not grabbing hold of Ethan when Kylie approached him. Yet here I'd made out with Ethan Barbanel a third time. I'd initiated it. I'd poured myself gleefully down a slippery slope leading to a cliff.

The problem was—I *liked* Ethan.

I wanted to drop my walls; I wanted to let Ethan in, to say *full steam ahead*, to believe *this* time it would work. Even if all signs pointed to the contrary. I even thought it might be worth it. So what if I fell for him and had my heart shattered into a million pieces? I'd done it before and survived.

But I couldn't watch my dad go through my messy sorrow again, looking helpless and as heartbroken as me. And I *definitely* couldn't make him watch me be heartbroken over his protégé. What if, god forbid, he felt caught between us? Nantucket made him happy. Ethan made him proud.

So this couldn't happen. Even if a large part of me wanted it to, it couldn't.

I just had to keep reminding myself of that.

* * *

Two days later, I stepped onto Golden Doors' lawn to find it transformed into a botanical wonderland. Flowers were ar-ranged in colorful bouquets: green myrtle and white gardenias and pink peonies and blue hydrangeas. Helen Barbanel stood at one end, directing two people to move vases around to the desired perfection.

I'd rarely interacted with Ethan's grandmother this summer. I saw her plenty—she presided over dinners and Shabbats and the occasional birthday, and every afternoon she and her husband sat on the deck and drank two fingers of amber liquor. But I mostly stayed out of the way of the Barbanel adults, except for Ethan's mom, who seemed determined to have genuine conversations about my day at least three times a week.

Now, however, Mrs. Barbanel and I were essentially alone together. I'd arrived early for the tour she'd be giving of her gardens, partially because I'd told Cora to come directly here instead of to the public meeting spot downtown. But I'd beat both her and my dad and now had to face the immaculately groomed consequences.

Mrs. Barbanel regarded me like I might regard a sea urchin—briefly interesting, but none too intelligent. "Ethan tells me you're playing matchmaker."

"He does?" I tried not to audibly gulp. "Uh . . ."

She raised her brows. " 'Uh' is not a sentence."

In my defense, she hadn't asked a question, though I bet she thought she had. "I thought my dad and my boss might like each other."

Mrs. Barbanel looked thoughtful. "The young lady who studies astrophysics?"

"Right."

"I assume they'll both be here today."

I nodded.

"Hm. And what about you? And beaux?" She frowned. "Or ladyfriends? My grandchildren tell me everyone likes everyone these days."

Oh, wow, okay, not sure I wanted to explain being queer to the Barbanel matriarch. "Uh, no, none of the above. Just—me."

"What about Ethan?"

What had I done to deserve this conversation? "Er—Ethan?"

"He seems to like you."

Hoo-boy. How did I tell someone's grandmother their grandson liked to hook up with me, not date me?

Actually, easy solution, I didn't have to talk about this. "Ethan and I are just friends."

Mrs. Barbanel gave me a skeptical look. "Why?"

"Why . . . are we just friends?"

"Young lady," Mrs. Barbanel said, "you should not spend an entire conversation repeating what the other person said."

Wow, love this talk for me. It seemed truly unfair old people could be rude and young people could do nothing in return. "I don't think Ethan and I see each other that way."

"My dear." Helen Barbanel sounded pitying. "You stare after him like a moonstruck calf."

Cool!

As though our conversation had summoned him, Ethan bounded onto the lawn. "Grandma! Jordan!" He wrapped an arm around my shoulders and gave me a hard side hug, knuckling my head as though I was a Little League player. I wanted to shove him away and also press my lips to his. "What's up?"

Mrs. Barbanel raised her thread-thin brows at me.

I smiled weakly. "Let's get ready for this garden tour, huh?"

"I'm pumped," Ethan said. "So ready. Grandma, can't wait to learn about flowers."

"I'm so glad after eighteen years you deign to come on a tour," Mrs. Barbanel said, but even she succumbed in the face of Ethan's good humor, a smile twitching at her lips.

Dad and Cora soon arrived, followed by the official tour of thirty people, both locals and tourists. A professional facilitated the tour, though Mrs. Barbanel did most of the talking, leading the group though the carefully tended groves and gardens created by generations of the women in her husband's family. By dint of not knowing anyone else, Cora and Dad gravitated together, though first I had to summon Ethan away so Dad couldn't use him as a crutch. "*Pst*," I said to get his attention while Mrs. Barbanel explained about beach grasses and other native plants she'd introduced to help fight dune erosion. When he glanced at me, I flapped my hand. *"Psst!"*

"You would make a terrible spy," Ethan said after finally coming over to my side.

"How can you say that? I would make an *excellent* spy." I gestured at my outfit, a black shirtdress. "I always blend with the shadows."

"A good spy blends with the crowd, not the shadows. If you really wanted to succeed at espionage, you'd be wearing Nantucket red."

This was not a horrible point. "True, but only if I was a daytime spy, not if I was a nighttime stealthy spy."

He glanced pointedly at the garden party. "Are you a nighttime stealthy spy?"

"No. But I'm not trying to be a spy, I'm trying to be—" I belatedly remembered the origin of this conversation. "Are you trying to say I'm not subtle?"

Ethan ruffled my hair and grinned. "There we go."

I pulled my head away and scowled, smoothing my hair back into place. "I am too subtle. *You're* oblivious. You were gonna spend the entire day hanging out with those two."

Helen Barbanel shot us a look, and I realized we weren't behaving like the captive audience she expected for her tour. I elbowed Ethan. "Shh."

"*You* shh," he whispered back.

For the final leg of the tour, Mrs. Barbanel led us to the small rose garden encircled by a tall hedge. We moved to the back of the crowd, and Ethan whispered in my ear. "Your boss is smiling."

"I'm a genius," I whispered back.

The rose garden had a gazebo in the center, and everyone wanted a picture as the tour ended. Cora glanced at it wistfully. "Dad, take a picture of Cora."

"Oh no, I'm fine," she protested, but I'd seen her Instagram. I knew her aesthetic.

"Dad," I insisted.

He turned his palms up. "I don't mind."

Smiling a little sheepishly, Cora went up the gazebo steps. At work, she was usually no-nonsense and when she joked, her humor was faintly dry. But now she laughed brightly, loosening up as she struck a few poses. And maybe she was just grinning for the camera, but her easy smile was still directed at my father. Dad grinned too.

Afterward, everyone returned to the lawn for a small selection of tiny quiches and miniature pound cakes, the cream fresh-whipped and the strawberries glistening with beads of juice. Mrs. Barbanel had also made a few treats specifically from her garden: rose-hip tea and a cake soaked in rose syrup.

Dad beckoned me and Ethan to join him at the table where he and Cora had taken a seat. He was, unfortunately, talking around a mouthful of food, but with great animation, pulling up images on his phone. "They're amazing. Did you see the latest ones?"

"Yeah." Cora nodded enthusiastically. "The third one? Wild."

"You kids see this?" Dad turned his phone toward me and Ethan. Red-orange wisps—the color of candle flames—spread across the black of space, pinned down by a smattering of orange-white pinpoints.

"What are we looking at?" Ethan asked.

"The Large Magellanic Cloud. It's a satellite galaxy of the Milky Way," Cora said.

"New pics from the James Webb telescope," Dad said, proud as though he'd taken them himself.

The James Webb Space Telescope was NASA's flagship infrared observatory. As the Harvard Computers had studied glass plates, modern astrophysicists could use images from the telescope to observe the formation and evolution of stars, planets, and galaxies.

Dad and Cora were talking up a storm about the images. Dad seemed thrilled to have an expert to talk to. Usually he was the passionate amateur expounding to his audience, but now he drank up everything Cora had to say.

"We have a framed photograph of the Pillars of Creation on

our living room wall," I told Ethan, watching Cora out of the corner of my eye. She had a postcard of the Hubble photo pinned to one of her corkboards. It showed interstellar gas and dust in the process of forming stars.

"You do?" she said.

The tips of Dad's ears reddened. "Kind of dorky, I know, but I think it's beautiful."

"No, I love it," Cora said. "I have it in my office."

Ethan kicked me under the table. I kicked him back, happily.

Everything was going well until Ethan's parents wandered into the backyard. I hadn't seen his father much over the summer; he popped on and off the island, mostly over the weekends. Now, the two came straight over, introducing themselves to Cora and making Ethan's back straighten.

"Just here for the weekend," Dan Barbanel said cheerfully when Dad asked. "But I'll be back for the conference and the comet party in August, of course."

Ethan's head whipped toward his parents. "You're coming to the conference?"

"Of course." His mom smiled. "We wouldn't miss your talk."

Ethan blinked several times, looking horrified.

"Wonderful," Dad said.

After the adults dispersed, I turned to Ethan. "You okay?"

"Sure." He looked dazed. "Why not. I love the added pressure of my parents coming to my talk."

"At least it means they want to support you."

"Or they're so baffled by the idea of me doing anything intellectual they need to see it to believe it."

I gave him a little nudge with my shoulder. "You're gonna kill it."

He still looked stressed.

"Wanna do some yoga?" I offered, my go-to stress killer.

He perked up. "Is that code?"

"It's code for 'doing some yoga.' Come on, there's some extra yoga mats in one of the closets."

"Fine," Ethan said with a sigh, following me upstairs.

For the next hour, Ethan mangled sun salutations and downward dog, fell over during tree pose and tickled me until I lost my balance. We laughed so hard my stomach ached. We stayed there until the white ghost of moon rose high in the blue sky, the smell of roses still clinging to our skin from the afternoon, and I wished for a moment that we could stay there forever.

Fourteen

D ad came over the next day to cook dinner. While Dad cooked at home—soups and stews and tofu bakes—I knew he didn't like impinging on the Barbanels' hospitality to use their kitchen, so it meant a lot that he'd come to cook dinner with me. We made gazpacho, enough for us and the half dozen fastest Barbanels (truly, a force of nature and of consumption), and a peach and arugula side salad.

"Come on," Dad said after we put everything away. "I have a surprise for you."

"A surprise?" I echoed. "What, here?"

"Follow me."

I did, confused, and also a little surprised he knew where he was going. After half the summer here, Golden Doors felt very distinctly mine. I recognized the route he was taking through the large, rambling house and was surprised he knew to take it.

"Just another minute," he said. "It should be right—aha!"

Dad opened the door to the roof walk. "How did you know about this?" I asked. It was nine fifteen, an hour past sunset.

"I asked," Dad said, pausing as I did.

Because I had stopped in astonishment. Usually, the roof walk was just me and my yoga mat (and sometimes Ethan). Now a telescope stood before us, its squat body perched on a tripod, pointing hungrily toward the sky.

"It's supposed to have sharp, high-contrast views," Dad said happily. He moved closer, adjusting an arm and a knob.

I stared at the telescope, baffled. "Is this—did you get this?"

"The Barbanels did, for their comet-viewing party at the end of the summer," Dad said. "It just arrived. We won't be able to see the comet by naked eye until September, so this way all the guests will be able to take turns looking at it."

"Cool." I remembered a few times, lying in starry fields, when Dad had produced a pair of binoculars for viewing the night sky. How fast the night spun when I moved even the smallest bit, like I was falling through the stars. Now I realized it'd probably been the unsteadiness of my child-hand, the impatience of wanting to find whatever Dad pointed out. I hadn't used binoculars in years, and I didn't think I'd ever looked through a telescope.

"Since you were interested in Maria Mitchell, I thought we'd try a little bit of what she did," Dad said.

He wanted to do for me what he liked to do himself, and it warmed me to my toes. "Like how you try to re-create nineteenth-century marine mapping. This would be nineteenth-century— sky mapping?"

"Sky sweeping," Dad said. "Which is pretty similar. In Maria Mitchell's day, astronomers used to sweep the skies daily, looking for anything out of the ordinary."

"Like what?"

"Like comets," he said. "She'd look at segments of the sky every night and note what was in each, and if she saw anything different, she knew it was out of place. I thought we'd give it a try."

"Think we'll find a comet?"

He laughed. "If we're lucky."

We did not find a comet; we didn't even sweep the skies for very long, only long enough to get a taste of the slow pace Maria Mitchell and other early astronomers must have lived. I imagined coming out in the evenings to the roof walk of her family's home in the center of Nantucket, studying each quadrant of the sky and noting each familiar star. Organizing the entire dome of the heavens into an orderly space, and getting to know each one.

Waiting for a comet.

"Do you think Gibson did this? Or would he have calculated the orbit without seeing it?" I asked Dad. From reading Andrea Darrel's diaries and researching the Harvard Computers, I'd learned some comets had been identified from photographic plates. A huge part of discovering comets also included calculating their trajectories; while all comets were parabolic, comets like Gibson's—and Halley's, and any other returning comets—were elliptical, periodically bringing them back through the inner solar system.

"He might have. It's a naked-eye comet, so he would have seen it at some point—but he caught it earlier than most people, either by photography or by telescope, as the first discoverer."

We carried the telescope back inside, to a little room across the hall from the roof walk where it would be safe from the elements, then headed downstairs. Dad slid his sandals back over his socks at the door. "I'll see you tomorrow for dinner."

"Pizza?"

Dad rolled his eyes, but only because it was his job to pretend he wasn't as excited about pizza as I was. "Why am I not surprised?" He smiled. "Yes, I think I can handle pizza."

* * *

The next day, I told Cora about the telescope and the sky sweeping over lunch. "Cool," she said. "Have you been to the observatory yet?"

I hadn't, though I knew two existed: the downtown Vestal Street Observatory, where the Maria Mitchell offices were, and the Loines Observatory a bit outside of town. "I keep meaning to go to one of the Open Nights but I haven't quite made it."

"I could take you over some time," Cora said. "Give you a tour."

"Really?" My eyes widened. "I'd love to."

"Ask your dad if he wants to come," Cora said, eminently casual. "Sounds like he'd also enjoy it."

"Sure." I tried to match her tone while inwardly wanting to scream in excitement. "Sounds great."

A few days later, Dad and Ethan and I headed to the Loines Observatory at nine o'clock. I'd enlisted Ethan because if there was even the slightest chance Cora wanted to hang around my dad, I would make that happen. With Ethan around, I'd have an excuse to leave Dad and Cora to their own devices.

"We could play romantic music, too," Ethan had teased, waving his phone back and forth like at a concert. "Serenade them."

"You mock. But wait until you see how effective my methods are."

The observatory was a few blocks north of town, across from a graveyard. I peered into the cemetery as the three of us walked along the sidewalk. One of the things I'd learned from night excursions was Nantucket did not invest in streetlamps as regularly as I'd like. Maybe rich people drove everywhere? Or maybe I was used to pollution warmly lighting the night sky?

"I think that's it." Dad looked from his phone to a steep driveway hidden in the trees across the street. A chain blocked the entrance, but at the top we could make out two domes peeking out from the forest.

"Very welcoming," I said.

We jogged across the street and up the drive. It ended in a small area with two round buildings covered in cedar shingles, their domed roofs metallic. A large deck connected the two, and more endless woods surrounded them.

"Hey, guys." Cora popped out of one of the buildings, its door propped open. "You found it!"

Inside, a massive telescope took up the majority of the space. It towered above us, pointed toward an open panel of sky.

"This is amazing." Dad walked a loop around the telescope. "Thanks for letting us in."

"For sure." Cora patted the base of the telescope fondly. "This is a twenty-four-inch Ritchey-Chrétien. There's Maria Mitchell's historic seven-point-five-inch Alvan Clark refractor, too—it's used for public stargazing."

"What's a refractor?" Ethan asked, hands in his pockets. I'd noticed that about him—he never pretended he knew something if he didn't. He'd always ask for more info, unafraid—as I was—of looking foolish.

"It's a type of telescope," she said. "Popular in the eighteen hundreds. This one's a reflecting telescope, we got it in 2006. Reflecting means it uses mirrors."

"A Cassegrain reflector, right?" Dad peered closer.

Cora grinned. "That's right."

"Ethan, I want some photos on the deck outside," I said, despite it being pitch black. To Dad and Cora, I said, "We'll be right back."

Ethan heaved a sigh. "My work is never done."

It was halfway through July; even late at night, the summer warmth lay like a blanket over us. We could hear the hum of cicadas, the low hoot of an owl. Above us the waning moon shone brightly in a cloudless sky. We'd be lucky with the Arborids this year; it'd be a new moon in two weeks, when they peaked.

"Now what?" Ethan asked. "Do you actually want me to take pictures?"

"Sure." I hopped up on the railing of the wooden deck. Ethan snapped a photo, then brought it over for me to see.

"I wonder if Gibson looked through the older telescope," Ethan mused, hopping up on the railing next to me. "He took an astronomy class here, so if the telescope was around then, he probably did."

I swiveled toward him. "Are you serious?"

Ethan blinked. "Yeah, why?"

"When did he take an astronomy class?"

"I think . . . 1906? Seven? Eight?"

"Annie Cannon *taught* those classes."

"Who?"

"Andrea Darrel's—the astronomer I'm researching—boss. Harvard sent Cannon over to help launch the Maria Mitchell Association. Do you think—what if Andrea Darrel and Frederick Gibson met?"

"Maybe they did. I can't imagine the astronomy community was that big."

"How old do you think he would have been?"

"Midthirties?"

In 1906, Andrea would have been thirty-three. "Interesting."

"Yeah." Ethan looked distracted. He ran his forefinger over the lace strap of my black romper. "This is also interesting. What is this?"

"It's a romper." I tried to ignore the flush of desire running through me. "I refuse to believe you don't know what a romper is."

"Whatever it is, it's wicked sexy."

It was, in fact, a very sexy romper. "Thanks."

He traced a line along the netting as the waist. "Bet you could get an interesting tan here."

Wouldn't you like to see? I almost replied, which didn't even make sense as a tease because Ethan saw me three-quarters naked almost every day at the beach. But the sensation of his finger running back and forth made it harder for me to think, and I couldn't manage any other words, so we sat locked in place, my breath coming harder and faster.

"Kids!" Dad called. "Come look!"

Ethan gave me a rueful look. "I guess they're not making out."

Neither were we, which was good. Right.

We stepped back inside the domed building, where Dad and Cora stood close to the eyepiece of the telescope. Dad gestured at it. "Come on, we want to show you something."

"What's it pointed at?" I asked, but Dad grinned and didn't answer, just gestured me closer while Cora made an adjustment. I stepped into place so my field of vision was filled with first darkness, then space.

At first, I wasn't sure what I was seeing—not a star, nor a planet, which I'd been expecting. No, this was distinctly human in make, modules connected by tubes, two long wings flaring out. It flashed across the field so quickly I barely understood what I was seeing.

"Was that the space station?" I felt a little stunned. People had done that, had created something capable of soaring through space. There were *people* up there, living and breathing and going about their lives, and we could look directly at them from thousands of miles away.

Cora readjusted the telescope. "Fast, right? It orbits Earth every ninety minutes." She motioned Ethan up.

"Pretty fucking cool," he murmured, and neither of the adults said anything about language, just smiled.

"Here." Cora tweaked the view again. "Now look."

I looked back through the eyepiece and sucked in a breath.

Now came a very different kind of awe, the kind created by witnessing something in nature so much larger than yourself. Jupiter. Dusty brown, the color of sand both pale and dark, striations circling the planet. A whole *planet*, something I could see simply by the effects of curved glass and mirrors. It made my breath shorten, even as my chest felt overwhelmed by air.

I could have stared at it forever, but I moved aside so Ethan could look, and Dad. Then Cora adjusted the telescope again so we could see Saturn, an even more foreign planet with its great rings.

"It's pretty amazing, isn't it?" Dad said. There was a soft yearning in his voice, an earnestness that came when he talked about the vastness of space or history. Like he was an explorer who knew he would never reach the other side of his journey.

I leaned my shoulder into his. "It really is."

An hour later, Ethan and I dropped Dad off at his apartment, then returned to Golden Doors. We parked in Ethan's usual spot, but instead of heading up the porch stairs, I tilted my gaze toward the stars, toward all those far-off balls of gas and plasma. Energy whirled inside me, a galaxy of motion, like I too hurtled through space on an unending mission. I turned to Ethan. "Wanna go swimming?"

Ethan looked at me for a long moment, then a smile burst out of him. "Heck yeah, I do."

We went down to the beach. The surf was rough and loud, waves taller and more forceful than usual. I drank it in, the way the night was unending here, the way we were two minuscule specks in a world of blue, the way anyone in any time could have stood on an empty shore and been overwhelmed by the crash of the waves and the diamond sprinkle of stars.

"Can you recognize the planets?" Ethan leaned back his head.

"Sometimes," I said. "There's not so many during summer nights, though. More in the mornings, and more in the winter. But I know some constellations. There's the Tree, see? Those three bright stars in a row, with the fan of faint stars at the top? That's what the Arborids are named after, because it looks like the meteors are coming from the Arbor constellation."

"Really? I didn't know that." He looked out at the rippling black water, at the pinpricks of light hanging above. "I've always thought the sea and sky are similar. They're both so wild. Dark and vast and cold and amazing." He nodded into the distance. "When I'm at sea, I can . . . I don't know, *feel* how connected the two of them are."

I nodded. "Cora told me when NASA looks for life on other worlds, they talk to marine scientists. Since the likeliest place for life would be a water world, and who best knows how to look for life in water? And Dad told me one of the space shuttles was named after a famous British explorer's ship."

"The *Challenger*?"

"Oh! The *Endeavour*, actually. James Cook?"

He laughed. "I guess there's a few. The *Challenger* did the first global marine research expedition."

"I like it." My gaze drifted to the ocean, the white-edged waves, the streak of moonlight. "The synchronicity of the two. Even the articles I've been reading use nautical references for space. 'The cosmic sea' and so on."

"They go together," Ethan said. "And even though they're wildly different, they're also wildly alike." Ethan gazed at the sky, the water, then me. "Jordan . . ."

"Yes?"

"Can I kiss you?"

He'd never asked before; asking made it feel more serious, intentional rather than accidental. A contract we'd agreed to. I couldn't tell myself, *Whoops, just slipped up, overcome by hormonal longing.* This made it 100 percent my fault. I'd looked at the choppy waters, said fuck it, and dived in.

But oh, I wanted to kiss him. Desire slid over me like a silken web, trailing shivers over my shoulder and down my back. Like a whisper at the ear, a kiss on the neck. Ethan looked at me with his sure, strong gaze, not hiding how much he wanted this, his desire and intent clear.

And I had never been very good at saying no to things I wanted. "Yes."

He slid his hand up my neck, his fingers finding their way through my hair, tugging my head gently back as he touched his lips to mine. I pushed myself closer, my hands over his shoulders, rising on tiptoe, holding him tight.

Oh no.

I had fallen head over heels for Ethan Barbanel.

Fifteen

The next morning, Ethan dropped down across from me at the outside table where I'd taken my coffee. His eyes gleamed. "I have an idea."

"Okay," I said cautiously. This seemed like a lot of energy, which I distrusted. "What kind of idea?"

It was one of those perfect summer mornings, with fat, lazy bees bumbling about. The sky was blue, the grass dark green, and everything smelled the way it had when I was a little kid at summer camp. If I could bottle this day, I would.

"Why don't we get your boss to come out on the ship?" He waved a hand at my blank expression. "You know, Gary Dubois's tall ship?"

"Gary—who? What ship?"

Ethan's surprise quickly morphed into embarrassment. "I thought you knew. It's in a few weeks. There's this guy, Gary, who's spent the last ten years building a replica of a nineteenth-century sailing ship. He's a tech CFO and this is his hobby, I guess. Your dad and I are going out on it for a few nights."

Right, yes, of course they were. Why was I still surprised they did things without me?

"Anyway, you and Dr. Bradley should come. It'd be guaranteed quality time for them."

I was too busy trying to stomp out my spike of resentment to respond. Fine, my dad and Ethan still had their own relationship, but did it have to include a *trip on a millionaire's boat*?

This was why anything romantic between us was a bad idea. I couldn't make out with someone who made me simmer with jealousy.

Well, apparently I *could*. But I *shouldn't*.

"Would they let us come?" I finally asked. "Is there room?"

"I think so. It's pretty big."

I didn't hate the idea: a trip, after all, would create many repeated, unplanned interactions. But . . . "How would I convince Cora?"

"I dunno. It's during the Arborids, so it's supposed to be great for seeing them. Maybe she'll care about that, because of astronomy?"

During the Arborids?

During the meteor shower Dad had always taken me to see as a kid, the one I'd assumed we'd watch together this year, on Nantucket. But Dad didn't plan to be here. No, he planned to be off at sea, with Ethan. "I see."

"I'll show you the ship." Ethan, unaware of my ire, pulled up a photo on his phone, and I blinked in surprise. Even though Ethan had called it a nineteenth-century replica, I hadn't expected to see something straight out of *Pirates of the Caribbean*. Sails billowed atop a deep brown hull, edged in endless rigging.

"It's a gaff-rigged schooner," Ethan said. "He's been working on it for years, and it's finally seaworthy."

It looked ridiculous. It looked amazing. "How long are you going?"

"Three nights."

"Huh." I bit my lip. "Maybe I'll talk to Dad."

I spent all day trying to psych myself up to ask Dad about the trip. He'd made a picnic dinner, which we took to Jetties Beach: avocado sandwiches with roasted red peppers, tomatoes, and red onions; pickle spears; salt and vinegar chips. It was windy, and the seagulls were out in full force—guarding our meal was an endless battle.

"So," I said, once we'd demolished most of the food and the seagulls forswore us in order to attack two couples sharing a bag of chips. "Ethan says you're going on a boat trip."

"Er, yes."

"Were you going to tell me about it before you left?"

"Actually . . ." Dad cleared his throat. "I was hoping you'd want to come with us."

I blinked. Then blinked again. "Oh."

"Only if you're interested," Dad said quickly. "I know you have your own plans and things to do here—"

"Dad, of *course* I want to come!"

He looked inordinately pleased. "Really?"

"Yes! Obviously!" I hadn't planned my strategy out this far, so I blurted, "You should invite Cora, too."

Dad froze.

"She'd love it," I forged on. "Think how well we'll be able to see the meteor shower."

Dad looked torn. "Well—I wouldn't want to overstep. But if you think she'd be interested . . ."

"Who wouldn't be? A free cruise? I mean, as long as the rooms aren't historically accurate."

Dad smiled. "No, the inside is modern. Gary was only willing to forgo so much."

"Great. Ask her."

"Maybe you should ask—"

"No," I said firmly. "It's a better, more real invite if it comes from you."

* * *

As it turned out, Dad had the opportunity to ask Cora the next day. I'd confirmed she'd be coming to a charity beach barbecue, and so I told Dad to join me and the rest of the Barbanel clan there.

Even though the days were routinely in the eighties, with hot, humid air keeping my hair in a decade to match the temperature, I knew better than to go to the beach without a sweater. I slung one over my shoulder as we joined a dozen people spread out over the sand, their colorful blankets and extensive coolers creating a city on the beach. A folk band had set up. Restaurant tents served bite-size burgers, caprese skewers, fruit salads filled with plump, gleaming berries. I tried a surprisingly delicious cucumber and grilled plum salad and summer squash with pesto.

"Do you remember when we boarded the ferry, and all those people asked about the arugula on your pizza?" I said to Ethan as we sat at a picnic table, licking strawberry lemonade popsicles.

"Oh, yeah. That was kind of weird."

"Right? It *was* weird. Why did all those strangers talk to you!"

"I guess they were really baffled by the arugula." He grinned. "I was busy trying to think of how to get the hot girl nearby to notice me."

"Oh?" I bit back a smirk. "What was your plan?"

"Aim my hot presence in her general direction. Luckily, it worked."

"I'm pretty sure you said, 'I want to show you something.'"

"In retrospect, not my best work. Ten out of ten results, though."

When Cora arrived, Dad joined her circle fairly quickly. I squeezed Ethan's bicep. "My god, do you see that? They're interacting. I didn't even manipulate them this time."

"Ow," Ethan said. "Didn't you tell your dad he had to ask her about the boat?"

I snorted. "Please, he's not going to until I make him."

We went over to join them, and sure enough, they were discussing a book they'd both read. Then mutual friends they had at the Media Lab, then techniques for cooking eggplant. Honestly, they weren't getting anywhere.

Eventually, Cora turned to me and Ethan. "How are you guys liking the barbecue?"

"It's great," I said, and, in a not particularly smooth transition, "Ethan was telling me about a really cool trip next week. Dad has this friend who built a replica of a nineteenth-century sailing vessel. We're going to go out on it for a couple of nights."

"Sounds fun," Cora said politely.

"Yeah. We'll be able to see the Arborids on the open water. They're probably really clear, with no light around." I gave Dad a pointed look. Really, was he going to make me do this whole thing myself?

Dad took a deep breath and turned toward Cora. But somehow—*how?*—he managed to trip over his own feet. In motion slowed by the sheer power of my horror, he lost his grip on his plate. It flipped in the air, food majestically staying affixed to it, before landing with a loud, wet *splat* on the beach, the crema-drenched sweet potato and corn salad flying everywhere, halted in their airborne escape by the nearest object.

Cora's feet and calves.

I covered my eyes, mortified.

"Oh, gosh, I'm so sorry." Dad dug several crumpled napkins out of his back pocket. His cheeks were bright red as he knelt to raise the napkins toward her legs.

"*Father,*" I hissed. Beside me, Ethan quaked with silent laughter.

Dad froze, still crouched. He glanced at me, then glanced at Cora, who stood just as frozen, before immediately shooting to his feet. "Here." He offered her the napkins, before looking down and realizing they were covered in food. "I'll be right back, let me get more."

He dashed off and I hunched my upper body down. "*Ugh.*"

Ethan rubbed my shoulder. "It'll be okay."

"It will never be okay."

"It's fine," Cora said, and when I looked at her she was laughing.

Suffice to say, Dad did not invite her on the boat trip that night.

* * *

I was undeterred.

On Monday, I had Dad pick me up at five o'clock and insisted he come in. He knocked on the doorframe to get our attention. When he had it, he lifted his hand and waved like he was auditioning to be the next Mr. Rogers. "Hello, there."

I muffled a groan but couldn't stifle a full-body wince. Why did my father have *zero game*? Why did I have *any*?

Cora swiveled in her chair. "Oh, hi. Picking Jordan up?" Unlike Dad, she sounded light and casual.

"Yeah. Yup."

We were doomed.

"Okay," I said slowly. "Let me grab my stuff." I gathered my bag and fussed around on my desk as though I had notes to throw in.

"My friend Gary's trip," Dad said. "It's, uh, there's a bunch of extra cabins. Empty cabins. He's inviting people he knows on Nantucket to come along, it's for three nights. This coming Thursday through Sunday. Anyway, if you're interested, you'd be welcome to join us."

I held my breath.

"You're inviting me on the trip?" Cora's voice gave nothing away, not whether she considered this good or bad, if she was thrilled or baffled or utterly uninterested.

Dad swallowed. "Jordan mentioned you might like it. And you—since you're interested in astronomy. Zero light pollution."

Those sentences hadn't been entirely logical, but they hadn't been the worst. And he'd only thrown me under the bus a little bit.

"Hm." Cora said. "I wouldn't want to be an inconvenience."

"You wouldn't be, not all. The more the merrier. Gary—the guy running it—loves having new people around."

They stared at each other.

"Yeah, okay," she said. "I'll think about it."

But she smiled, and I knew *I'll think about it* meant yes.

Sixteen

The night before the trip, Grace sent me the next batch of Andrea Darrel's diary entries. *I think we'll need one more trip to finish this off,* she wrote. *Planning for next week so Sierra and I can have a normal dating rhythm lol unless you desperately need diaries earlier.*

I answered right away. *This is perfect!*

Curled up in bed, I went to work deciphering Andrea Darrel's handwriting. Now I recognized the loops and dips of her words, the way her *n*'s bled into the letters around them. These journals covered the years when Andrea would have accompanied Annie Cannon to Nantucket to help on her astronomy course—the years when Andrea might have overlapped with Frederick Gibson.

June 3, 1906

I'm of two feelings, heading home. I'm thrilled to see my family, but I'm nervous about my professional and personal worlds mixing. Annie and I will be staying with my parents, whom I have given strict instructions to in regard to their behavior. Specifically, they are not to make rude comments about spinsters. At thirty-three, I am solidly in the spinster category (and yet they still have hope), but I know Annie, ten years my senior, will baffle them.

June 15, 1906

Home, and it is mostly fine. Annie charmed Papa. Mama is, for the first time, acting as though my career is worthy of interest. Hattie has made a few snide remarks about age and children, but she has sympathy for anyone who has lost their mother. She does often forget to face Annie so she can lip-read, and when I remind her acts as though it is a trial, but Hattie also acts as though feeding her own progeny is a trial.

We have started the summer class, and it is going quite well. The students are mostly locals (many I have known my whole life). Annie is an excellent teacher, and we have been asked by Mrs. Albertson, the curator of the Maria Mitchell Association, to give talks at the end of August open to the whole community. It is nice, the people I have known all my life finally seeing me shine.

August 27, 1906

The talks went well! Yesterday, Annie spoke about the constellations, and today about the 1900 eclipse we saw in Virginia. There was a lively atmosphere, especially as this served as the culmination of our summer classes, and I believe everyone enjoyed themselves. Afterward, my parents' friends Mr. and Mrs. Thomas came to chat. They introduced me to a Mr. Gibson, who has been visiting the island for a few days. He is very tall and lanky, and he made me laugh, twice, which generally men do not.

In Cambridge, it's easy to talk with the men I meet through work, but here I'm always on my guard, aware it is my parents' greatest wish I acquire someone else's surname through any means possible. I'm reluctant to give them any reason to think it a possibility, so I was more reserved with Mr. Gibson than I'd usually be with someone so handsome.

"I enjoyed your talk very much," Mr. Gibson said.

"Thank you," I said, and if Mr. and Mrs. Thomas hadn't been there, I might have flirted, but instead I asked him about his own career. He was very charming as he told me and the Thomases about his work with the Coast Survey. We talked for almost an hour, and at the end everyone insisted they had had quite the best time. Mr. Gibson said, very sincerely, he hoped to see me again.

It's been years since I was so taken with someone. I am happy with my independence and have no desire to relinquish it, but I must admit I might have a desire for something else. It is too bad I am leaving for Cambridge in a few days, and he lives in New York.

A delighted grin spread across my face. I *knew* it! They'd met. They'd met, and she *liked* him. I wanted to tell Ethan, but it was near midnight, and knocking on his door at this hour wouldn't lead to anything good. I went back to reading, skimming furiously for mentions of Gibson, but Andrea rarely mentioned him after returning to Cambridge. Instead, she talked about the endless search for variable stars, the publications of her colleagues, and the catalogue of stars she, herself, was working on.

Then, the next summer, Andrea and Annie Cannon returned to Nantucket.

July 3, 1907

Frederick Gibson is taking the astronomy course Annie and I are teaching.

I haven't thought of him (very much) this year, but I occasionally daydreamed of running into him again. Now I will be teaching him for eight Wednesdays in a row.

He came up to me on the first night. "I'm sure you don't remember me," he said with a crooked smile, as though I make a point of forgetting attractive men who make me laugh. "We were introduced last summer by the Thomases."

"Mr. Gibson, how do you do," I said. "I remember you. We're glad to have you here."

I know he's probably taking this course out of an interest in astronomy, but part of me hopes it's also because of me. Or that it might become because of me.

July 10, 1907

After class today, Mr. Gibson lingered until everyone but Annie had left. Then Annie (with a bit of a smirk) said good night, leaving me and Mr. Gibson alone.

So much of my conversation with men happens at work or at dinner parties—rarely alone at night. I can't remember the last time I was nervous to talk to anyone. To make up for it, I tried to be brisk and businesslike. But soon he had me laughing, telling me about a woman who is suing her hairdresser for burning her hair while trying to create a marcel wave. "They brought a hairdresser into court to show how it is properly done," he quipped. "I don't believe the judge was impressed."

Frederick Gibson often lingered after class, under the stars on late summer evenings, but nothing further ever happened. Andrea clearly developed a massive crush, but by the end of the summer she had no idea where he stood, and she resolved to put thoughts of him out of her head during the rest of the year.

But the next summer, and the summer after, Frederick Gibson reappeared on Nantucket. Like the first summer, Andrea and Frederick had plenty of flirtation and little follow-through. It was frustrating for Andrea—and for me as a reader, honestly. By the time she returned to Cambridge at the end of the summer of 1909, Andrea seemed done. *It is irritating how much I think about Mr. Gibson,* she wrote. *I am starting to want this to be more than it is, and I don't have the time or energy to waste if it won't be. He has made no move to visit or write to me in Cambridge outside the summers. I need to stop spending so much time thinking about him, and spend it instead on my work.*

Fair enough, Andrea.

She returned to Cambridge, refocused, and filled her journals with scribbled equations and verbal sketches of daily life. And for the first time, in 1910, Andrea didn't go home to Nantucket—

instead, her family came to visit her in Cambridge for a few weeks in May. And in August, the local astronomy scene ramped up for a gathering of the Astronomical and Astrophysical Society of America.

August 1, 1910

One cannot turn a corner in Cambridge these days without bumping into a famed astronomer. It seems everyone in the world is here for Dr. Pickering's meeting. Hale is determined to convince Dr. P to join his Solar Union, which I think would be a good thing, and so a whole collection of astronomers will be taking the train out to Hale's Mount Wilson Observatory in Los Angeles so he can properly entice him. Until then we are overrun with royal astronomers and the like. We're whisking them all about the city, showing them telescopes and plates and the observatory, and I haven't had so much fun in a long time.

August 2, 1910

Tonight Dr. Pickering hosted a gathering at his home for the astronomers in town. As soon as I entered the parlor, I noticed a pair of broad shoulders, a finely shaped head. Even before I saw a quarter profile, I knew it was Mr. Frederick Gibson. It made my chest ache and my head feel light.

I have not felt like this since I was in college. I don't particularly enjoy it.

I turned to face my friends. I refused to approach Frederick first; if we spoke, I wanted him to approach me, some validation of his interest.

My friends noticed me behaving oddly. "What is it?" Melony said.

"Who is it," Claire corrected, with a sly glance toward the knot of men containing Gibson. "Did one of them catch your eye?"

"It's the man I was telling you about," I said, so quietly they had to step closer to hear. "From back home."

"Mr. Gibson, from the summers?" Melony glanced toward the men, even though I made hushing noises at her. "But you said he never wrote."

"He didn't."

"Then what is he doing here?"

"The same thing everyone else is," I suggested. "He is interested in astronomy."

"He's coming!" Melony said. "Our way!"

We burst into giggles, as though schoolgirls instead of fully grown professionals.

His low, smooth voice cut through them. "Miss Darrel? Is that you?"

I turned. In my daydreams, I pictured myself being cool and aloof, but in fact I smiled terribly brightly. "Mr. Gibson! Hello!"

He smiled warmly. "I thought I recognized you. But then, this is your stomping ground, not mine. And these are your colleagues?"

I introduced everyone and I'm sure we had a very pleasant conversation, but I floated through it. I'm not even sure it's a good thing Frederick is here, but I cannot deny I feel light as hydrogen.

August 10, 1910

Mr. Gibson called on me to see if I would like to go for a walk on Sunday, and so we are going for a walk, and all I can think about is us on a walk. I am supposed to be combing through my quadrant for faint variable stars and helping Mrs. Fleming prepare her manuscript, and I cannot. Is this why so many successful women are unmarried, romance decays the brain and makes you spin in circles?

Andrea didn't write for several weeks, and I wondered if Gibson had taken over too much brain space.

September 3, 1910

Three days ago Frederick kissed me and I was over the moon about it, so filled with joy and delight I couldn't even write. But I have not heard from him since, and now I think I'm starting to go mad. What is the protocol for talking to someone who kissed you, and said they would call on you, but did not? I asked Claire and she laughed (bitterly) and said I should track him down and make him tell me his intentions. But Melony said I should under no circumstances do so.

I am too old to be so stressed about whether a man likes me. I am too happy with my life to want to dramatically change it. And yet.

But he *did* call on her; that week, and the next, and the next. They attended Red Sox games and played tennis and discussed infrared photography and the Wright brothers. Andrea sounded happy, but also irritated Frederick Gibson's intentions weren't more clear. I'd had no idea such irritation was so universal throughout history.

November 13, 1910

Somehow, on a perfectly normal evening, I found myself asking (after one too many beers) "Why have you never married?"

Freddie flashed me his crooked grin, like this was a joke rather than a question I'd been harboring for ages. "I've never found a woman who could keep up with me."

"How strange," I said archly, "given how many brilliant women I know. Perhaps you were looking in the wrong places?"

He laughed. "Perhaps I meant keep up and keep me in my place. I suppose the truth is, I wasn't ready."

And then—again, I blame the beer—I said, "Wasn't? Or aren't?"

His eyes gleamed, and he leaned forward, and he called me on my implication. "Why, Miss Darrel," he said, "are you making a proposal?"

The mortification I felt. I don't know why. I suppose because

I am never sure of Freddie. We go for coffee and automobile rides but I'm never sure he wants anything more. And even though I am not sure I want more, I might. Yet I never want him to think I want him more than he wants me. I don't want to give him that kind of power over me.

I leaned back in my chair and said, "I'm not a goose of a girl, Frederick. I don't long for marriage. But I am a scientist and I trade in facts, and so I would like to have some. Are you looking for a companion, which we have been to each other over the summers for several years now? Or are you looking for a wife—and if so, are you considering me, or am I a convenient pastime until you find the correct lady?"

I rather think I shocked Freddie. Which I enjoyed.

"You have always been too quick for me," he said wryly. "And more blunt than I expect. It keeps me sharp, I suppose."

I waited.

"I think you are brilliant," he said slowly. "The most brilliant woman I've ever met. But you seem married to your career, and I always pictured my wife would be more . . . married to me."

I did not snort, but I came close. "To tend your house and raise your children?"

He gave me his wry smile. "Is that so wrong?"

"It is so typical. I would have thought a spouse should be a partner, an equal, not an employee."

"Maybe you're right. But . . . I never expected my wife to have a career."

I looked away. It hurt, even though I knew it shouldn't,

"That doesn't mean she shouldn't," he said. "Just I've never

thought about it. I'm not sure I would have expected a woman with a career to want a husband. After all, you've never married, either."

"Maybe I've never met anyone who can keep up with me, either," I said.

(This is not true; plenty of the men at the Observatory can keep up. But it sounded good.)

"And you think I can?" he asked, smiling.

I shrugged. "Mostly."

He laughed. Then he looked at me, his eyes that perfect mottled brown-green that I find so beautiful, that I am very afraid that I love. "And—just to make sure I understand—are you saying you are interested in the institution of marriage?"

"I might be," I said, though it felt like scraping rocks out of my throat to admit it. "Yes. I suppose I would be."

"I'll make note of it," he said, and we did not speak of it again.

I feel like I have swallowed a storm and it is churning my insides in great, wild waves. Do I want to marry Frederick? Do I want to marry at all? I don't want to give up my career. I don't want to stop sweeping the skies or searching for a comet, but what if I could have both?

I rather think I would like both.

Seventeen

The ship was much more dramatic than I'd expected.

Sails the color of old parchment billowed from the tall masts. A complicated web of rigging draped from one wooden post to another, like someone had forgotten to erase the architectural lines in a drawing. All it needed was the Jolly Roger flying to put viewers in mind of pirates.

Cora craned her head back. "How long did this take to build?"

"Five years," Dad said. "There's a pretty good documentary about it. They followed Gary as he built it."

A hearty-looking man barreled toward us. "There's my intrepid adventurers!" he cried, which sounded like the type of thing one might say if used to being followed by a film crew. He wore a vest and khaki shorts, and had a large, bulbous nose, ruddy skin, and watery blue eyes. "Glad you could make it."

"Thanks for having us." Dad clasped the man's hand. His warm tone made it clear he liked the guy. "Wouldn't miss this for the world." He placed a hand on my shoulder and indicated the rest of us in turn. "This is my daughter, Jordan. And Dr. Cora Bradley, and do you remember my assistant, Ethan?"

"Ah, one of the Barbanel brood!" the man said in his louder-than-life voice. He bent his knees—he was tall, maybe six five—to smile at me. "And Jordan, you look just like your mother! So glad you could make it." He turned to greet Cora more formally, but I was too stunned to take anything else in.

This guy had known my mom? I'd been under the impression Dad had met Gary Dubois—and this had to be him—because they both spent summers on Nantucket and were into old boat stuff. How was my mom involved?

I had no time to ask. Gary hustled us along a theoretically stable gangway connected to his ship. I craned my head back to take in the huge masts and the crow's nest high above, then exchanged a wide-eyed, impressed look with Ethan.

"Mike will bring your things to your cabins," Gary said, introducing us to a crew member. "I'll give you the grand tour, and then you can get settled in before dinner."

Gary led our quartet around, patting the rail fondly as he gave us the ship's biography. "She's one hundred twenty-five feet. Just finished her two years ago. This is the first time we're out to Nantucket, though—I kept telling Tony I would come." He nodded at my dad.

"What do you do with the ship the rest of the year?" Cora asked.

"We keep her out of Philadelphia most of the time. I've got a team running tours on her—day trips for schools and tourists, and we do five-night trips, too. We can accommodate a dozen guests along with our crew on those longer trips, and the day classes are often fifty or so."

He'd built the ship because he wanted a ship, we learned, but it was also a business. And it wasn't all historical. While the deck and spars were made of Douglas fir, the hull and masts were steel. He led us through the decks, pointing out all the different sections: the fore, midship, and aft; then the bow, the front, the stern, the back. He named the masts—main, fore, and mizzen—and the parts of each mast, but by then I was starting to get a little loopy.

To make our way downstairs—excuse me, "below deck"—we descended steep stairs. Weren't sailors notoriously drunk? Wasn't the ocean, you know, not steady? This seemed ripe for disaster.

"You lot are in our midship cabins." Gary pointed to doors where aesthetically pleasing and functionally useless gilded life-buoys encircled our names. "Over here's the crew quarters." We peeked in at a room full of bunks and suitcases and people in their twenties, who waved. I imagined what it would be like to be them, headed off to sea on their own, on an adventure.

The largest part of the lower deck looked like an old-timey hotel restaurant, with a long bar along one side and skylights letting in natural light. "This is the grand salon. When we're not on deck, we're hanging here. Meals, socializing—and come look," Gary said, with a wink at me.

He opened a door into a small, cozy room shaped like an octagon with books lining its walls. The ceiling lights resembled stained glass and glowed with a candle-warm light. Four armchairs nestled around a small coffee table in the center of the room, and two side tables held lamps whose stained glass shades complemented the ceiling. "My husband insisted," Gary said. "Said if I got a ship, he got a library."

Cora peered at the titles. "Is this whole shelf . . . murder mysteries set on cruise ships?"

Gary grinned. "You gotta give the people what they want. The people being my husband, Brent."

Gary showed us back to our quarters and told us the ship would depart in forty-five minutes. My cabin was the size of a postage stamp, barely large enough to turn around in, but charming all the same. Pink and teal throw pillows and blankets enlivened the crisp white linens. The bed was beneath a round port window. I kicked off my shoes and scrambled up to peer out, smiling involuntarily at the wash of blue before me. There was also a mirror, a dresser, and a TV screen bolted to the wall—so much for historical accuracy. My suitcase had been rolled neatly into a corner.

After unpacking, I knocked on Ethan's door. I wanted to tell him about Andrea and Frederick, and everything had been such a scramble of packing this morning I hadn't gotten a chance. He didn't answer. I found him on the upper deck, excitedly talking with Gary and my dad about the experiments they had planned for the trip. Of course. But I wasn't as bitter as I might have been a few weeks before. In fact, it struck me as cute, how excited they all were.

Soon, everyone had gathered for the official departure. Gary stood at the front of the crowd. "Hello! Hello, everyone!" he cried. "I'd like to welcome all of you to the *Salty Fox*—yes, I named the ship after the bar where Brent and I met," he said to a few chuckles, nodding at a blond man smiling abashedly. "Some of you have been sailing with me for a bit, but I'd like to welcome our newcomers for the next few nights. We've been joined by my neighbors from New York, who are spending the summer on Nantucket, Doctors Ishikawa and Wrisberg, along with my old friend Tony Edelman, his daughter, Jordan, and his student, Ethan. We also have Dr. Cora Bradley with us, a brilliant astrophysicist."

Everyone waved and called out hellos.

And I thought, *Old friend?*

"Tony here is responsible for this little adventure to see the Arborids in the darkest skies imaginable, away from light pollution. He's been 'lightly' suggesting this for two years now."

The adults laughed politely.

Gary introduced the people already onboard: his sister and brother-in-law and their college-aged kids, an old colleague, a writer and a tech bro, whose connections to Gary I missed. The crew came next, most of whom were professionals, and a few students and volunteers. "As for the person actually in charge," Gary said, gesturing to a woman beside him, "Captain Laskshi runs the show around here, along with First Mate Wójcik and Second Mate Foster."

"You run the show, I think," Captain Laskshi said with a smile. "I run the ship."

With introductions done—and a few safety measures imparted to us newcomers—we set off. Gary popped a bottle of champagne and everyone cheered as Nantucket dwindled behind us. Then, with the sun only now starting to lower, we headed into the lounge for dinner.

The newcomers ate together, and Gary and his husband, Brent, joined us. The food was better than I'd expected: sweet potatoes and tofu marinated in a soy-and-honey sauce, plus a spinach side salad and fresh-baked roll. Conversation inevitably circled to the meteor shower, which would peak for the next few nights. "We're lucky to have our very own expert," Gary said to Cora, smiling broadly. "Will you mind being peppered with questions?"

"Not at all."

"The Arborids come from Gibson's comet, isn't that right?" one of the doctors asked. "We were wondering—why aren't they named after the comet?"

"People knew about meteor showers long before they connected them to comets," Cora said. "They're usually named after the constellations it looks like the meteors originate from."

"Where'd people think meteors came from?" Ethan asked.

"That's outside my realm." Cora looked at Dad. "Maybe our resident historian knows?"

I swear Dad blushed. "Ah—well. For a long time, people thought meteors were religious signs, or rocks falling from thunderstorms. Scientists were skeptical, since they didn't think rocks could fall from the sky. But in the eighteen hundreds, a dramatic shower in France made people start thinking they were credible." He tilted his head. "I'm not sure when people figured out they came from comets."

"On that note," Gary said. "Shall we go watch rocks fall from the sky?"

We arrived back on deck just as the sunset's hues brightened into a spectacular lightshow. We watched the sun sink into the waters and the meteor shower begin as the streaks of white grew in vibrancy. We lay on the deck, a scattering of humans on a few planks of wood in the middle of the open sea, surrounded by shooting stars. For a dizzying moment, I imagined them falling into the water, sizzling as burning rock hit the icy waves.

Everyone stayed out for hours, but Ethan and I stayed out later than most. It was like we'd been waiting for a chance to be alone together, and now here we finally were, lying on a picnic blanket in silence as the deck emptied out around us.

"Are you ready to have your mind blown?" I asked.

"In a good way or a bad way?"

"A good way! Andrea Darrel and Frederick Gibson *did* know each other. He took her astronomy course, she writes about it in her diary. And . . ." I waggled my brows.

"And what?"

"They were in love."

Ethan leveled up, propping himself up on one elbow. He looked delighted. "Seriously?"

"Yeah. They hung out during the first summer, and over the next few, and then he came to see her in Cambridge. I thought . . . I don't know, I want it to work out for them. Do you know if he married, who he married?"

He shook his head. "I think he married a New York socialite."

"Ugh." The hope drained out of me. "Well. He didn't seem sure he wanted a wife with a career."

Ethan winced. "Wow."

"The nineteen-tens, man." I leaned my head back to take in the pinpricks in the sky above us. "She must have been so jealous."

"Of his wife?" Ethan asked.

I laughed. "No—of his *discovery*. She was the astronomer,

right? She wrote about sweeping the skies at night—that's what you do, when you're looking for oddities, like a comet. It's how she calmed herself down when she was stressed; it's how Maria Mitchell discovered her comet. But it was *Gibson* who discovered a comet. That would have sucked."

"Maybe she was happy for him."

I scoffed. "She'd have to be a bigger person than I am. What are the odds, right, that the professional astronomer doesn't discover the comet but her amateur boyfriend does?"

"I guess he got lucky."

"Guess so. When did he discover it?"

"Nineteen eleven."

In 1911, they might have still been together; they'd been sharing their thoughts on marriage at the end of 1910. I remembered the beginning of the summer, watching Ethan get all my father's attention. I'd felt like I'd been stabbed. Andrea Darrel, watching Frederick Gibson make the discovery she'd always wanted? She must have been ablaze with envy.

Maybe that *was* what had broken them apart. Love conquers all, they said, but did passion for a person exceed passion for your own goals?

I glanced at Ethan, realizing I wasn't as resentful as I'd been a few months ago. It turned out all I had needed was for Dad to make space for me, to tell me he wanted me to come on this boat, to carve out time for me throughout the week. I still wanted him to be proud of my work, but I didn't mind him being proud of Ethan, too. Partly because *I* was proud of Ethan, weirdly. I wanted everyone to be proud of him, including my dad, including his parents. "Your talk is in a week, right? Are you excited?"

He looked away. "Not really."

"Why not?" I asked, surprised. "Are you nervous?"

He shrugged.

He *was* nervous. "When was the last time you did a talk in public?"

"Uh—my Torah portion in my bar mitzvah?"

"Seriously? What about school? Didn't you have to give presentations?"

He shook his head.

Okay. Baffling, but . . . "Practice on me."

He gave me a look, skepticism only barely outweighing hope. "You're joking."

"I'm not. It'll make you feel better."

He hesitated. "It's not ready."

"It'll never be ready," I said, having watched my dad prepare plenty of book talks throughout the last few years. "It's important to practice before a live audience."

His mouth quirked. "You're a bit of a tyrant."

"Tell me I'm wrong, then."

He couldn't. Taking a deep breath, he flicked through his phone and propped it on his knee so he could read off it. "Here goes." He plunged in. "Hi, there. My name is Ethan Barbanel, and I'm excited to talk to you today about Frederick Gibson's work. Famously known for discovering a comet, Gibson devoted his earlier career to wire-dragging alongside Nicholas Heck, some of which work he did here, on Nantucket."

Despite his nerves, he'd crafted a compelling speech. I could see my dad's print in the flow of sentences and the insertion of anecdotes, but other parts were all Ethan—the humor, the excitement, the energy. When he finished, I applauded. "That was great!"

His lips twitched. "You're just trying to make me feel better."

"Maybe. But I'm also being honest. Dad's dragged me to enough talks I know a good one when I see it."

He relaxed. "I bet you have suggestions. Your dad always does."

"One or two. But it really was good."

"I can take it."

"Let me see the speech."

He offered me his phone. I scrolled to the beginning. "Okay, so you have a really strong opening, but then I'd move this paragraph up above this one . . ."

We spent an hour on his speech as the meteors flashed above us. Eventually, we faded into silence, watching the darting light against the darkness. Tomorrow would be the best day for watching, since we'd be at the farthest point from land, before turning back the day after. Still, tonight still topped any meteor shower I'd ever seen.

"Gary knew my mom." The words slipped out. I hadn't meant to say them, but now they floated between us.

"Really?" Even in the darkness, I could see Ethan's head turn toward mine. "How?"

"I don't know. He said my dad was an old friend. And that I looked like my mom."

"Wow. Are you going to ask him about it?"

I gave a half shrug. "I was thinking I'd ask my dad first. I just . . . haven't."

"How come?"

I wrapped my arms around my knees and pulled them close. "I guess I'm not used to talking about her? It feels like there's two different worlds, this one and the one before my mom died. And it's a world I know very little about, but everyone else knows, everyone else visited, so they don't need to talk about it because they already know it. But I don't. So I want to talk about it, but I don't know how."

Ethan sat up too, nodding as though my rambling made sense. "She died when you were pretty young, right?"

"Four."

"Do you remember her?"

I gazed at the sky. "Sometimes I think I do, but sometimes I wonder if I just remember stories my dad and aunt have told me. But I think . . . I remember her reading me Spot the Dog books. I remember playing dress-up and showing her each of my new outfits—a princess or a firefighter or whatever—and she was like, 'Wow, where did my Jordan go?' and I was worried because I thought I'd disguised myself too well and now she was scared."

Ethan laughed.

The sound made me relax into a small smile. "I remember sitting next to her on the futon when I was little. I don't think I remember her face outside of photos, but I think I remember her body? Cuddling into her. But I wish I remembered more."

"Do you miss her?"

I squeezed my legs closer. "Sometimes I think I remember the missing more than her. I remember so much crying and confusion after she died. Like a limb had been cut off."

"I'm so sorry."

It was what everyone said, but I was still glad to hear it.

Ethan and I stayed out for another hour, watching the streaks of white light across the dark sky. Even knowing they were rocks burning up in the atmosphere, the meteors were magical. What would it look like if we pushed all the space debris into Earth's atmosphere so it burned up? Small lines or fireballs dashing across the sky? I wondered what Gibson's comet would look like. I'd never seen a comet before.

At some point, we lay down and our hands found each other's. We didn't kiss, but this felt almost more intimate, lying side by side, comfortable with no words or motion between us. We watched until our eyes started to drift closed more than once, then made our way quietly down to our cabins.

We paused outside our doors. It was very late—or very early—and like Andrea Darrel, I didn't entirely know what I wanted. I didn't want to say goodbye, I knew that at least. Maybe I wanted to just lie together, to sleep side by side, to feel Ethan's arm around me.

But I didn't say anything, and neither did he. Or at least, not what I wanted him to.

"Good night, Jordan," Ethan said, and kissed me gently, and turned away.

Eighteen

"Ahoy, matey!" Dad said the next morning at breakfast, and I didn't even roll my eyes. "What have we here?"

"It's pretty good," I told him. My plate overflowed with scrambled eggs, spinach quiche, and a tiny cinnamon roll. "Not bad for a ship."

"Much better than in the eighteen hundreds," Dad agreed. "They'd be eating hardtack and salted meat."

"Ew. What's hardtack?"

"It's an unleavened biscuit sailors ate, made from water and flour."

"Like matzo?"

Dad smiled. "A little worse. It was twice-baked for short voyages and baked four times for long trips, to make it last. You couldn't eat it by itself. Sailors dunked it in liquid to soften it up."

"Gross."

"But," Dad said, on a roll now, "the salted beef and pork the navy gave sailors was high quality. Better than they'd get if they stayed home, where most people only ate meat on holidays. Sailors were lucky in a way, guaranteed protein. American sailors in the early eighteen hundreds ate an average of four thousand calories a day."

"Dad," I asked, curious, "what are you getting out of this trip for the book? You can clearly do some of your research elsewhere. And we're not eating hardtack."

"No, though I have made it and eaten it before."

Of course he had. "How was it?"

Dad tilted his head. "You know, I didn't mind it."

"Yeah, well, people don't mind matzah, either, on the first night of Passover."

He smiled and returned to my question. "A lot of my writing is atmosphere. This ship helps me accurately paint a picture of what life would have been like for the people I'm writing about. If I haven't tasted the salt wind, felt how chapped my lips get, seen the scatter of the stars—I can't describe it as well. And then my writing isn't as good."

"So you're doing it for the vibes."

He grinned and said, with great relish, "Yes. I'm doing it for the vibes."

Oh no. I knew that tone, which appeared any time he'd learned a new phrase. He'd say he was doing it for the vibes for the next two years. "Do you have particular things you're trying to get here?"

"Well, I'm working on a section about how the US Coast Survey mapped the coastline. When we come back, we're going to sail around Nantucket—we need to make a circle to avoid the shoals—so I'll be able to see what it's like, trying to map the coast. And right now, I'm trying to pinpoint the exact feeling of finding your sea legs."

He turned his notepad around, and I read his list:

SEA LEGS

Tremulous

*Like taking a step down and finding you've reached a landing
    instead of another stair*

Like drinking sprite instead of water

"I like it," I said. "Is that how you feel?"

"I'm a little wobbly. I'm better at writing about the sea than being on it."

"I've already got my sea legs," I mock-bragged. "I'm a natural sailor. Queen of the sea."

" 'Queen of the Sea,' " Dad echoed. "All-girl band playing—sea shanties?"

I shook my head, grinning. "All-girl, yes, but more regal. Maybe, like, a melancholic rock band."

"Like the Cranberries."

"Yeah! We'll find another name for your sea-shanty band."

We paused, and I knew Dad was coming up with names, but before he could offer any, words tumbled out of my mouth. "Gary said he knew Mom."

Dad looked momentarily surprised before settling his face into neutral-but-positive. "Yes. We all knew each other in college."

In college? "I've never heard of him before."

"We haven't been in touch for years. Not since—" He hesitated, then plunged forward. "Mom died. We ran into each other a few years ago on the island and reconnected."

I nodded slowly, drawing a line through my eggs with my fork. "Was he always so rich?"

Dad laughed. "Not this rich. But I think his family was always wealthy."

"Were there other people you and Mom were friends with in college? Who I don't know?"

"Let's see." He looked at the ceiling. "I guess so. Miguel and Trever, Kristy and Jen—Jen and Miguel dated, though Jen dated Trever first. A complicated love triangle." He smiled briefly. "And there was Gary and his roommate Omar. Omar was part of the group before Gary, I think, and brought him in. I think a few of them were in—oh, student government together?"

"Are you in touch with any of the others?"

He shook his head. "Everyone moved after school. But we still get holiday cards from a few of them."

"Huh." I'd never thought about the people behind the cards stuck on the fridge every year. "I thought I'd ask Gary about her."

Dad nodded emphatically. "Yes. You should."

Wow, he'd really agreed there. "Cool."

After breakfast, I joined Gary's niece and nephew and Ethan on the deck. Because of some strange desire to keep us entertained/out of mischief/away from the adults' main activity of day drinking, we'd been conscripted into what Gary described as "Intro to a Nineteenth-Century Sailing Vessel." I couldn't complain; it was another clear, bright blue day, and I was pretty hyped to learn whatever they wanted to teach us.

"My new recruits!" Gary pressed his hands together and rubbed them. "Are you lot ready for your tasks?"

Beside him, Brent looked like he couldn't decide whether to find his husband's behavior endearing or painful. Honestly, a mood. I glanced at Ethan, and we glanced at Gary's niece and nephew, and then we all shrugged.

"Tough audience." Gary gestured forward a woman around my dad's age. And Gary's age, I supposed, if they'd all gone to college together. "This is First Mate Wójcik. She's gonna take it from here."

"Hey, guys," the first mate said. "I've been with the *Salty Fox* since she launched, and she's one of my favorites. We're going to get you familiar with a few of the basics sailors have done for centuries, and then we'll give you a bit of hands-on experience."

Despite knowing I'd likely forget all this in a week, I dove into learning, game to try adjusting the sails and climbing the rigging. By lunchtime, my arms were sore, but so was my stomach from laughing, which I hadn't really expected. And I needed the break—I was worn out and sweaty. Ethan was too, if the way he pulled up his shirt to mop his face was any indicator. I blatantly stared at the expanse of muscles he'd exposed.

Ethan noticed and smirked. "Checking me out?"

"You should be so lucky."

"I should," he said, giving my ponytail a flick.

We had lunch on the deck, paninis for the most part—tomato and mozzarella and pesto for me. It was *delicious*. Gary waved an arm grandiosely. "The spice of the open seas."

Brent gave him an indulgent smile. "And the ridiculously expensive pesto you insist on buying."

After lunch, everyone split up into their preferred activities: learning more about rigging or sailing, performing experiments, chatting in clusters around the deck. Gary checked in on his guests, moving purposely from one group to the next. As he left a clump, I intercepted him. "Hi. Mr. Dubois?"

"Hi, Jordan." He smiled broadly and focused on me, as opposed to looking like he needed to dash off elsewhere. "How are you enjoying the trip?"

Kudos for remembering my name; I didn't think I'd have remembered someone I'd barely spoken to. But then again, he'd apparently known my dad—my *parents*—for a long time. Maybe he'd even heard my name seventeen years ago. "I wondered if you had a moment?"

His bushy brows skyrocketed above his eagle eyes. "Sure thing. Want to sit?"

We chose a shady part of the deck. I sat across from him, concentrating on not fiddling with my hands. "It's a really nice ship."

"Thanks." Gary launched into a loving homage before abruptly reining himself in. "But I'm guessing the ship's not what you wanted to talk about."

I nodded quickly, bracing myself. "My dad says you knew my mom in college."

Gary smiled. "I did, yes."

"I wanted to ask—What was she like? What was my dad like with her?"

The question seemed to startle Gary, though it was what

I wanted to ask everyone who'd known my mom. I wanted to ask her friends who still dropped by on occasion, my aunts and uncles, even my dad. But I felt embarrassed. They'd known her so intimately, so well, and she'd been my mother, after all. I shouldn't need to ask.

Only my mom's parents told me stories, but so wistfully I almost preferred they didn't.

But this man, Gary, had stopped knowing my mom before she got sick; he didn't have bitter memories of her illness shading the sweet memories of her life. When he'd last seen her, she'd been ebullient and alive, and his memories of her were probably no different from the memories anyone had of a friend they'd fallen out of touch with.

"The two of them . . . Well, she was a ball of energy, I'll tell you that." Gary settled comfortably into his chair. "Your dad was a nerd, head in the clouds. We all met around the same time—we were in the same dorm freshman year, and I remember us as a giant clump—but the two of them were instant friends. She was the faster walker, he was the slowest, but she'd drop back when he was around to talk with him."

"Really?"

"Yeah. And she was *loud*. She had giant crimped hair and was always bossing everyone around. Freshman year, she joined a dozen clubs, then quit them all. Took up too much time, she said. She wanted to be with her friends, you know, she didn't want to be writing articles or organizing events. She had a really strong sense of self. She was good at reaching out, at making sure she spent quality time with the people who were important to her. I think half the kids in the dorm had a crush on her. She only had eyes for your dad, of course."

"Really."

Gary laughed. "Didn't he tell you? He'd been pining after her for, oh, two years. She'd been dating other people on and off, but one day she looked at Tony. They were close, we all knew that, but they'd only ever been friends. The two of us were sitting on the quad, and your dad was playing Frisbee with some of the others, and she turned to me and said, 'Do you think I should marry Tony?'"

I stared. "What?"

He laughed. "That's what I said! She gave this decisive nod—she was always giving that nod—and said, 'Yes, I think so.' Then she got up and interrupted the game and asked him out."

I gaped at Gary. "And what did *he* say?"

Gary laughed again, harder this time. He had one of those laughs that was mostly a snort, and he had to catch his breath to recover from it. "He said, 'Uh, we're in the middle of a game.' And she walked away, and he kept playing for about three more minutes, and then he turned around and ran off the field and chased her down. And never left her side again. Best thing that ever happened to him, he said. She drew him out of his shell, and he calmed her down."

I'd never heard that story before. "Wow."

"Yeah. She was a great person, your mom. Knew exactly what she wanted and went after it. Took me a long time to learn to do the same thing."

"Thanks for telling me." I paused. "Crimped hair, huh?"

He laughed. "The nineties were a trip. And you should have seen our Y2K parties. We went wild."

* * *

After talking to Gary, I headed to the little library below deck. It was empty, so I took my time scanning the shelves. I hadn't asked if it would be here, but I had a hunch. My gaze latched onto the blue-and-white spine soon enough.

The book was as familiar as Dad: a tiny piece of his soul in physical form. It didn't matter which physical copy of the book it was, whether one in our living room or Dad's study, or in a library or bookstore or here on the ship. They were all the same, all part of Dad.

I flipped the book open. There, the dedication:

To my wife, Rebecca, who believed in me long before
I believed in myself. I will miss you forever.

And to my daughter, Jordan, who has my whole heart.

My heart lurched. I'd remembered he'd dedicated the book to Mom, but I hadn't remembered a dedication to me. It made my eyes strain with tears, made my stomach roil and my chest feel tight.

No wonder I'd never read further. I wanted to snap the book shut right now and start crying.

Instead, I flipped to the first page.

* * *

Several hours later, the door cracked open. "Oops," Cora said. "Didn't mean to interrupt."

I tore myself away from a surprisingly riveting description of my dad attempting to use a sextant to measure the distance between the moon and a star to determine the longitude. "Just reading."

She spied the cover. "Your dad's book. I read it a couple of weeks ago."

"You did? You didn't say anything."

She flushed. "It felt a little funny, like I was spying on him. I didn't want to be weird about it."

I grinned. "It's all stuff he decided to put out there." I looked at the book in my hand. "I didn't know how much he wrote about me."

"Does it bother you?"

Maybe if I'd been reading the current manuscript, detailing me right now, I'd be bothered, but these were stories of me at around age thirteen and kind of sweet. "I guess not."

She nodded, dropping down in the armchair across from me. "You and Ethan looked cozy last night."

"Yeah. He's . . ." I looked out the porthole, two domes of blue cut through with a clear line. "It was nice."

She cast me a slightly smug look. "He's very cute."

"We're not—" I started, then faded away.

Cora lifted her brows. "Not?"

"Nothing," I said, in a tone designed to flatten further inquisition.

"You're not nothing." She looked far too amused. "Got it."

I cleared my throat. "Are you liking the trip?"

"I am." She picked up the book, which I'd placed on the table between us, and flipped through it. She paused on Dad's author photo on the back flap. We'd pored over options from the photo shoot he'd done with the art teacher at the high school and settled on one where he half smiled. Well, *I* settled and Dad indulged me. He'd wanted a serious, no-smiling photo, but I'd insisted on this one.

"It's funny, though," Cora continued, in one of those trying-to-sound-casual-but-not-feeling-casual voices. "I'm pretty sure everyone thinks I'm here because your dad and I are dating."

My gaze whipped toward her. "Really?"

"Mm-hm."

Okay. Wow. How to handle this? I probably shouldn't blurt out interrogating questions like *And would you date him? Shall I make you dinner reservations as soon as we get back?* "I could tell people to stop, if it, you know, makes it uncomfortable." I stared at my hands. "Does it make you uncomfortable?"

She shot me an unreadable look. "I was wondering if it made *you* uncomfortable."

I stared at her. "I'm sorry," I finally said. "Was I being subtle by accident? Because Ethan once told me I *wasn't* subtle, and honestly, I agree."

She looked startled. "What?"

Wow. Maybe I *had* been subtle. Or maybe adults were astonishingly obtuse? I returned to her question. "No. It doesn't make me uncomfortable."

She nodded. "Does your dad date a lot?"

"Does my *dad*—" I snorted a laugh, then broke it off at the look on her face. "Oh, you're serious."

Cora raised her brows. "I was until you laughed in my face."

"He doesn't date *at all*. I don't think he's been on a single date since my mom died." At Cora's expression, I realized this was probably not the right way to signal Dad was emotionally available. I backpedaled. "Which doesn't mean he's not ready to date! Just, he hasn't. But he's not anti-dating, I'm sure."

"Hm." She straightened. "I'll leave you to your book. Good talk."

I saluted, because I was a weirdo. Oy.

"And don't worry," she said as she left the small library. "You're not subtle."

* * *

I read until dinnertime, which was another loud, boisterous meal. Afterward, like the day before, everyone watched the sunset from the deck. Ethan leaned next to me at the rail. Our arms pressed together, his skin warm against mine.

"I never get bored of looking at the ocean," I said. "Or the sky. They're always different. Always interesting and beautiful and changing."

"And always connected," Ethan said.

My mouth quirked in a smile. "How poetic."

"Am I wrong?"

I took in the vaulting sky, the endless dark sea, the way the horizon circled us in a stark line of dark and light blue. Our ship was the only small thing in the center of the blue world. "No. I guess not."

"Two halves of one whole." Ethan sounded satisfied.

I opened my mouth to tease him about better halves, but my lips stretched into an unstoppable yawn. "'Scuse me." I covered my mouth.

"You better not fall asleep," Ethan warned. "Tonight's the best night for the meteors."

He was right; not only was tonight the peak of the shower, but tomorrow we'd start heading back toward land and light. "I don't know if I'm gonna make it. All this exercise stuff really got to me."

He angled his body toward me. "Well. The best viewing is at three a.m. Total darkness."

"Is it?" I arched my brows. "Maybe I should go to sleep now, then."

"Maybe you should," Ethan agreed. "Maybe I should, too."

"Maybe we should both just happen to come up here at three."

"I'm in if you're in," Ethan said, and when I nodded, he grinned at me. "It's a date."

A date. My whole body tingled as I watched Ethan walk away. Not a *date*-date, I knew—it was just a turn of phrase—but the word caused me to shiver.

Dad joined me. "Don't look directly at the sun."

"*Dad*," I reprimanded, because I was too old to receive such parental advice. Even though, admittedly, I had been looking directly at the sun. Just a peek! It glowed orange, perfectly round, and it was amazing you *could* look at it and see anything besides blinding light.

Dad held up his hands. "I have no choice. It's in the rulebook. See someone seeing something, say something."

I rolled my eyes but then leaned into his side. "I started *Mapping*."

Dad looked confused for a second, though we traditionally called his first book *Mapping*—the whole title, *Mapping the Atlantic: A History of American Maritime Cartography*, was too much of a mouthful. And often, we didn't even say that, just "the book" or "book one." Slowly, he realized what I meant, and his expression looked torn between happiness and terror. "Really?"

"Yeah." I expected him to ask what I'd thought, but he didn't, instead continuing to look astonished. "I'm halfway through. It's good."

"*Really*," he repeated. "You like it?"

"Yeah. It's fun. And smart." I ducked my head, feeling almost shy. "I really like it."

I once again expected a different reaction—for Dad to joke and say, "I am really fun and smart." Instead, he smiled widely. "Thank you, Jordan."

"I'm sorry I didn't read it before."

Dad looked scandalized. "Why would you be sorry?"

"I don't know. I feel like I should have? To support you."

"Jordan." He leaned toward me, a crease in his brow. "I'm really glad you're reading and liking the book. But there is no pressure or expectation for you to *ever* read any of my work. You support me by being a great daughter. You don't have to do anything else."

I blinked rapidly and looked away. I wasn't entirely sure I was a "great" daughter—I was fine, I supposed. Definitely adequate at the daughtering. Could do better. Six out of ten, tops. "Thanks."

He kissed the top of my head. "I'm glad you came out here. Not just on the ship, but to Nantucket." He hesitated. "It hasn't been all bad, has it?"

My throat closed a bit at Dad's earnestness. "No. It's been nice." I nodded at Cora, laughing with a group of other people across the deck. "I like working with Cora."

"You seem to have learned a lot."

"And she's great." I tilted my head. "Don't you think so?"

Dad frowned. "I know what you're doing."

I looked up at the night sky, the pinprick stars and whirling clouds. "Hm?"

"With Dr. Bradley."

I gave him an oblivious smile. "Categorizing space trash?"

He sounded sober and disapproving. "She's too young."

"She's thirty-eight. I wouldn't call her young."

He flinched. "Brutal."

"For *you*, Dad," I said, finally admitting what we were talking about. "You're only forty-four. That's not even middle-aged. I mean, hopefully."

"I'm ancient. And I'm balding."

"True." I patted the thinning hair on the crown of his head. He made a face; clearly I'd been supposed to defend his diminishing hair. "But you have a job, and you're smartish."

"Jeez, are those the requirements these days?" He struck a pose. "What about how I'm debonairly handsome?"

I tried to rein him in by flatly saying, "Dad."

"And I'm witty. I've got a great sense of humor. I have a great car—"

"From 2007."

"It's still alive! It's amazing!"

"Hm."

"I have a beautiful daughter—"

"This is true," I allowed. "But you have a severely lacking love life."

"Which is none of your business."

"Fine. Whatever." I leaned against the rail. "So, ignoring my evil machinations, what do you think of Cora?"

"She's very smart," he said primly.

I rolled my eyes. "She's smart, she's hot, and she's a nerd. I honestly don't know what more you could want."

"For my daughter to back off," Dad said firmly.

"Whoa." I held up my hands. "Strong words."

Dad sighed and rubbed the bridge of his nose. "Just—will you let me do this how *I* want to do this?"

I perked up. "Does that mean you *want* to do this?"

"Jordan!"

"Dad, you're out of practice. You haven't—you haven't dated since Mom."

I held my breath. I'd never said anything so blatant before about his dating life.

Dad didn't say anything.

"If you don't want to date, fine," I said. "As long as it's because *you* don't want to, not because you're concerned about me. Because I'm okay, Dad. I'm good. You don't need to worry about me."

He looked at me for a long moment. "Of course I have to worry about you. You're my daughter."

I swallowed hard. "Okay." I refused to lose sight of the goal, even if that'd been an emotional sucker-punch. "You can worry about me, but you shouldn't *also* avoid living your own life because of it. You can't use me as an excuse."

He sounded astonished. "I'm not!"

"Good. Don't. I want you to be happy, Dad. I want you to date, if it makes you happy. I think it might."

For a moment, he was silent. We listened to the roar of water. Always here, out on the ocean, but so ever-present it was easy to forget it, despite how loud it really was.

"Okay," Dad finally said. He reached out and hugged me to his side. "I'll think about it."

"Good."

We stayed there and watched the shooting stars for a long time.

Nineteen

At 2:55 a.m., my alarm went off. I flailed wildly, then re-membered I was awake on purpose. And on a boat. Flop-ping out of bed, I brushed my teeth and pulled on a cozy old sweater. The sleeves fell past my hands and the hem fell to the top of my thighs.

A quiet knock sounded on my door, and I opened it to Ethan. "Hey," he whispered. "You ready?"

I nodded and followed him, still half bundled up in sleep, un-til we stepped out onto the deck. "Oh." I turned my head to the stars. "This is *wonderful*."

Above us, meteors streaked across the black-velvet sky. I'd never seen so many at once, or so easily. Out here, in the dark of night, there was no competition for their brightness.

Ethan tilted his face up too. "Wow."

For a moment we watched the darting light, too absorbed to speak. Then Ethan spread out a blanket he'd had the foresight to bring, and we lay down on it.

Side by side, yet with a careful border of space between us, we watched the meteors. Yet for the first time, they couldn't hold all my attention. I was too aware of how much I wanted to bridge the gap between me and Ethan; my desire to touch him was so strong I felt almost paralyzed by it. Why was it so easy for me to make a move on a stranger, but almost impossible when I genuinely liked someone?

And god, I liked Ethan. So much.

"Are you cold?" he asked after a minute.

I eyed him. "Maybe."

"Lift up." He nudged at my shoulders, and when I did, he slipped his arm under them and pulled me closer. My whole body seemed to exhale, relieved to finally be in contact with him. My head rested on his chest, and I curled toward his side. I could feel my heart pounding. Could feel his, too, and the hard press of his chest against my cheek, and the edge of his chin against my head.

"Much better," he said softly.

Too oddly shy to speak, I nodded, and crept my hand across his chest so I was hugging him. We lay there, breathing, figuring out how to fit into each other. Watching the light above us.

"Make a wish," I said.

"You too."

What would I wish, on a shooting star, on a dozen of them? There were enough to grant every wish I'd ever had, if I could pull them all together.

At the beginning of the summer, I would have said I wanted my father to spend the summers at home. With me.

During the middle, I would have said I wanted him to respect me. To be impressed by me.

But now . . . I wanted him to be happy.

And . . . I shot a glance at Ethan, who stared firmly at the firmament. I wanted to be happy, too. I wanted to be with Ethan, I wanted it to work between us. But in all practicality, I knew it wouldn't. I was a good time, not a long time.

"What's your wish?" he whispered.

"What's yours?" I whispered back.

He didn't say anything. Instead, he traced the curve of my cheek, my ear, my chin. His eyes were almost black in the darkness, but his touch was tender. He bent his head and kissed me, sweet, then fierce, his hands pulling me closer, his body blazingly hot. An answering heat burned in my own body, a kind of desperation, and I pressed myself as close to Ethan as I could. It didn't feel possible to get close enough. I wanted his hands, his touch, everywhere. I felt as though my body contained the stars in the sky, jolts of fire, wild and reckless. I wanted to devour him. He wanted the same, I imagined, from the press of his body, the low groan in his throat.

We stayed out there, under the blanket of night and fire in the sky, for hours. When I fell asleep, it was with my head on his chest, listening to the steady beat of his heart, that strange bloody muscle to which we attributed so much.

* * *

"Good morning."

I opened my eyes, sticky with sleep sand, and found Cora's face looking down at me from above, the rising sun gilding her crown of braids. "Err," I said, and yawned.

"Ah, to be young," she said glibly, sipping from the cup of coffee she cradled in both hands. "My back would never survive a night on a ship's deck."

"We came up to watch the meteor shower." I rubbed my eyes. "Good morning." I poked Ethan in the side. I hadn't expected to fall asleep again, but what could I say, I was no match for the lulling motion of a ship and slept debt. "Wake up."

"They're pretty great." Cora nodded to the east. "So's this."

"Wow," I said, catching sight of the sun on the horizon. I patted Ethan's cheek. "Wake up, you don't want to miss this."

"Sleeeep," Ethan groaned, eyes still shut.

"No, wake up." I took his hand and pulled him to his feet. He staggered—I couldn't tell if he was feigning or only half conscious—so I looped my arm around his waist, letting him lean on me.

"Wow," he agreed.

In silence, the three of us watched the sun rise, a molten-gold globe slowly emerging from the sea. Reds and oranges formed a dark seam at the horizon, while the sun pushed back the darkness above. The water itself was a ripple of dark blue, so dark and glossy the untold depths seemed truer than usual, an ache in my heart, not just a fact in my head.

We watched until the sun had cleared the horizon. Then, yawning, Ethan and I stumbled below decks for the only acceptable way to drown: in caffeine.

That morning, like the one before, the crew showed us the literal ropes of the ship. Ethan and I joked and laughed with Gary's niece and nephew, and I felt for the first time like I really understood it, what my dad and Ethan liked to do—being out on the water, wearing yourself out under the hot sun, trying something new and different and failing and laughing and trying again.

And all morning, my heart kept pounding out a song, the same song, with the same lyrics, and it went, *I really really really really like Ethan Barbanel.*

Too much.

In the afternoon, I went back to the library and kept reading Dad's book. Maybe I should have talked to Ethan, pulled him into one of our cabins for privacy, but I didn't know what I would say. And he didn't try to talk to me, either, so he must have been fine with our lack of clarity about what we were doing. He was happy, I could tell, by the way he smiled at me and placed his hand on the small of my back. I was happy too. I just wanted . . . more.

After dinner, everyone came back to the top deck to watch the sunset. Tonight, the sky glowed more smoothly than yesterday; instead of bright streaks of clouds and gold cutting sharply through each other, the colors melded into one another like an opal, smooth and rolling pink here, then purple, then yellow. Maybe this was what people had done before TV; they had watched the sky every night, an endlessly repeating lightshow.

Or maybe people had toiled in the fields and then collapsed in exhaustion, ignoring the sunset entirely.

"I remembered a few more stories about college," Gary said, joining me and Ethan and Dad and Cora as night fell. He looked at Dad. "Do you remember when we lost that bet and had to audition for *The Full Monty . . . ?*"

They told stories about their group of friends, and about Mom, more stories than I'd ever heard before. About stealing a deconstructed table from the dining hall, about being peer pressured into joining their dorm's intramural soccer team for one terrible season. About good professors and bad professors and funny friends and sulky ones.

I drank their stories in, thrilled by every new detail I learned. It felt good, these stories; they felt easy, and Dad felt open, and I felt, for the first time in a long time, like Mom wasn't a tragedy I kept locked away but something good and bright.

Slowly, people peeled off for the night. Ethan and I walked to our rooms together, arranging it so no one else was around. Ethan stopped in front of his door. "Do you want to come in?"

How strange, that though we lived in the same hall, we'd never been further than the doorway of each other's rooms. It felt like a boundary.

But boundaries felt less real here, at sea. "Yes."

Inside, we reached for each other as the door shut, hands on skin, lips on lips. Ethan pressed me up against the wall, and my arms instinctively wrapped around him.

I wanted this, and I wanted him, but something Andrea Darrel had written popped into my head. *I am a scientist and I trade in facts, and so I would like to have some.* She'd wanted clarity from Frederick, and she'd been willing to be blunt to get it. She'd been willing to have an awkward—even tense—confrontation about her career and marriage.

And maybe she hadn't ended up with Frederick Gibson. But hopefully, asking him what they were doing, making the conversation happen, had helped her figure out their future. Maybe it had kept her from spending four more summers dangling after him.

I placed my hands on Ethan's shoulders and pushed him back. "Ethan."

He smiled at me, a smile that had become so very familiar, so very dear. "Jordan."

Okay. Okay, I was going to do it. I had found myself an internship and started my own research project and learned to be less jealous; I could communicate with the boy I liked. "What are we doing?"

And there they were. I was terrified, but also kind of proud of myself.

"What?" Ethan looked startled.

Okay, maybe I should have built up to this, instead of simply blurting it out. "Like, um"—I waved a hand between our bodies—"us."

Ethan went very still and spoke cautiously, as though not to scare off a nervous deer. "What do you want to be doing?"

I wanted Ethan. I wanted a steady, serious relationship with him. And I didn't want to keep wanting that if he'd never want the same from me. I didn't want to take what, for him, might be casual crumbs of affection, when to me they meant so much. "I think I mentioned I've had some . . . bad relationships. Where I get invested in them and they don't get invested in me. I'm trying to keep from doing that anymore."

". . . Okay." Ethan took a step back. Now there was space between us in this tiny room, and I couldn't tell if I wanted it there or not.

"I guess I . . . don't want to do anything casual right now."

"Ah." He nodded a few times. "So you'd want us to be . . . not casual?"

My chest felt tight. Was he checking in about what I wanted or saying what he wanted? "Would *you* be interested in something not casual?"

He tilted his head and studied me. I could feel my heart beating, a persistent *thump-thump, thump-thump*, though I couldn't tell if it was going to stop entirely or burst out of my chest. I felt like we were in a standoff, two Wild West cowboys waiting for the other to draw first.

Then Ethan said, "Yeah. I would be."

Oh my god. Oh my god, oh my god. "Um. I need a moment." I sank down onto his rug, the same white cotton rug as in my cabin, and curled my knees to my chest.

This was exactly what I wanted. This was everything I wanted. So why was I freaking out?

Ethan knelt across from me. "Are you okay?"

Because I had tried this before. I had done this before. And it never, ever worked. It would almost be easier *not* to try, because how could I believe this could end well?

"It's complicated," I managed. "You're my dad's assistant."

"True. But honestly, he loves me. I think he'll be psyched."

255

I let out a startled laugh. "You're so full of it."

"With good reason."

I grinned, and god, I wanted to reach out and take what he offered, but—there was this horrible sinking feeling in my stomach. He was. My dad's. Assistant. We could try, but I had tried before, and it hadn't worked.

My smile slowly fell away.

"What?" Ethan asked.

"It's—what happens when we break up?"

Ethan's brows flew up. "What?"

"You work with my dad. We won't stop being in each other's lives. It'll make everything so much messier."

"Why are you already breaking us up?"

"Because that's life," I said. "Because I've done this before, and it never works. I have a pattern, where I fall for guys I'm obsessed with and it never works out. It's stupid for me to ignore my past experiences and imagine the future might be different."

His lips quirked. "So you're obsessed with me."

I dealt him a sarcastic look. "That's not supposed to be your takeaway."

"But it is. Come on, Jordan. Let's give this a go."

"How?" I whispered. "Ethan . . . Every time I like someone this much, it ends with my heart getting broken. And I'm sick of it, Ethan. I'm fucking sick of getting my heart ripped out and stomped on, and having to patch it up and paste it back together. Each time I do, there's more missing pieces, and eventually I'm going to have more patches than heart."

"I won't break your heart."

"You can't promise that."

He was silent a minute. "Okay. True. So what do you want to do?"

I leaned my head against the wall and stared at the ceiling. What did I want to do? My whole body—my whole *being*—strained toward Ethan all the time. If I thought there was the smallest, slimmest chance this would work, shouldn't I throw myself into it with my entire heart?

But wasn't it the stupidest thing in the world to think this would work? I'd tried dating boys like Ethan. I'd dated John and Tarek and Louis, and I'd been wild about all of them. And I'd cried my eyes out on a park bench over John, stopped enjoying food for a week after Tarek, and been bone-achingly sad about Louis. Why do that to myself again?

Or, who was I kidding, I'd do it to myself in a heartbeat. But I didn't want to do it to Dad.

"I don't know," I finally said. "I want to be with you. I just . . . I have a hard time trusting it'll work."

He ran a hand through his hair. "Do you want to keep being casual then?"

"No," I said fiercely. "God, no, I can't. I'd rather just be friends."

He reared back. "Friends. Okay."

"No! I don't mean that's what I want. I want . . ." I smiled wryly. "Not to sound like a mid-two-thousands rom-com, but I want you."

He grinned. "Good. Then we're together."

"But I think . . ." I said slowly, trying to figure out my actual hesitation, "I don't want anyone to know we're dating."

He winced.

I winced too. "Sorry. It sounds shittier out loud. I just want to make sure it's real, before my dad finds out." Because if this imploded, I wanted to be able to hide it. "Dad puts up with a lot. Every time I go through a breakup, he's there. He's the one who hugs me and watches Netflix and makes popcorn with mini chocolate chips. I don't want him to have to do that again." This time, if my heart broke, I'd keep it hidden.

Ethan stood, pacing the few feet the room allowed. I stood too, and sat on the edge of his bed.

"Look," Ethan said. "I don't want to get between you and your dad. But I also don't want your dad to get between you and me." He looked embarrassed and frustrated. "I don't want you to decide it's not worth being with me because we might break up and it'll be hard on your dad. He's an adult. He'll be fine."

"I know," I said softly. "I just don't want him to think *I'm* not fine."

"Maybe you *shouldn't* be fine if you go through a breakup. Maybe that's okay."

I groaned. "Why do you have to be so sensible?"

"That's me." He sounded a little happier. "Sensible Ethan, that's what they all say." He brightened even more. "I guess if no one knows we're dating, no one'll keep an eye on what rooms we're in at night."

I rolled my eyes and bit back a smile. "You're incorrigible."

He grinned. "You love it."

I knew he was just tossing out the word, but it made something deep in my stomach clench, like I'd been called out in a way I hadn't been prepared for.

Ethan didn't notice. "So basically, we're gonna . . . keep doing what we're currently doing?"

When he put it that way . . . "Well, yeah. But exclusively."

His brows shot up. "Have we not been exclusive all summer?"

I blushed. Ethan Barbanel, making me blush! "I guess. I have. Have you?"

He laughed and dropped down to sit next to me. "Yeah."

"Oh." I felt a flood of relief and delight. So he *hadn't* been hooking up with the girl from the dunk tank or the beach party. At least, not this year. "Okay. Good. Well, now we'll be exclusive intentionally. And . . ."

His brows got even higher. "And?"

"And now it's not . . . just . . . physical." The words got harder and harder to push out of my mouth. God, it was hard to be emotionally vulnerable, who signed up for this? "Now we're doing this with the acknowledgment that we . . . we . . . like each other."

He grinned. "So you're obsessed with me *and* you like me."

I scowled. "If you don't say it back I will shove you off this bed."

He laughed and slid his hand up my neck. "I like you so much, Jordan Edelman," he murmured, and he kissed me again.

Twenty

The next day, I stood on the deck next to Dad as Nantucket became a raised line on the horizon. *Home*, I thought, with a swell of fondness, though of course Nantucket wasn't home. But it felt like it, after almost two months. Maybe because the island was so small, so easy to know quickly; maybe because natural beauty had a way of burrowing deep inside your heart.

Dad showed me and Ethan how to map the coastline as we circled the island. We sat by the rail, trying to draw the dips of coves, the sweep of cliffs. All too soon, we glided into the harbor, said goodbye to Gary and Brent and the rest, and climbed into cars waiting to take us back to Golden Doors. I felt unexpectedly nostalgic—it had only been three nights, but they'd been good ones.

"Welcome back!" Ethan's mom said when we arrived. "You're just in time to help with dinner."

Ethan looked at me. "Should we go back out for a while?"

"Very funny," his mom said. "Shira and Noah could use some help on the mango-avocado salad."

Five minutes later, Ethan was squeezing limes for the vinaigrette and chopping cilantro, and I was peeling mountains of fruit. While I'd loved being on the *Salty Fox*, I loved this, too: laughing with the Barbanel cousins, listening to the adults chatting in the great room, eating outside as the sun set, breathing in the scent of jasmine and listening to the coo of mourning doves.

I couldn't believe it'd be August in a few days, and a few weeks after I'd head to UMass. I could barely conceptualize college, despite visiting campus and texting my new roommate and forcing Dad to sit through the tedium of AlcoholEdu with me. I remembered Andrea Darrel's nerves about going to college. I'd been further from home than she ever had, but still couldn't imagine leaving home and living in dorms, surrounded by strangers. I still wondered what I should expect.

And what would happen to me and Ethan?

I pushed the worry out of my head. Later. I would deal with that later.

Grace texted around 10:00 p.m. Sent the rest of the paper pictures, sorry to send so late! Just got home from a VERY GOOD DATE with Sierra

Like a legit date

We went out for dinner and then there was a dance party (??) in the street and so we danced

And then we MADE OUT against a MURAL and part of me was in my body but part of me was outside and like "I wish I had a photo of us making out in front of this mural"

That sounds weird now that I type it out

Don't worry I was fully in the moment

Anyway should I ask her if she wants to be my girlfriend? how does one do such a thing

Before my phone could ping any more, I called Grace. "Yes!
You should ask her."

"What if she says no?" Grace's face was illuminated only by
the twinkle lights around her bed. "What if she's like, no, you
freak, I don't want to date you seriously?"

"Then *she's* the freak. And you'll know, and won't waste any
more time on her." My new mantra.

"How very mature," she said skeptically. "What's gotten into
you?"

A smile tugged at my lips. "Since you ask . . ."

We talked for ages, until neither of us couldn't stop yawning.
After we hung up, I opened the images she'd sent of Andrea's
diaries.

Andrea was *happy*. Blissfully, devotedly, ecstatically happy. To
be honest, it was a little boring.

It also clearly made her less inclined to journal. For several
months she stopped altogether, except for one line in March
1911 saying *terrible news about the Triangle Shirtwaist Factory fire*,
which I vaguely remembered being a Bad Historical Disaster.

And then—

April 8, 1911

I don't even know what to write. I think I might cry.

She'd written two lines of numbers below. I tried to make sense of them. She'd scribbled mathematical equations in the margins before, but she'd never written anything so deliberately, as though she had already worked it out elsewhere and was copying it over here in a neat, careful hand—far more careful than her usual—for posterity.

What could make her want to cry?

I flipped the page. I half expected a time-jump, given Andrea's erratic journaling. Instead, the following entry was dated the next day.

April 9, 1911

> *How dare he.*
> *I thought we loved each other.*
> *I thought he respected me.*

Cold trickled through my body like slivers of ice. I read it again. *How dare he.*

There were no further pages.

What had happened? Grace had said she'd taken pictures of the rest of the journal available. Had all the journal's pages been filled, or had Andrea stopped writing in it? Had she censored the pages she gave to Harvard? Or had Harvard censored her?

How dare he.

Who was "he"?

But of course he, to Andrea Darrel, always meant Frederick Gibson. And Gibson had discovered his comet in 1911.

I'd expected Andrea to be envious about her boyfriend discovering a comet, but to be furious . . . to sound betrayed . . . How dare he what? How dare he . . . break up with her? Discover a comet first? Say something cruel?

I wished I could talk this out with someone—and then I realized I could. Ethan was right down the hall. Ethan and I were dating, and I could go to his room if I wanted.

Without letting myself think about it too much, I slipped out of my room and knocked on Ethan's door. "Hello?" he called, his voice croaky and sleepy. Shoot, I hadn't even checked the time. After midnight, for sure.

I pushed the door open, then shut it behind me and leaned against it. "Hi."

He blinked, then sent me a bone-melting smile. "Hi."

"That is not why I'm here," I told him, trying not to pay attention to how good his messy hair looked. "Grace sent me more of Andrea Darrel's diaries."

"Okay . . . ?"

I sat at the foot of his bed. "The last two entries are weird. Something happened, and I don't know what—but I think it was about Gibson." I showed him my phone, flipping between the two entries.

"What are these numbers?" Ethan asked through a yawn, nodding at the string attached to the first entry.

"I don't know. But—Ethan, when did Gibson discover the comet? Was it—it wasn't *then*, was it? It wasn't April eighth or ninth?"

"Huh?" Ethan rubbed his eyes. One of his curls stood straight up.

"Something big happened, to Andrea. And the next day, she was furious. In 1911, the year of the comet's discovery. Maybe Gibson dumped her . . . or said something rude . . . I'm trying to figure out why she was crying and speechless and furious."

"I dunno." Ethan still looked sleepy.

I worried at my lip with my teeth. "I feel like it was about her work, since she said *I thought he respected me*, and Andrea desperately wanted to be respected for her work. She was so ambitious. But also . . ." I looked at the first page again.

I don't even know what to write. I think I might cry.

"Sometimes, you don't cry out of sadness or fury." I worked through it out loud. "Sometimes you cry out of joy. Sometimes you're speechless from awe." A shiver danced across the base of my neck. "Isn't it funny? An amateur astronomer discovering a comet, instead of his girlfriend, a professional astronomer, who's been sweeping the skies for years?"

I raised my gaze to Ethan's and found him staring straight at me, completely awake now. His eyes widened. "You think . . ."

"I don't know," I said. "I think she felt a very strong feeling on the eighth, and then she felt betrayed on the ninth. What if . . . she was speechless from awe? What if this string of numbers . . . What if the reason she felt betrayed . . ."

He said the words out loud because one of us needed to. "You think Gibson's comet—one of the most famous comets out there—wasn't discovered by Frederick Gibson. You think Andrea Darrel discovered the comet, and Gibson took credit for it."

The words settled over me, heavy and blunt and real. I couldn't be sure, of course. But in my gut, the words rang true. "Do you know when, exactly, Gibson discovered the comet?"

"Let me see." Ethan rolled out of bed—seriously, he rolled over and landed on the floor in a cross-legged position, like a supremely sleepy acrobat. He pulled his laptop toward him, and I sat at his side, my back against his bed, as he tapped away.

He turned toward me and kissed me.

For a moment, I kissed him back, lost in the taste of him, in the feel, in the fact that we were *together* now, if secretly, and I got to touch him as much as I wanted—

And then I realized we were sliding horizontal. I pushed him up and pointed at his computer. "Ethan! Concentrate!"

"I'm concentrating." He swept my hair back behind my ear.

"On the wrong thing."

He groaned. "I can't believe you're only using me for my research abilities. Use me for my body, please."

"Later."

"Promise?" he asked hopefully.

I jabbed my finger once more at the screen. "Comet!"

He sighed, then continued poking around. The date wasn't easy to find. Wikipedia only said: "Frederick Gibson discovered Comet C1911d during a routine search for comets." No further details on timing, just information about the Arborids and the comet's orbital period. "I'm not seeing it. Did you say people had to file for a discovery? Where?"

"I'm not sure—the local powerhouse astronomy center? Which would probably be Harvard."

Sure enough, we found a website with serious nineties vibes, declaring that the Harvard College Observatory Bulletins were the Western Hemisphere's main way of announcing discoveries of comets and novae between 1898 and 1926. They had PDFs of scans of their old bulletins. "There's one from April ninth, 1911," I said, my stomach clenching.

We opened it. In bubbly handwriting, like mine at thirteen, it read, "A cablegram received at this observatory from Mr. Frederick Gibson states that a planet has been discovered, positions of which are as follows." A few lines of numbers followed.

"Planet?" Ethan asked.

I could barely hear him over the pounding in my ears. "That's how they referred to comets." I remembered how Andrea had written about Witt's planet. How she'd longed to discover a comet herself. "Gibson filed for a discovery. The same day Andrea wrote *how dare he.*"

"But—Jordan, Andrea worked at Harvard, she basically *lived* at the observatory. If she discovered the comet, how would he have been able to file for it before her? She would've had to tell him the positions and everything first, and why would she do that before telling Harvard?"

"I don't know. But these numbers—look, they match the ones she wrote down in her diary."

Ethan let out a low whistle. "Looks bad. Though it's possible, right, they both independently discovered it?"

Like Witt and the other dude. "Yeah," I admitted reluctantly. "But why would she be so mad if he genuinely found it?"

"Like you said. She'd been trying to do this her whole life.

He'd only been interested in astronomy for a few years. I bet it'd still make her furious if he scooped her."

"True." But I thought about Rosalind Franklin, who did ground-breaking work on DNA only to watch two men win the Nobel Prize. And Lise Meitner, who didn't get any credit for nuclear fusion. And the Harvard Computers, called Pickering's Harem, whose names were below men's for their own work, or absent. "But this kind of thing happened. A lot."

"I'm just saying, it could've gone down differently."

Irritation spiked through me. "Why are you trying so hard to defend him?"

"I'm not! I'm trying to make you see we don't have absolute proof. And I think we need absolute proof before spreading this around too much. I mean, this is a pretty big accusation."

"Wait." My eyes narrowed. "Is this about—you?"

He looked confused. "Huh?"

"About your research on Gibson? About the speech you're giving, the work you've done? You think it'd look bad for you if it turned out he was a thief?"

Ethan's eyes widened. "Are you serious?"

"I don't know! Why else would you care?"

"Because I'm trying to protect your dad," he half shouted. "The conference we're presenting at next week? It's run by the *Gibson* Foundation, Jordan. Your dad's trying to get a grant from the *Gibsons*, and the chair is the great-grandson of Frederick Gibson. You think they'll like it if you call their founder a liar and a thief?"

"Oh." I suddenly felt very small. "I didn't know."

"Now you do. And it's what I was trying to tell you, so you could have waited before jumping down my throat."

I swallowed. "I'm sorry. But—if they knew Gibson was wrong, wouldn't they want to acknowledge it? It'd be the right thing to do."

Ethan scoffed. "Because adults have such a great record of doing the right thing. Like cleaning up the environment. And the ocean. And space."

My stomach sank. Given the choice between the right thing and the easy thing, society had made it very clear what it'd choose. But—"I shouldn't have to choose between my dad getting a grant and a woman getting credit for her discovery. That's ridiculous."

"No," Ethan said, softening. "We need more proof. Proof they can't dismiss out of hand."

"Okay." I felt a little reassured. "Makes sense. But—Ethan, at some point, we have to tell people. Even if we don't have proof. We have to at least say what we know."

"Agreed," Ethan said. "But maybe we wait until after the conference? I have papers the foundation let me read for my research. We can look though those, see what we turn up. And obviously tell your dad if you want, I just meant you shouldn't charge up to the Gibson Foundation and accuse them of fraud."

"Yeah." I thought about it. "Maybe I won't even tell Dad until we have a few more facts. I don't want him to feel like . . ." I smiled wryly. "I don't know, like I'm making mountains out of molehills. Like I'm being messy."

Ethan nodded. Then he closed his laptop, put it aside, and

turned to me. "You can trust me, you know. I'm not going to defend a guy who stole work from another scientist."

"I know." I bowed my head and stared at my feet.

"And—I know you're nervous about the two of us. Being together. But I'm on your side. Always."

I nodded, feeling sick. Why had I yelled at him? Had I ruined things between us immediately? "I'm sorry. I'm bad at this. I guess—I should go now. Give you some space."

"Jordan." His voice was gentle. "Do you want to stay?"

I looked back at him.

"It's your call. But you can. If you want."

I swallowed over the lump in my throat. "Yeah," I said. "That sounds nice."

Twenty-One

The Gibson Foundation held their conference at a seaside hotel. The weather was exceptional—mideighties but not too humid, giant puffy clouds in the sky. Ethan and my dad's talk would be at four, two hours before the dinner and keynote speech by the foundation's chairman, Mr. Charles Gibson. It would be a full day of talks devoted to the sciences. Nantucket's status as a summer destination made the foundation lean into Frederick Gibson's tenuous connection with the island, and people from all over had come.

I'd asked my dad about the grant the day before, when we were watching TV in his tiny apartment over dumplings. "Is this grant important? The one from the Gibson Foundation."

"It would certainly help."

"What do you think about the foundation itself?"

He smiled wryly, paused, then said, "They're very generous with their grants."

Sounded a lot like *If you can't say anything nice, don't say anything at all.* "What about the chairman? Do you know him? He's the one looking at your grant?"

"There's a whole committee," Dad said. "But yes, he has final say. He . . . Well, he's very proud of his foundation. It's very well-respected. And I think for some people, it's fun, to get to make a big speech and give out awards."

I narrowed my eyes. Dad was being very circumspect. "Do you hate him? Is he the worst?"

Dad laughed. "No. No, he's fine. I think he's perhaps—less interested in knowledge for knowledge's sake, and more interested in the foundation for prestige. Which is—differently than I think."

Cool. So we hated him.

But it also sounded like Dad wanted this grant, and like Mr. Charles Gibson might not be an altruistic science dude who would immediately be on my side if I brought up Andrea Darrel. If I wanted to be a good daughter—if I wanted Dad to be able to focus on writing instead of taking tutoring gigs and teaching summer school—I shouldn't make it difficult for Dad to get this grant. Maybe I let this go. It was a hundred years ago, and Andrea and Frederick were both dead. Was bringing this up worth ticking off Charles Gibson and ruining Dad's chance at this grant or future ones? Was righting a wrong in the past worth taking away something real and tangible in the present?

But thinking about letting go of this made the walls of my stomach squeeze toward my midline. It made a difference to everyone ever who hadn't received the credit they deserved. It wasn't right. I shouldn't have to choose.

Ethan knocked on my door at nine o'clock the morning of the

conference and didn't wait for an answer before bursting inside. "How do I look?"

I'd never seen him nervous before. I'd also never seen him dressed so sharply, in a blue suit and skinny tie. "Really nice."

He let out a breath of relief. "Thanks."

"How are you feeling? Ready?"

Ethan dropped to sit on the foot of my bed. "For all my family to stare at me with the expectation I'm going to mess up any minute? God no."

"They won't be thinking that. They're going to be proud of you."

"Yeah." He sounded skeptical. "Should we head out?"

I stifled a laugh, waving at my state of undress—my tank top and shorts. "I'm not exactly ready."

"Right." He bounced his hand off his forehead. "I'm a dummy. In my defense, you look great."

I laughed. "Give me ten and I'll be down."

I took twenty because I decided to wrest my hair into a gentle twist and braid it over one shoulder. I'd selected my outfit ages ago, an old favorite I'd thrifted back home: a black dress with golden stars embellished on it. I had earrings to match, and I'd saved a silky golden strip of ribbon from a present I'd once received and now wore it as a headband.

It wasn't often you got a Cinderella-at-the-top-of-the-stairs moment. I hadn't at prom, where I'd gone with my friends, or for any school dances. I'd never stood at the top of any stairs, someone's face craned toward me, washed over by amazement.

"Wow," Ethan said, standing in the foyer and gazing up at me on the second-floor balcony. "You look amazing."

I grinned down at him. "Thanks."

"Maybe we should skip this whole thing and stay home?" Ethan asked hopefully, stepping forward and sliding his hands around my waist as I reached the bottom of the stairs.

I gave him a quick peck and slipped away. "Not a chance."

Ethan tapped his fingers nervously against the wheel as he drove, his whole body vibrating with tension. I placed my hand on his arm, trying to offer some amount of comfort. When we arrived at the resort hosting the conference, Ethan turned the engine off but kept his hands on the wheel, breathing deeply.

"You're going to do great," I told him.

He straightened his jacket and his tie. "Yes. Okay." He gave me a lopsided smile. "But if I need to run, will you be my getaway driver?"

"Yes. But you're not going to need to run."

We found the check-in stand, where a sea of laminated name-tags greeted us. We put on ours. Ethan looked like he might throw up and kept tugging at the cuffs of his sleeves and taking deep breaths. I took his hand, and he didn't let go.

People streamed through the venue, dressed in blazers and ironed pants and sheath dresses, and lanyards for all. They crowded around coffee kiosks and strode purposefully down the halls. I didn't see anyone close to our age, and I felt very young and even a little silly in my star-spangled dress. "Wow," I said. "Kind of a lot."

"Yeah." Ethan tugged at his tie. "Not that many people will be at my talk, right?"

I squeezed his hand. "I'm sure it'll be great."

"Should we find your dad?" Ethan still sounded unsure of himself.

Honestly, I felt the same. I pulled out my phone. "Definitely."

Dad was in the speakers' green room, which turned out to be a large conference room with round tables in the center and a long rectangular table at the front, covered with snacks, coffee, tea, and easily transportable fruit.

"You made it!" Dad said, beaming up at us from his table, where he was chatting with two women and a man.

"Hi," Ethan said, then couldn't manage anything else.

"This is my daughter, Jordan." Dad said. "And my assistant, Ethan."

The man's gaze lit up, raking over Ethan's appearance. "Ethan—Barbanel, is it?"

Ethan's usual buoyancy cooled in the way all members of his family seemed to when anyone got too excited by their last name. "Nice to meet you."

"This is Charles Gibson," Dad said, and both Ethan and I straightened. I looked closer at the man. He was older than Dad but younger than my grandparents, with a thick shock of gray hair and bright blue eyes. Was there anything of Frederick about him, any resemblance in appearance or spirit?

"I hear you'll be talking about our founder, my great-grandfather. The one who brought us all here," the man—Mr. Gibson—said to Ethan.

"Yes, sir," Ethan said. His gaze flicked to me. But I could hold my tongue. I wouldn't say anything, not here, not now. No matter how much I wanted to.

And I really wanted to. *Who brought us all here?* Well, my dude, it wasn't your umpteenth grandpa. If he'd wanted something cool on his résumé, he could have put in the effort like the rest of us.

"If you'll excuse us," Ethan said, like the calm, well-trained person he'd been brought up to be, "there's a panel we wanted to see."

* * *

A few hours later, Ethan and I headed to the conference room where he and Dad would give their talk. It wasn't very large, with space for about eighty people, but I thought that was better than a giant room with only a trickle of audience.

Ethan and I took seats in the first row as Dad and a conference organizer fiddled with the projector and microphone. Ethan was fidgeting, and about an hour ago he'd almost entirely stopped talking. I ran my hand up and down his shoulder. "You're going to do great."

"I'm terrified. Is it normal to be this terrified? I feel like my tie is trying to strangle me."

"Then take it off. No one's going to care if you're wearing a tie. And yes, I think it is. Stage fright."

"Okay, well, it *feels* like I'm the first person who's ever experienced this in the entire world." He bent in half, placing his head on his knees. His voice came out muffled. "I am a child."

I laughed and placed my hand on the back of his head, twining my fingers through his thick, glossy curls. "You're nervous, it's normal. But you know this stuff backward and forward. You could riff on Gibson even if you hadn't written everything down."

"You hate Gibson. You think he's a shitty person."

I pressed my lips together to muffle another laugh. "Maybe. But that doesn't mean your research is shitty. And I suppose shitty people are capable of also contributing to science."

He groaned slightly and straightened. When I started to move my hand back to my lap, he caught it and pulled it into his. His eyes met mine. "My family is going to think I'm ridiculous."

"No, they won't. They're going to be super proud of you."

He opened his mouth, but before he got any words out, we heard his mother behind us. "Ethan! There you are!"

We turned. The room had started to fill as people took seats in ones and twos. Now a whole wave of people entered. The Barbanels had arrived.

"Maybe you should've given a pre-talk just to them," I whispered to Ethan as they poured in, aunts and uncles and cousins and, in the middle, both Helen and Edward Barbanel, matriarch and patriarch.

"I'm going to be sick," he whispered back.

"Ethan Barbanel. You are a badass, adventurous, brilliant person. You can handle your family."

"Nope," he groaned. "I can't."

"Then look at me," I said, and he did, his eyes wide and scared. "During the talk, you look at me, you tell me what's going on, and don't think about anything else. Imagine we're sitting on the roof walk or at the beach. And you're telling me a story."

He nodded, and the panic started to leave his body. "Okay. I can do that." He brightened. "Give me a kiss for good luck?"

I leveled him with a look. "Maybe after. If you're lucky."

His expression turned speculative. "Isn't one tip for feeling comfortable picturing the audience in their underwear?"

I stuck my tongue out. "Feel free. But while you might get me, you're also going to get your grandparents."

His laugh turned to a wince, and then his family descended upon us in a cloud of well-wishes and advice.

For someone not participating in the talk or doing any speaking whatsoever, I felt abnormally nervous when the clock struck four and the audience quieted down. At the front of the room, Dad and Ethan sat in two plastic chairs like the ones for the audience, their nameplates and water bottles on the table in front of them. They were joined by one of the women Dad had been talking to in the green room, who clicked her microphone on and nodded to someone in the back, who hit the lights.

Polite applause rippled through the room, and the woman smiled. "Thank you, everyone. I'm Farah Irfan, and I'm pleased to be joined by Tony Edelman, author of *Mapping the Atlantic: A History of American Maritime Cartography*. His other publications include articles in *The Atlantic*, *The Boston Globe*, and more. Let's all welcome him—"

The room applauded again. Dad waited for it to die down, then leaned toward his mic. "Thanks, Farah. Thanks for having me. I'm so glad to be here, and to get a chance to share some of my research. I've spent this summer working on my second book, and today I'm going to talk about . . ."

After years of giving talks, Dad had perfected it, and thank god—in the beginning he'd been as nervous as Ethan, and when Dad was nervous, I was nervous. Now Dad was a pro, timing his water sips for when he knew the audience would laugh or need a moment to process his stories. His body was relaxed, and he never once glanced at his notes.

Ethan, on the other hand, sat stiffly at Dad's side. He kept still save one hand drumming against his thigh, and his eyes were unfocused, as though internally going over his own words.

And then Dad said, "To talk about Frederick Gibson himself, we have my assistant, Ethan Barbanel—a student at the University of Chicago."

"Hi," Ethan said into the microphone, his voice breaking. He'd leaned too close and feedback cracked through the room. He jerked back, eyes widening.

And then they found me.

I smiled encouragingly, even though now *I* felt like I might be sick.

Ethan visibly took a deep breath—one of my yoga breaths—and let it out. "Hi," he tried again. "I'm Ethan Barbanel, and I'm excited to talk to you today about Frederick Gibson's work for the US Coast Survey."

It went fantastically. He was, for all he'd been so nervous, a good speaker. He landed a few jokes, and when the audience laughed he relaxed. Sometimes he sped up too much when he got excited, but when his gaze landed on me—as it often did—he seemed to remember to take a breath, a sip of water, and slow down.

When he finished, Ethan let out a long breath and attention

switched to my dad, who picked up with an unexpectedly humorous anecdote about getting lost while trying to use a homemade compass. I kept watching Ethan, who'd sat back in his chair. The tension seemed to finally drain out of him, his stiff shoulders relaxing. He met my gaze and beamed.

Afterward, the usual post-talk shenanigans occurred; most of the audience filed out, while a few approached my father—and the Barbanels descended on Ethan. "My sweet little boychik," Ethan's mother said, kissing him on his forehead. "Look how well you did! We're so proud."

"Good job," his father said, and Ethan smiled so broadly I thought I might cry.

I stood a little way off, grinning as Ethan's family peppered him with praise. Finally he broke free. "I'll see you at the keynote speech," he said when they tried to pull him back. "I'll see you soon!"

Then he swept past me, my grabbing my hand along the way. "Come on."

I tossed a look behind us. "What—don't you want to be with your family—"

He pulled me outside, to a quiet hotel courtyard. Riotous hydrangeas bloomed, the air heady with their perfume, and a fountain splashed and burbled. He pushed me against the gray-shingled wall and kissed me, a long, searing kiss that left me melting into his body. I looped my arms around his neck and hung on for dear life, my knees no longer working, held up by the wall and Ethan's body.

He pulled away. "Sorry. Sorry, I know you don't want anything public—"

"No, *I'm* sorry." I pulled him back. "I'm sorry I've been so scared. God, Ethan, I want you so much. I want this. I want us. I do trust you, you know. We don't need to be secretive. We can tell people."

"Really?" He perked up. "You're sure? You're not just over-whelmed by hormones? Because I could totally stop kissing you if you need to think about it more clearly."

"Don't you dare."

He pressed a kiss to the base of my neck. "Thank god."

And then we were kissing again, our lips pressed together, my arms twined around his neck, and I *liked* this boy. I felt good about this. I wanted him, only him. I wanted us. The sea and the sky. The horizon.

* * *

For dinner, we joined my father, Ethan's parents and grand-parents, and Cora at one of the white-clothed tables set up on a stretch of lawn. Cora, it'd turned out, had always planned to attend the conference, though she'd told me earlier in the week she hadn't submitted a grant proposal. "None of my research fit. Next year, maybe," she'd said. "The grant committee likes a Nantucket connection."

The rest of the Barbanels had absconded. Shockingly, hanging out at a conference wasn't the highlight of their summer. But, I thought with a glance at Ethan, who sat at my side, talking earnestly with his grandfather, it might have been the highlight of mine. I couldn't stop smiling, didn't *want* to stop smiling. I had been so scared this wouldn't work, that I made the wrong calls and choose the wrong boys, and Ethan would be like the rest. But Ethan wasn't like them; Ethan wasn't like anyone but *Ethan*. He was goofy and ridiculous and loud and sweet and soft-hearted. And a little arrogant and ridiculously hot, but hey, I couldn't *completely* go against type. And I didn't want to. I wanted Ethan.

We held hands under the table, hidden in the cloth falling over our laps. I beamed at Ethan, at everyone, and so did he.

"It's impressive, everything you two have done," Ethan's dad said as the waiters poured water and wine and served tiny plates of salad covered in sheets of parmesan. "I didn't realize the level of research involved."

No? I wanted to say archly, but I let Dad take that one, diving with excitement into a description of the work necessary for his latest chapter, concerning the invention of the stern-post rudder during the Han dynasty and its introduction to and impact on worldwide technology.

I hoped Ethan's family would be more appreciative of how hard Ethan worked after hearing about Dad's extensive levels of research.

As the salad plates were cleared and servers started their elaborate dance of delivering the main courses, I noticed Charles Gibson, the chairman of the foundation, circulating throughout the tables. Eventually, he reached ours, bracing his hands against the corners of Cora's chair as he paused. "How we all doing to-night?"

I didn't like the way he smirked down at Cora or the way his gaze narrowed in on the Barbanels as Dad made introductions around the table.

"You must be so proud of your grandson," he said, and I didn't think it an exaggeration to call his tone ingratiating. "I know I am. It's rare people realize my great-grandfather was a scientist in his own right. We'd love to see more work about his contributions."

I resisted rolling my eyes, glancing over at Ethan to see his response—but he was drinking it in. Which, okay, made sense. He'd been so nervous about this talk, and he'd worked so hard on it. He deserved praise. Even if I wasn't convinced Frederick Gibson did.

"If you'll excuse me," the modern Mr. Gibson said, after a few more comments to the elderly Mr. and Mrs. Barbanel and to Ethan's parents. "It's time for my speech."

Charles Gibson climbed to the low stage. Behind him, twinkle lights sparkled. The audience quieted down, covertly digging into their entrées. "Welcome, everyone, to the eighty-ninth annual gathering of the Gibson Foundation." He paused for a round of applause. "I'm excited to introduce our newest initiatives and members, but first, the announcement we've been teasing for the last few weeks . . . As you know, my family's foundation has been a proud supporter of the sciences for over a hundred years, and we're delighted to fund so many deserving causes. We support innovation in all stages, but I have a special spot in my heart for those who accidentally stumble into their life's work. And so I'm particularly proud to announce the Frederick Gibson Award, a new award for early career scientists."

The applause was enthusiastic, and I joined in, muddled as I felt. On one hand, it was great the Gibson Foundation would be sponsoring more research. On the other hand—

"As you may be aware, the Gibson Foundation was founded by my great-grandfather, Frederick Gibson, who is famous for his discovery of Gibson's comet—which we'll all enjoy viewing in a few weeks. But he began his career in coastal surveying and only pivoted in his late thirties after accidentally discovering a comet."

On the other hand, I didn't exactly love the story being furthered here.

"Frederick was the third son of a rather demanding family, who didn't think he'd amount to much." The chairman allowed himself a small chuckle. "But he was fascinated by the stars, and so he set himself to work learning everything he could about them. He took astronomy classes here on Nantucket, and often in the evenings, he'd go outside to look at the sky. His hard work and research paid off: Within a few years, he'd accomplished something few others had. He'd discovered a comet."

My hands closed in small fists beneath the table, but I made myself breathe deeply. It wasn't like the chairman *knew* Frederick Gibson had been a liar; he thought the story he was telling was true. Besides, it wasn't like I had hard-core proof yet, either.

"The discovery of the comet and the fame that came alongside it changed Frederick's life. Instead of a normal career, Frederick was catapulted into an extraordinary stratum of scientific society at the time, and could make the connections necessary to launch this foundation, which has helped encourage and support research to this day. He is a sterling example of the way passionate new researchers can make a difference in the world, and we hope others will follow in his example."

Despite myself, I let out a disgusted snort. It would have been nice if *Andrea* had been launched into an extraordinary strata, if more women had her footsteps to follow in.

Dad looked at me. "What is it?"

"It's nothing." I flattened my hands against my knees. Ethan shook his head warningly. *Keep it together, Jordan.*

Onstage, Charles Gibson wasn't done. "In fact, I'm excited to announce that next year, during the ninetieth annual gathering of the Gibson Foundation, we'll be giving a retrospective of the man himself. Let's all raise a glass to the new Frederick Gibson Award—and to Frederick Gibson himself!"

Everyone did, but it was beyond me to join in. In fact, my mouth dropped open, and I stared at Charles onstage. "Are you kidding me?"

"Jordan, are you okay?" Dad asked.

"Yeah, I'm okay. It's just—" I snapped my mouth shut, glancing again at Ethan.

"Just what?" Ethan's mom asked.

Everyone was looking at me so expectantly, except Ethan, who gave me a searching look. But—it wouldn't hurt to mention it here. It wasn't like Charles Gibson could hear me, so it wouldn't get in the way of any grants. I wasn't making a big deal of this publicly, just at our dinner table. "Gibson didn't discover the comet."

Ethan closed his eyes.

I suddenly had the attention of the entire table, from Dad and Cora to Ethan's parents and grandparents. "Excuse me?" Cora said.

Oops. After the words had burst out of me, I felt halfway deflated. "I mean, I'm ninety percent sure he didn't. So this whole thing, holding up Frederick Gibson like some kind of hero"—I waved at the stage, where Charles Gibson was still talking—"feels like a farce."

Helen Barbanel was perhaps the only person not regarding me with shock. Instead, she cut into her moussaka. "I, for one, hate farces. Very tedious. How does this one go?"

Beneath the table, Ethan took my hand and squeezed. I shot him a grateful look, then turned to everyone else. "I've been researching this woman, Andrea Darrel. She was an astronomer in the early nineteen hundreds." I looked at Dad and Cora. "One of the Harvard Computers. She helped Annie Cannon teach astronomy classes, and Gibson took one. They fell in love." I took a deep breath. "I think Andrea Darrel discovered the comet, not Frederick Gibson."

Everyone stared at me, then the table burst out in a babble of questions.

"You read this in her diaries?" Cora asked. She sounded like she believed me. "She wrote it down?"

I winced. "Uh—close. But it could be . . . more conclusive."

"Jordan figured out that Andrea Darrel wrote the position of the comet in her diary the day before Gibson filed the discovery with Harvard," Ethan said. "And the next day, she wrote how furious she was with Gibson."

A murmur went around the table. Everyone looked at each other, then started talking, too loudly and quickly for me to keep track of what they were saying. A few people at neighboring tables glanced over.

Then, in a dose of excruciating bad luck, Charles Gibson's speech ended to a rousing round of applause. We had to pause to join in, to wait as Gibson smiled and said goodbye several times and walked offstage. He shook a few hands as the applause continued, but did he keep looking at—us?

Oh no. He was coming toward us now, too.

"Hello, again." Gibson couldn't keep the curtness out of his tone, despite the smile plastered on his face. Honestly, I couldn't blame him. If he'd glanced over, he'd probably noticed we weren't paying any attention, and we might even have caused a small disturbance. "What's the excitement over here? More exciting than my speech, I could tell." He forced a chuckle.

I should have made something up. I should have said we were playing a rousing game of, I don't know, Scattergories. But I didn't, and it turned out Ethan's grandmother was an agent of chaos. Helen Barbanel nodded at me. "This young lady says your ancestor stole the comet discovery from a young woman."

Wow. Damn. She really laid it out there.

Gibson froze, then slowly turned to me. "Excuse me?"

I wanted to sink into the floor. Oh no. Oh no, this is what I *hadn't* wanted to do. I hadn't wanted to call Frederick Gibson out, not yet, not until I had proof and the grants were settled and I could frame this exactly the way I wanted.

But also—

Frederick Gibson *did* steal Andrea Darrel's discovery. And male scientists had gotten away with taking credit from their female colleagues for way too long.

"I'm not trying to insult anyone," I said. "But I've been reading these old diaries and, well, yeah. It looks like this woman, Andrea Darrel, found the comet first."

"She says so? In her diaries?"

"Well—she doesn't exactly say it." I swallowed. "Not explicitly. But she wrote down the comet's position first."

Gibson smiled pityingly. "Even if she did, part of being the first discoverer is filing the correct paperwork."

"Right, I get that. But I don't think they each independently discovered it. She was his girlfriend. I think he stole her work."

"His girlfriend!" Charles Gibson laughed, as though this fact undermined the others. "Maybe she wanted him to get the credit."

Oh my god. Who would ever think that? "Uh, no. She was really proud of women's achievements. And she was really mad at him after."

He raised his brows. "And she says she was mad because of this?"

"Well, no," I admitted, frustrated. "But the timing works out."

"Maybe she was mad because they broke up," Gibson said. "After all, he didn't marry an astronomer."

"No!" I said. "Like I said, it was the same date as when he filed for the discovery. That's when she was mad."

But I could see the way he was looking at me, the way I was afraid Dad would be looking at me, and the rest of the table too, though I was too mortified to look at them. Like I was spinning mountains out of molehills. Coming to ridiculous conclusions.

"I can see you're very passionate about this." Gibson's voice dripped with condescension. "But it seems like you have a theory, and you're trying to find proof to fit into it."

"I'm not." I stared at my lap. "Or, at least, I think there's enough evidence we should consider the possibility. I'm trying to figure out the truth."

"I think the truth," Gibson said firmly, "is what happened: my great-grandfather discovered a comet. We'd have heard about it in the past hundred years if he hadn't. You're spinning yourself a fairy tale."

Heat burned in my cheeks and swelled up in my stomach and chest, like great bellows washed anger and embarrassment through me. I tried to swallow it down, but it was too much, too explosive, and it rushed out of me in a swell of loud, angry words. "You're hearing about it now. I'm trying to tell you. And I don't think it sounds like a fairy tale to think a guy might have taken credit for a woman's discovery. I think it's pretty fucking common."

Oops. Shouldn't have sworn.

Mr. Gibson stared at me, then smiled, and it dripped poison. "If you're going to make accusations like this, young lady, you need evidence." He glanced at my father. "And I have to say, it's very poor manners to do this here."

I pushed to my feet, my chair skittering loudly backward in the pool of silence that had spread around us. "Don't make this about my dad."

Gibson let out a sour laugh. "Sweetie, relax. No need to get emotional."

My chest felt like an overinflated balloon about to burst, and I was afraid that when I did, I would collapse. I didn't know what to do next, didn't know how to face anyone after making such a big scene.

So I didn't. "Excuse me," I said tightly, and I turned on my heel and walked out.

Twenty-Two

I had fucked up.

Breathing in jagged, panicked breaths, I ran through the hotel and out the front doors. Now, where to? Dusk had fallen, casting everything in blue and purple shadows.

What had I done? Why had I made such a scene? Should I go back in and apologize? No; it would be easier for Dad to smooth things over if I was gone.

Besides, I didn't want to apologize or smooth things over. Maybe I had laid everything out wrong—I hadn't been prepared to try to convince anyone about Andrea Darrel—but shouldn't Mr. Gibson have been willing to hear what I'd found out? He'd been *so* dismissive of Andrea, and of me. I shouldn't have been written off as emotional.

I needed to get out of here. Scanning the parking lot, I caught sight of a car with a Lyft sticker. I ran toward it, Cinderella to her pumpkin, hoping it wouldn't melt away. "Hi!" I yelled, waving my hands. "Are you free?"

The driver rolled down her window. "You running from someone, honey?"

"Embarrassment. Humiliation. Shame."

The driver winced. "Can't outrun melodrama," she said under her breath. "All right, get in. But you gotta find me on the app."

In minutes, we were speeding away. I'd put downtown as my destination, uncertain of where I wanted to go but certain it wasn't where anyone could find me. I watched the trees dash past, tall pines heavy with summer moss. Where should I go? Not Golden Doors. The Atheneum? But it would probably be closed now.

Abby or one of her friends?

Not Abby's. She was dating Noah Barbanel, and I didn't want the Barbanels to be able to find me until I was ready. Stella, then. I texted her. Any chance I could crash with you for the night? I'm having a bad day

Sure, she texted back immediately, followed by the address. I've got lots of ice cream.

* * *

Stella did have lots of ice cream.

I'd never been to her place before. It was a tiny room in a building with a bunch of other tiny rooms for rent, filled with summer employees. Like my dad's room, it was located in a forested mid-island neighborhood; I redirected my driver there, and she dropped me off at Stella's doorstep.

We collapsed on her rug and devoured a pint of Ben and Jerry's. "What's going on?" she asked. "Did you and Ethan have a fight?"

"No." I belatedly realized this meant she thought Ethan and I were together. So much for our theoretical secrecy. "I made a total idiot of myself, though."

As I told her about the accidental confrontation with Mr. Gibson, Stella looked infuriated on my behalf. "What a jerk."

"Yeah. But I should have kept it together." I was too mortified to look at my phone, though it kept buzzing in my pocket. I put it facedown on Stella's bed, hoping to ignore it.

"Now what are you going to do?"

Now? "I don't know. I was sort of hoping to avoid thinking about that for a while."

Stella's phone buzzed. She glanced at it and grimaced. "Ethan wants to know if I've seen you. What do you want me to say?"

I fell over backward on the floor and flung my arm over my forehead. "I don't know. I feel . . . humiliated. I embarrassed my dad, and maybe risked his chance at an important grant. I was a disaster in front of my boss. And Ethan already thinks I'm jumpy and wary about dating him and probably a weirdo and he told me—and I agreed—to not make a big deal out of this until later and then I went off the rails—"

"I'm just not going to say anything."

I nodded.

"Did you know that cheetahs are very anxious and zoos give them their own emotional support dogs to help them feel comfy and model social behavior?"

I blinked. "No. I did not."

She turned her phone toward me. A golden retriever puppy and a fluffy little cheetah were flopped on top of each other.

"Wanna watch TikToks of baby cheetahs cuddling with their emotional support puppies?"

Yes. I did.

* * *

We were deep down the rabbit hole of baby animal friendships when a knock sounded at the door. "Stella! Stella, are you there?"

Stella and I stared at each other. "I swear I didn't text him anything."

But maybe not texting had given us away; maybe everyone else had responded in the negative. My chest felt both heavy and hollow, and my ears buzzed in a way that seemed to slow the world down. "I'll talk to him."

"Are you sure?"

"It's fine," I said faintly. "I don't even know why I ran away. I have to face him—everyone—at some point."

As though in a fog, I crossed to the door and swung it open. "Hi."

Ethan stood there, arm raised and poised to knock again. He breathed heavily, as though he'd been running (though from where? His car to the door?), and his eyes widened, like he hadn't expected to find me. "You're here."

"I am," I agreed. In case, I don't know, he needed verbal proof. We stared at each other.

Creeping shame burrowed its fingers through me. I couldn't believe I'd *run*. Like a child. I should have stayed, I should have borne the brunt of whatever conversation occurred, I should never have gone off like that in the first place—but I had, and now Ethan thought I was an idiot and a fool and the kind of mean, stupid child who was willing to throw her father's career away.

I didn't want to threaten Dad's chance of getting a grant. I just wanted to stand up for Andrea Darrel.

"We should talk," I said abruptly. I leaned back into the room. "Thanks, Stella. We're gonna go for a walk."

"Okay." She popped her head out. "Let me know if you need me. Hey, Ethan."

He nodded at her, and then we headed down the hall and out of the building. I led him across the street from Stella's, where a grassy trail led into deep woods. Around us the trees shot up tall and lush, dark green moss dampening their bark.

"I'm sorry," I said. "I shouldn't have run. I was overwhelmed."

"*He* should be sorry," Ethan said immediately. "Gibson. He was a jerk."

My gaze shot toward him. "What?"

"He shouldn't have been so patronizing."

"You thought he was patronizing?" *I* thought he'd been patronizing, which should have been enough, but I felt weirdly validated Ethan agreed.

"Yeah, of course. He called you sweetie and said you were emotional."

I ducked my head. "Yeah."

We were silent a moment. "You should let your dad know you're okay," Ethan said. "He's really worried about you."

And after I had spent all summer trying to make him *not*

worry, trying to prove myself adult and capable and not messy. So much for that. "He's probably really disappointed, huh."

Ethan looked at me curiously. "Disappointed about what?"

I gave a little shrug, as though that lessened the impact. "In me. At my behavior."

Ethan frowned. "I don't think he was disappointed. I think he was worried. And confused."

But he had to have been a little disappointed, didn't he? He didn't come after me, after all. I stared up at the moon, half obscured by clouds.

"What?" Ethan asked.

I shrugged again. "I guess I wanted him to follow me."

"But he did," Ethan said. "I mean, he stayed long enough to tell off Gibson and then he went after you. We all did, me and Cora too. But by the time we made it outside you were being whisked away in a car, and we've spent the rest of the night searching for you."

"He told Gibson off?" I don't know why I was so surprised— or why I wanted to cry. Except I wasn't sure I deserved my dad standing up for me.

But I was really glad he had.

"Yeah. Well, in your dad's very polite way of telling someone off. He said Mr. Gibson couldn't speak to you like that, and he was being rude and inappropriate, and his reaction shouldn't have been to be challenged but to find out what your whole case was."

Oh. "But why didn't he say that when we were fighting?" I asked in a small voice. "Why didn't he back me up?"

It was Ethan's turn to shrug. "I don't know, I think he was

listening. Processing. Your dad doesn't always jump into the middle of conversations."

This was true. It probably did not mean he thought I was the worst, but rather too rapid-fire. Maybe. "Oh."

"You should let him know you're okay," Ethan said again.

A terrible and painful idea. I winced, then pulled my phone out. Ignoring the cacophony of alerts, I called Dad. He answered right away.

"Hi, Dad," I said in a small voice.

"Jordan?" Dad sounded panicked. "Are you okay? Where are you?"

"Yeah, I'm fine. Sorry for bolting. And—exploding."

"Where are you?"

"I'm at my friend Stella's."

"I'll come pick you up."

Of course he would. Which I hadn't quite been ready for. "Okay," I agreed, and gave him the address.

Hanging up, I turned back to Ethan. "He'll be here in fifteen minutes."

"Cool." Ethan opened his mouth, hesitated, closed it, then tried again. "Are we okay?"

I looked down at the moss and the forest floor and the ferns, then up at the sun casting its last rays of light through the forest canopy. "What do you mean?"

"I didn't speak up, either." He paused. "And you left me behind."

Struck, I stared at him. I hadn't realized *Ethan* might be afraid *I* might leave. That he might have a hard time trusting me.

"Ethan. I'm so sorry." I stepped forward, cupping his cheek with my hand. "I'm sorry I freaked out. And I don't want to break your heart either. I think you're amazing."

He smiled at me, a soft smile that made his entire face glow with a golden light. "I think you are, too, Jordan. I'm wild about you."

Something hard and tight broke apart in my chest, leaving breath coursing freely through me, my heart pumping hard enough I could hear it, feel it. I rose on my toes and kissed him.

He smiled down at me. "What next?"

I leaned my head back, gazing through the tree branches above us. In the dusk, only the brightest stars could be spotted. I sought Polaris, steady and bright. What could anyone ever do but follow their own north star? "I'm not ready to give up. I want to figure out what really happened. Maybe later on, I'll be too tired to try to right wrongs. Maybe at some point I'll be exhausted and burned out, but right now—I have the energy. If we want to make the world better, we have to try."

"All right. Then that's what we'll do."

"That's what we'll do," I agreed. "We'll show the world what Andrea Darrel of Nantucket discovered."

Twenty-Three

D ad picked me up in front of Stella's. "Your dad loves you," Ethan reminded me before he left. "You'll be fine."

Yet I felt like I was pushing through Jell-O as I walked to the passenger side of Dad's borrowed car, like a deep fog had muffled my ears and brain. I wanted to do anything but this. I'd never been afraid to see Dad before. But I'd behaved like a brat, and probably embarrassed him in front of his friends and colleagues. For all I insisted I had my act together, I'd acted like a child throwing a temper tantrum, and I didn't know how to apologize.

I opened the door. "Hi, Dad." My voice was small and I couldn't bring myself to look at him. I stared at our feet—my polished toes in flip-flops, his besocked feet in sandals—and spoke to them. "I'm sorry."

Dad was silent. I snuck a peek up and found him frowning at me. My heart started racing and it was getting harder to breathe and I thought I might cry—

And then he reached across the divide and pulled me into a hug.

I let out a surprised, shaky gasp and drew in a shuddering

breath. I clung to him, feeling like a little kid. "I'm so sorry," I started blubbering. "I don't know what got into me—"

"Jordan." He set me back a little bit, concern written in every line of his face. Had I placed any of those lines there? "Are you okay?"

"What?"

"I've been so worried."

"Oh. I mean—yes. I'm fine."

"Okay. Let's get home, and you can tell me what happened."

I pulled myself mostly together on the short drive to Dad's studio apartment. Upstairs, he made us mint tea and we settled into the two armchairs. Dad stirred sugar into his drink. "What happened?"

Obviously he'd been there; he wanted it from my perspective. "I guess . . . I've been getting pretty invested in Andrea Darrel. And I think I'm right," I said firmly, "about everything I said. She *did* discover the comet. But I never meant to go at Mr. Gibson. I just got worked up. I don't like being told I'm wrong."

"No," Dad says evenly. "No one does."

"I wasn't even going to bring it up with him there, but then Mrs. Barbanel mentioned it—" I closed my mouth. I couldn't blame a ninety-year-old woman for my loss of temper. "I got mad. I hate how often women in science have been dismissed. It's ridiculous. It shouldn't still be happening. But I'm sorry I lost my temper. Do you hate me? Did I ruin your chance at a grant?"

Dad's brows shot up. "What?"

"Ethan and I thought—I don't know, if I made this fuss about

Andrea Darrel, the Gibson Foundation might be pissed off and not want to fund your grant."

Dad stared at me a moment, his mouth twitching. He raised his fist to his mouth and let out what was clearly supposed to look like a cough, but was really a poorly muffled laugh. It went on a little too long.

"What?" I echoed, irritated.

"You two have . . . quite the imagination," Dad said in his diplomatic voice. "It's possible you watch too many movies."

"So I didn't ruin your chance at a grant?"

He looked amused. "I won't lie and say grant committees can't be petty, but I don't think this'll have an impact."

I sagged in relief. "Oh. Good."

He furrowed his forehead thoughtfully. "Jordan, I want you to be able to talk to me about anything. Is there anything else this summer you've been . . . stressing out about?"

Overheated, I tugged at my collar and looked out the window at the misshapen low moon. I thought about staying silent, but if there was ever a moment to admit to what had bothered me over the past several summers, it was now. "I guess I was a little . . . stressed about Ethan."

God, how humiliating. I couldn't believe I was admitting to my father I'd been *jealous* he'd paid attention to someone else more than me.

When I didn't say anything else, Dad finally prompted, "Because you like him?"

My head whipped toward Dad's. "What? No!"

Well, yes, but I'd been working toward a different point.

Dad looked as surprised by my response as I'd been at his suggestion. "You don't? But—I thought—Aren't you two dating?"

Oh my god, *mortifying.* "We're not—" Actually, we were. "I mean—yes." I squeezed my eyes shut. Did we have to talk about this? Were we done?

"That's great!" Dad sounded way too cheerful. "I always thought you and Ethan would like each other!"

I peeled one eye open, then the other. Please don't say *Dad* had been playing matchmaker? I refused to believe it. Also, Dad *wanted* me and Ethan to date? What?

Dad's excitement slowly faded into bewilderment. "Is that—not what's been bothering you?"

"No." I drew out the word. "It's been more . . . I was jealous of the attention he got from you the past couple summers."

"What?" Dad sounded perplexed.

Honestly, how could he be perplexed? Hadn't this been obvious? "Yeah. I felt like he was your replacement kid. Your summer kid."

Dad looked like he didn't know what to say. "He's not a replacement. Not at all."

"But—you were proud of him, Dad. He had his shit together, unlike me. I was messy and disastrous, and I know you love me because you're my dad, but you've never been proud of me in the same way. You wouldn't let me help with your work at all this summer. It felt like you thought I was incompetent."

"What? No! I don't think you're incompetent, I think you're brilliant. I—" He took a deep breath. "Jordan, I knew you didn't want to come here. I knew I was making you leave your friends and your job and your home. I certainly wasn't going to make you work for me. And look! You found a job you really liked! You're flourishing!"

"I found the job because I wanted to prove to you I could do what you do! Prove I could be a good researcher and figure things out and be as smart as you or Ethan."

Now Dad looked even more stunned. "I thought you liked astronomy? More than the history I research."

"Well—yeah." He had a point. I was probably happier having spent the summer studying the stars than I would have been studying navigational methods. "But I wanted to be closer to you, Dad. I thought—Why not *me*, Dad? Why couldn't I assist you? I wanted it to be me. I want to feel like you're *picking me*."

"You are my favorite person in the whole wide world," Dad said, his voice hoarse. "I will always pick you over everyone else."

Tears brimmed at the bottoms of my eyes and threatened to spill out. I sniffed. "Okay."

He hugged me, and then the tears did spill out, leaving wet tracks down my cheeks and damp stains on my shirt. My voice came out shaky. "You're my favorite person, too."

"Oh, Jordan. I love you so much."

That set off the waterworks, and I felt like I was ten. But it felt good, too, crying. I didn't feel sad or upset; I didn't feel like a hot mess. The tears felt cathartic, like I was finally letting go of all the stress and worry and jealousy I'd been carrying around. I knew my father loved me; I knew it was us first. But it was good to hear it, too, on occasion. Good to remember.

"The other thing, Dad," I said, once I had cried myself out and dashed away the tears, once my throat didn't feel tight and my chest didn't feel heavy. "I worry you're so busy focusing on me, because I *can* be a mess—"

"You're not a mess," Dad said. "You're seventeen."

I smiled wryly. "Okay, maybe. But I feel like you don't focus on yourself enough. And I want you to know—I want you to really know, it doesn't have to only be us, forever. You can pick someone else." I sniffed and pushed my hair back. "I want you to be happy."

"I am happy." Dad brushed my hair out of my face. "When you're happy, I'm happy. You make me so proud. I'm so impressed with the young lady you've grown up to be. You're strong, and adventurous, and brave. I think you're incredible."

I sniffed and rubbed at my watery eyes. "You *have* to think that. It's in the rulebook."

He laughed and hugged me. "I'm so sorry your mom didn't get to see you all grown up. I wish you'd had longer with each other." He hesitated. "Part of the reason I worry about you is because—I want to give you everything. But I couldn't give you two parents. I couldn't give you Mom back. I feel horrible about that."

"You don't have to feel horrible. I miss Mom, but I'm okay, Dad. I mean, I wish we talked about her a little more. I don't have memories like you and Gary and Grandma and Grandpa have."

"Oh, honey." Dad rubbed my back. "I know. I can do better at that. I worried about upsetting you by bringing her up. And when you were little—maybe I wasn't ready. And so I never got in the habit of it. But I can be better."

I took a deep breath. "And . . . I don't know, I wish we did a little more around Shabbat and the holidays. I guess that's when I feel connected to her."

Dad was quiet a moment. "Do you wish I'd raised you more Jewish?"

"I don't know," I said softly, because I didn't want to hurt his feelings. "It might have been nice. But I didn't make it easy, I didn't exactly want to go to Hebrew school as a kid." I hesitated. "Sometimes I'm a little embarrassed when I don't know anything."

Dad frowned and leaned forward in his seat. "What do you mean, not know anything? You know so much!"

"Well, I don't know how to read Hebrew, like the Barbanels, and sometimes I feel like I'm trying to fake my way through the prayers. I feel pretty fake a lot of the time, actually."

Dad looked gutted. Really, you should never tell fathers anything, they are sensitive souls. "You're not fake. You're as Jewish as anyone else."

A twist in my chest relaxed at those words. "It's not that I want to be more religious," I explained. "I want the culture. I feel left out of some parts."

"We can learn it together," Dad said staunchly. Dad, my anti-organized-religion father. "We could do Duolingo?"

"Really?" I said, a little amused.

"Yeah!" He brightened. "It'll be fun. I could use some brushing up on my Hebrew."

"Okay." I smiled. "That would be nice."

"I want you to feel like you can talk to me," Dad said earnestly.

"I do. I really do, Dad. I guess I've needed to—sort things out for a while. But I'm starting to feel pretty sorted."

"I want to help," Dad said. "However I can."

"You are helping," I told him, and I meant it. Because it was true; if there was one thing I knew in the world, it was that my father would be there for me, no matter what. "Just being with you helps."

Twenty-Four

I stayed the night at Dad's place. He borrowed an air mattress that took over the entire floor. I had to admit, I wouldn't have lasted the summer on it. (It had half deflated by the time I woke up.) In the morning, I took Dad's bike back to Golden Doors. The high today was supposed to be ninety degrees, but this early, the world was still cool, the light soft and birdsong gentle.

I walked inside Golden Doors, now so familiar it felt like home, and followed the scent of banana bread to the great room. One of the triplets waved me over. "Ethan's looking for you. On the roof walk."

"Thanks." I grabbed a coffee and two slices of banana bread and carried them upstairs. When I arrived, Ethan turned to me. "Hi."

"Hi." I sat down and handed him a plate.

"Thanks. How'd it go with your dad?"

"Really well. I got out everything I've been stressed about. Um—he knows we're dating."

"Does he?" Ethan looked half pleased, half apprehensive. "What'd he say?"

I rolled my eyes. "Apparently, he thought we'd be a good match."

"Ha!" Ethan let out a joyful shout. "I knew it!" He paused. "I suppose this is less great for the rest of our summer if he tells my parents."

"Hopefully they won't kick me out for the last few weeks," I teased.

"We should probably take advantage whenever we can, just in case." He leaned forward, and for a few minutes we indulged in drowsy, sweet kisses.

Then I pulled back. "The triplets said you were looking for me?"

"Maybe this was why I was looking for you."

I made a face. "I really hope you weren't using your thirteen-year-old cousins to arrange a booty call."

"Right. Fair. I wanted to make sure you were okay, and also . . ." A smile grew across his face. "Did I mention the Gibson Foundation sent me lots and lots of old documents at the beginning of the summer? For my research into his early work wire-dragging near Nantucket?"

"I think you did," I said slowly.

"Turns out they included a bunch of letters he'd sent. Including this one, to his brother, on April fifteenth."

He handed me a printed piece of paper.

As to the other matter, I assure you I am fine. The lady's unreasonable behavior makes me question my prior devotion. She behaved as though I had done something wrong. She always said these things must be done early, and as she was asleep I took it upon myself to act on her behalf, as a favor; as I sent the telegraph obviously I signed my name. Which was to be hers, so I do not understand her objection. We were to be a unit. I was going to provide and care for her. Honestly I consider myself lucky; this absurd outrage tells me she would have been a poor wife and mother of my children, and I should consider myself well rid.

Prior devotion.
I sent the telegraph.
I signed my name. Which was to be hers.

Well, *damn*, Frederick Gibson. A confession in so many words. Maybe not one other people would recognize, reading this paragraph—not if they didn't know the date of the comet's discovery, or about Andrea Darrel's fury, or about their relationship. Which, speaking of—"Were they *engaged*?"

"I don't know," Ethan said. "But if they were . . ."

"Then this is useful, right? This is corroboration?"

"I think so," he said. "It'd be better if we had proof he meant Andrea, but it seems like a clear connection."

"Maybe there is proof. Didn't historical people announce engagements?"

I pulled up *The Inquirer and Mirror*, Nantucket's oldest running newspaper, where I'd originally found mentions of Annie Cannon and Andrea Darrel teaching their astronomy course. I searched for *Darrel* and clicked forward further than I had last time, until I reached 1911. Then I read entries carefully until I reached one from April 4:

Mr. and Mrs. Darrel are pleased to announce the engagement of their daughter, Miss Andrea Darrel of Cambridge,
to Mr. Frederick Gibson of New York. Mr. and Mrs. Darrel
will be hosting an engagement party for the couple this
Friday.

I read it again. The engagement party was scheduled for April 7.
The happy couple would be in attendance.

They had both been on Nantucket, together. Which would
explain why Andrea hadn't been at the Harvard observatory,
able to file her discovery immediately. Perhaps Andrea had spotted the comet when sweeping the sky late at night, the day after
their engagement party. And perhaps, before she had a chance
to telegraph Harvard, Gibson had done so in her place. Perhaps
she'd told him about her discovery, or he'd read the entry in her
journal. *I took it upon myself to act on her behalf, as a favor,* he had
written. *She always said these things must be done early.*

"Now what?" I asked Ethan.

"The only better thing would be if we had it written in her own
hand," Ethan said. "She didn't leave any other diaries, did she?"

"None I know of. She left the Vassar ones to Vassar and the
Harvard ones to Harvard, so unless she worked somewhere else—
or left them to descendants?"

I paused. Ethan and I stared at each other. Descendants.

How had I not thought about descendants? Sure, Wikipedia
said nothing, but they could still exist.

Old letters and diaries. Weren't these things families had?
Family stories and legends and notebooks?

A few minutes later, we'd logged into a genealogy website Ethan's grandparents belonged to and found a family tree for Andrea Darrel. She'd had two children in the 1910s, one of whom married and had three children in the 1940s. Andrea Darrel's seven great-grandchildren had been born in the sixties and seventies. I stared at the names. "How do we pick who to contact?"

"The oldest?" Ethan suggested. "They're all cousins—they'll probably know who to go to."

I noticed something else. "Look, this woman has an account." I clicked on her name and saw she'd uploaded plenty of info over the past ten years. "I bet she's the genealogist in the family."

The website had a message function. After laboring painfully over my phrasing, I sent one.

Dear Dr. Trowbridge,

My name is Jordan Edelman and I'm an intern for Dr. Cora Bradley, an astrophysicist at Harvard working on an article about the Harvard Computers. I've been researching your great-grandmother Andrea Darrel for the past several months. I've read her diaries, and I'm trying to clarify her connection to her former fiancé, Frederick Gibson, who is best known as the discoverer of Gibson's comet. I'm also trying to understand Darrel's involvement in the comet discovery itself. I was wondering if you might be available for a call sometime soon?

Thank you,

Jordan Edelman

I received a reply half an hour later: *Hi Jordan—happy to chat. Are you free Sunday at 2? I'll send a link.*

I'd never been so nervous for a conversation in my life, but by 1:50 p.m. the next day I was sitting in front of my computer, perfectly coiffed and dressed, waiting impatiently for the call to begin. When the clock ticked over to 2:00, I made myself count to ten and clicked the Zoom link.

Dr. Trowbridge was already there, a woman in her sixties with short salt-and-pepper hair, thick-framed glasses, and a cozy-looking lavender sweater.

"Hi," I said. Panic immediately seized me. Who did I think I was, talking to actual adults?

"Hi," she said, then immediately shouted at someone off-screen, "Put the spatula down." She turned back. "Sorry, I have my grandchildren with me today."

"Oh, no worries. Thanks so much for talking to us. I'm Jordan, this is Ethan, and we're researching Andrea Darrel—your great-grandmother, right?"

"Yeah," she said vaguely, attention off-screen again. She snapped it forward. "What about her?"

"Do you know much about her?"

"Mm. She was an astronomer."

"Yes. And. Um." I took a deep breath. "Did you know she was connected to Frederick Gibson?"

"I didn't know they were engaged," she said. "I knew they were involved for a while, yes."

Better out with it all at once. "We think she discovered the comet. The one returning later this summer. Known as Gibson's comet."

For a moment, the woman stared at us. Her dark eyes pierced across screens and oceans into my own. Then she turned. "Samir! Get over here!"

A man's torso showed up in the screen: a buttoned-down cardigan with a mug held in front of his belly. "Yes, dear?"

"Sit down. These two think Grammy's mom found Gibson's comet."

The man lowered into the frame. He was the woman's age, with matching thick-rimmed glasses and frizzy hair haloing his bald spot. "Do they?"

The woman turned back to us. "And why do you think so?"

"Well," I said, a little nervously. I didn't quite understand the energy between the couple, their air of almost amused curiosity. "I was reading her old diaries, and she talks a lot about wanting to contribute to astronomy. And then she fell for Frederick Gibson."

A clatter sounded on the other end of the call, and a disembodied voice floated through. "I'm here! Sorry I'm late, Mom, the T was—oh sorry, I didn't realize you were on a call."

Dr. Trowbridge looked up. "Come in, dear. Dad and I are talking to some students who think Andrea Darrel discovered Gibson's comet."

"Really?" the woman said with relish before coming on-screen, squeezing her face in above her parents. She looked around Cora's age, and a friendly smile tweaked her lips. "How come?"

"Um." I cleared my throat.

"I'm sorry," Ethan said, leaning forward. "Are you guys—not surprised?"

"It'd be very strange if we were." Dr. Trowbridge's smile invited us to join her in the joke. "We've been celebrating her discovery since I was a baby."

* * *

This is what they told us.

Andrea Darrel had always told her family about her discovery. She'd told her husband before they married; he'd believed her. When the comet came back almost forty years later, on its first rotation since Andrea identified it, their children had been grown and with their own kids; Andrea Darrel and her husband had thrown a giant party in the yard of their Cambridge home. Dr. Trowbridge sent me a few sepia-toned pictures, pointing out her own mother, a baby with a cowlick.

Andrea Darrel beamed in the photos. In the late 1940s, in her seventies, her face and body had filled out. But there was still something youthful about her, the headband in her hair, the way she'd been caught laughing.

"But why haven't you said anything?" I cried when Dr. Trowbridge told us. "Didn't you want her to get credit?"

"Said anything? To who? It's just a family story," she said. "We don't have proof."

"Do you, though?" her daughter pressed. "You have proof?"

"We have some things." I walked them through what we'd discovered: the diaries, the timing, the bulletin with the same numbers as in Andrea's diary, the engagement party, the letter from Frederick to his brother. "Was she bitter?" I asked. "Never getting credit for her discovery?"

"My mother said no," Dr. Trowbridge said thoughtfully. "Angry, sometimes. But not always."

"Why didn't she fight for credit, later on? The world had changed. People might have believed her. And in her diaries, from college—she sounded like she wanted, badly, to make a major discovery. A contribution to science."

"I don't know," Dr. Trowbridge said. "She said the people who mattered knew, and that was enough. And she did contribute. She published articles and spent thirty years as a professor. And I think—a comet discovery would have opened a lot of doors for her, but it wasn't the same level of work as what she did later on. I think she enjoyed her later work more."

I was glad to hear it; I wanted Andrea Darrel to have lived a long, fulfilling life. But at the same time, I also wanted to get her recognition for this. "Did she leave anything with your family in writing?"

"She kept journals."

"I thought so!" I yelped, then managed to control myself. "I mean, since she kept early journals, at Vassar and Harvard, I thought she might continue writing. But I couldn't find any more."

Dr. Trowbridge nodded. "Ah, yes—after she got married, she kept all of them."

"Who did she marry?" I asked.

"Another of the computers, actually."

"Really?" I wondered who—if she'd written about him in passing, if she'd known him before Gibson or met him after. "Do the journals mention her discovery?"

"Not directly. She alludes to it, occasionally. But she didn't like to dwell on it."

"And what—what happened?" I asked. "Did she ever write why he stole it?"

She smiled, half amused, half sad. "That's the oddest part. He didn't think he did."

According to Dr. Trowbridge, Andrea Darrel had been sweeping the sky from her childhood rooftop while visiting her parents. She caught sight of an out-of-place star blazing across the familiar map of the sky and realized immediately it was a comet. She noted the position, and a few minutes past midnight she had calculated the orbit.

Thrilled beyond belief, she told Frederick. Maybe he was also staying at her parents' house. According to my scant knowledge from reading Edith Wharton in school, they probably hadn't been staying in the same bed, but I certainly knew how easy it was to slip from room to room when staying at the same house.

Andrea went to bed and, despite her excitement, slept late. In the morning—perhaps at the breakfast table in her parents' house, where they'd so recently celebrated their engagement, perhaps, even, at her bedside as she awoke, if he'd snuck in to see her—Frederick proudly told her he'd taken care of filing for the comet. Furious, she told him to take it back, but he refused. And when Andrea reached out to the observatory herself, they said—politely, but firmly—what was done was done.

"She stopped working for them for several years," Dr. Trowbridge said. "But she went back to it eventually. She loved working there."

"Are you two planning to do something?" her daughter asked. "We always thought about writing an article, but it never seemed particularly urgent. Or like we had enough proof."

"I'm not sure what anyone else will think, but *I* think we have proof," I said. "And if you're interested in helping, I think we have a pretty good case."

Twenty-Five

Mr. Gibson met with us the next day.

Dad arranged the meeting. "Send him everything in advance. People hate to be surprised. He'll want a chance to prepare his response."

"But aren't we giving him more time to think about how to shut us down?" I'd asked.

"Maybe," Dad had said. "But he might decide—as I think he will—that you have too much evidence in Miss Darrel's favor. If you throw everything at him in the moment, his hackles might go up and he might get defensive. If you give him time to process—and bring him along on the journey of your discovery, and ask him his opinion—he'll feel like he has a say in what happens and more likely be agreeable."

I'd stared at my father, impressed. "Dad. You're kinda diabolical."

"Thank you?"

"Did you ever play mind games on me as a child?"

He'd looked harassed. "All the time. Do you know how hard it was to get you to eat your vegetables?"

Rude. "I *love* vegetables," I'd said, and flounced off.

Ethan and I headed back to the hotel where the conference had been, where Mr. Gibson was staying. The August afternoon was strangely crisp, as though fall lingered at the gate, waiting to come in whether invited or not. I spent the morning smelling things more strongly than usual, as though the cool air carried scents more clearly: the honey in my oatmeal, the scent of dead, scorched grass.

Mr. Charles Gibson waited for us in a windowless conference room. He sat at the head of a long table, tapping away at his laptop. When we entered, he smiled pleasantly. I wasn't sure how much to distrust his smile and tried to withhold judgment.

"Good afternoon, Jordan, Ethan," Mr. Gibson said. "How are you two doing?"

Ugh. Did we have to do polite small talk? But I guessed this wasn't a denouncement in a movie; no chance for me to point my finger and cry "J'accuse!" (Besides, as Dad had labored to instill, pointing was rude.) "Good, thank you," I said instead. "How are you?"

"Have a seat." He gestured at the chairs; Ethan and I took the first two to his left. "Are you two excited to head to college? It's your freshman year, is that right, Jordan?"

I nodded.

"And what will you be studying?"

"If you don't mind," I said, "can we talk about Andrea Darrel?"

He stilled, then smiled again. "Of course. It's an interesting story you've sent me."

It's not a story, I wanted to burst out. Instead, I reminded myself what Dad had said, about how I needed to bring Mr. Gibson along on a journey, make him feel like we were in this together. I had to make him feel like the easiest thing to do would be to acknowledge Andrea Darrel, as opposed to feeling like I was an enemy combatant. "It is," I said, my voice so calm it pained me. "I was surprised by a lot of stuff I found out."

He nodded. "And you talked to Andrea Darrel's descendants. Interesting they've never said anything before."

"I think they felt like they didn't have a case. But with the statements from Andrea's diaries, and the date when Gibson claimed the discovery, and Gibson's letter to his brother, the story seems pretty clear."

"Hm," Mr. Gibson said. "All right."

All . . . right?

I blinked. I looked at Ethan. *He* blinked. We both turned back to Mr. Gibson.

"Excuse me," I said. "Um—all right, what?"

"I've read the deck you put together. You've convinced me."

"We've—what?"

"I believe you. Andrea Darrel discovered the comet."

"Oh," I said faintly. He *agreed*?

"So. That's that, then," Mr. Gibson said.

"We're glad. Thanks," Ethan said quickly, when Mr. Gibson seemed ready to send us on our way. Which was good, since I was so shocked I might have walked straight out. "Just to make sure—are you going to say something about it? I'm sure you get how important it is everyone know the truth, especially with all the attention on the comet in the next couple of weeks."

"Yes, of course." Mr. Gibson paused, but it felt more like a performance than a moment of thought. "I'll have the foundation put out a statement. Why don't you send along the contact info for Ms. Darrel's descendants, so we can get in touch with them, too."

"Uh, yeah." Ethan glanced at me, where I still sat, stunned. "We'll check with them."

"I'm sorry," I said, not an apology, but an *excuse me, wait just one moment*. True, Mr. Gibson had had a chance to sit and think on our deck before we arrived, and maybe Dad was right—maybe that was all he needed. Maybe powerful people were content as long as they believed they were the ones deciding the spin. And yet . . . "I didn't expect you to be convinced *quite* so easily." Dr. and Mr. Trowbridge's faces flashed through my head, their amusement, their lack of surprise. "Did you—know?"

Mr. Gibson stared at me.

I stared at Mr. Gibson.

"No," he said firmly. "Certainly not." He closed his laptop and slid it into his bag. "Very nice to see the two of you again, and thank you for bringing this to my attention. Good luck at school—and please give my regards to your families."

And he walked out the door and vanished down the hall.

I slowly pivoted to look at Ethan, who stared back at me, my own feelings reflected on his face. "Fuck," Ethan said. "He *knew*."

"He did, didn't he?" I couldn't close my mouth. It hung open by the gravitational law of astonishment. And something surfaced from the confrontation we'd had, which I'd replayed a hundred times in my mind. "He—had said Frederick Gibson didn't marry an astronomer. But I never mentioned Andrea was an astronomer to him."

"Jesus." Ethan shook his head. "No wonder he's going to put out a statement. There's probably more evidence if anyone digs for it."

Anger started to build inside me. "I hate this. And what if he kind of buries it? He's probably not going to want anyone to even notice."

Ethan grimaced. "Honestly, a big announcement would look good for him. Admitting and correcting a mistake like this? He'll look sympathetic and progressive."

Fury curdled inside me. Of course he would. No consequences for being condescending or keeping this hidden. "It's not fair."

"Let's beat him to the punch," Ethan said.

"What do you mean?"

"Let's put out something first. Why let him get the credit when you figured this out?"

For possibly the first time in my life, I considered *not* being impulsive. "Gibson might get mad if we say something before his official statement."

"What's he gonna do?" Ethan said with all the cavalierness of a rich white boy. "We've all agreed this should be public."

I thought about it. Maybe whatever we posted wouldn't make a splash, either. Probably it'd fly under the radar. But when I thought about this pattern repeating over and over, of women discovering things and men getting credit, I thought, well, screw that. I *had* figured this out. I wanted my name on this.

"Let's go, then," I said. "Let's break this story wide open."

* * *

Ethan and I spent the next few days making a video.

Or, technically, the triplets did. I wrote the script, but as soon as the triplets caught wind of what Ethan and I were doing, they wanted in.

"You need to make an impact," Iris said seriously. "You need to construct a narrative."

"We'll start with your arrival on Nantucket," Rose said, already making notes all over the handwritten pages I'd cobbled together.

"But it needs to be short," Iris said. "People don't have long attention spans. Under three minutes."

"Do you think we can shoehorn the romance in?" Lily pursed her lips thoughtfully. "People love a romance."

"What?" I flicked my gaze toward Ethan, who bit back a smile. "We're not going to shoehorn a romance in."

"Mm," Lily said, nodding slowly. "You're right. Nothing explicit, just enough to make viewers ship you."

"Ethan can touch her hand at one point," Rose said, still busy scribbling. "And she can bump his shoulder."

Truly, these girls were terrifying.

"We're going to need some establishing shots of you at Dr. Bradley's office," Iris said. "We need to make you look smart so people will take you seriously. Maybe wear a college sweatshirt. Does Dr. Bradley have any Harvard-branded stuff in her office? Or lots of books?"

"I'll do costuming and set design," Lily said. "I know you usually wear contacts, but wear your glasses for this. And no offense, but we're going to tone down your eyeliner."

I would have been offended if I hadn't been so mystified by the way the triplets took over.

"Only Shira can control them," Ethan murmured to me. "The rest of us don't even try."

"I'm truly astonished."

"Last Hanukkah they made us all do a play. Memorizing lines and making swords out of carboard and tinfoil. They're like a hurricane. A hurricane of triplets, that's probably their collective noun."

It took two days to shoot the video and another two to edit it under the exacting eye of Iris. I did exactly what the triplets asked, except for wearing a college sweatshirt. Instead, I wore my favorite black romper and bright red lipstick. But I answered the questions Rose asked and stood where Iris and Lily placed me. This included a gratuitous number of shots where I looked through the telescope on the roof walk or walked along the beach or gazed at the sky.

But by less than a week after Ethan and I had met with Mr. Gibson, the video was done, at two minutes and forty-seven seconds. We sent it first to Andrea's descendants, who enthusiastically signed off. Then, summoning all my nerve, I asked Dad and Cora if they'd like to see it.

We'd told them what we were doing, but I felt terrified all over again as I set up the video on my monitor at work. Dad came to

Cora's office so I only had to go through this once—after finding Ethan's stage fright kind of cute, it was embarrassing to realize I, too, hated the idea of having anyone watch anything I'd produced. I'd considered emailing it to Dad and Cora, but then I worried I'd be in too much agony knowing they *could* be watching it, but not knowing if they *were*.

I pressed play.

"I can't watch," I said to Ethan a mere five seconds in, from the back of Cora's office. "It's killing me."

"It's only three minutes long!"

"It's already been three hundred years." I backed out the door and into the hall, unable to watch my face on the screen for the zillionth time.

Ethan followed me as I curled up into a little ball on the floor. "Do you think they hate it?" I asked my knees. "They probably hate it."

I could hear him crouching down in front of me, feel his warmth and then his hand on my leg. "You stood up to Charles Gibson himself. I think you can handle a video."

"No. I cannot. It has defeated me."

Another three hundred years passed, then the door swung open. "There you are!" Dad said, a huge grin on his face. "What are you doing out here?"

My head jerked up so fast I swear I strained my neck. Ow. "What did you think?"

"It was great!"

My jaw dropped, weighed down by shock. "Really? You liked it?"

"I thought it was amazing," Dad said, and maybe he was contractually obliged to think/say so, but a warmth still spread throughout my body. I glanced at Cora.

She smiled. "I'm impressed. Short, to the point—you got everything across in an interesting and informative way."

"So"—I looked back at Dad—"you think we can post it?"

"I don't see why not."

I looked at Ethan. He looked at me. The video was loaded and prepped to go on my phone, and we were within the timeframe Iris had given me during which a video gained the most views.

"Are you ready?" Ethan asked.

I wasn't sure. It was *scary*, putting myself out there, not sure if the establishment would come yell at me or say I was a liar or be dismissive or put me down. But I had done the research. And I was right. Andrea Darrel had discovered that fucking comet.

"I'm not sure I'll ever be ready." I opened the app. "But. Yes."

I hit post.

✳ ✳ ✳

At first, there was nothing.

It was a letdown. Barely anyone viewed or watched it. It was tough to sit there, waiting for some grand finale, epic fireworks, and getting nothing.

"Come on," Ethan said an hour after posting, when we'd only gotten a handful of views, not enough to engage any social media

326

algorithms. "Let's go sailing. The important thing is, we know. And if Gibson makes his announcement, maybe the media will pay attention then, and notice our video."

"Yeah," I agreed, though I felt pretty down. Still, I pulled myself together and went out on the water with Ethan.

It had rained the night before, and the sky was that strange washed-out color that followed a storm—as faded as a pair of jeans, leached of color by the torrents of water. The clouds, though, had depth, a darkish purple on the bottom, the top a shimmery warm white, like the sunny glow of twinkle lights.

"Turn your phone off," Ethan said when I kept glancing at it.

"I might die of withdrawal."

He pulled me closer and kissed the breath out of me. "You don't think I can keep you entertained?"

"Nope." I turned my phone off. "I very much think you can."

* * *

"Where have you *been*?" Iris burst out when we returned to Golden Doors.

"Sailing," Ethan said. "What's up?"

But I knew. I could tell by the way she vibrated. "It's the video, isn't it?"

"It has *taken off.*"

"Like a comet?" Ethan joked.

Iris frowned. "Comets don't take off."

"They kind of do. Like from the Oort cloud," he tried.

The triplets stared at him. "No," Iris said, less, I expected, at his words than at him trying to joke in the first place.

I kissed his cheek. "I think you're funny."

"Look at this." Iris swiveled her phone toward us. "You've got three hundred thousand views. You've also got comments from news journalists asking to talk to you. I'd check your DMs, I bet they're crazy."

I'd already started powering my phone back on. I had several missed calls, including Dad and Cora. I called Dad first.

"Sorry I didn't pick up," I said when he did. "Ethan and I went sailing so I didn't obsess over the video. What's up?"

"That sounds nice," Dad said. "How was sailing?"

Just like Dad, to get distracted. "It was good. Why'd you call?"

"Ah. Well, I got an interesting call. From Charles Gibson."

I squeezed my eyes shut. "Is he furious?"

"Yup," Dad said cheerfully. "Luckily, you're a minor, so they have to be furious at me, not you. And they don't have any valid reason to be mad, they're just angry you stole their thunder. They still have a few bureaucratic hoops to jump through before they can put out their announcement tonight."

"Am I in trouble?" It didn't *sound* like I was, but best to make sure.

"Nope," Dad said. "Not at all! Let's go out to dinner to celebrate."

I called Cora next. "This is so fucking kickass," Cora said, sounding as cheerful as Dad. She paused. "Sorry. I feel like I'm not supposed to curse in front of you."

"Yes, you've ruined my impressionable young brain," I said. "Do you want to come out to dinner with me and Ethan and my dad?"

"I don't want to intrude . . ."

"Please," I begged her. "I'd love if you came."

"Then I'm in."

I spent the night with my three favorite people on the island, celebrating.

And when I got back home, the video had crossed one million views.

Twenty-Six

A week later, the Barbanels threw their end-of-summer comet-viewing party.

The lawn, once more, had been transfigured, this time into a cosmic theme done on a galactic level. The tablecloths were a stark white, a striking contrast to the heavy black plates glittering with star maps. The cards for the dishes were the night sky, embossed with gold print. There were iridescent, metallic details everywhere—in the decorations, in the food itself. Dark macarons with flakes of edible gold. Bouquets of blue and purple orchids interspersed with star-shaped ornaments. A dark and gleaming dance floor.

Around the lawn, metallic sculptures of each of the nine planets (the adults were very attached to Pluto) had been placed at estimated scale: the sun, Mercury, and Venus clustered close to the center, the rest scattered on rings further out.

In pride of place stood the telescope, waiting for nightfall. And beyond, a projection screen.

Yesterday, Ethan had knocked on my door, a dazed look on his face. "My parents—they asked me—" He'd plopped himself down on my bed, looking at me with a stunned expression.

"Yeah?" I asked. "Asked what?"

"If we want to share the video at the party. Like, they weren't doing it as a favor. They weren't giving me a pat on the back. They *like* it."

I didn't mention how, as of my last check two hours ago, so did four million other people. "That's great. Right?"

"Right. Yeah. I guess—I'm not used to them paying attention to me. Of being proud of me for more than, you know, existing."

"Well, they are, and they should be. Tell them we're in."

He had, and now we nervously eyed the screen set up at the top of the dance floor, facing the guests and family. "Who knew so much public speaking and performance went into being a researcher?" Ethan said.

"At least this time we can sit here silently."

"And hold hands."

I gave him a gentle nudge with my shoulder, unable to keep from smiling. "You're such a sap."

Ethan's grandmother swept by on her way to play MC. As she passed us, her gaze briefly dropped to our intertwined fingers. Her lips twitched, and she gave me an amused nod. I waved.

"Did I ever tell you," I whispered to Ethan as Mrs. Barbanel gained the attention of the crowd, charming them into silence and laughter, "your grandma said I looked at you like a moonstruck calf?"

Ethan beamed at me. "You're a sap, too!"

Guilty.

"And now," Mrs. Barbanel said, "before we turn our eyes to

the heavens, let's first turn our eyes to the screen." She nodded to Iris, who clicked play. Everyone fell silent at their tables, more than a hundred pairs of eyes focused on the video.

Across the black screen, white letters typed: WHAT IS GIBSON'S COMET?

In quick succession, the screen cut to strangers we'd interviewed downtown: a guy in his thirties, an older couple, a twenty-something woman. They all gave different answers.

"It's . . . a comet?"

"It's the comet, right, coming this month."

"Gibson's comet is a naked-eye comet with an orbital period of thirty-eight years, next appearing in a few weeks."

We'd been surprised but deeply appreciative of the twenty-something who gave us that exposition-filled explanation.

Next, across the black screen, the question: WHO WAS FREDERICK GIBSON?

"Honestly, no clue, but given your last question I assume he's the guy who discovered Gibson's comet."

"The man who named Gibson's comet?"

"He was an early twentieth-century astronomer who discovered Gibson's comet."

Back to the screen: *Frederick Gibson is known for having discovered a comet in 1911.* And the next question: WHO WAS ANDREA DARREL?

The same people were shown, their answers short and the same.

"Never heard of her."

"I don't know."

"Who?"

Then me. I sat in Cora's office, wearing my glasses, in front of a bookcase with a few astronomical trinkets arranged aesthetically. "My name's Jordan Edelman." My voice blasted from the speakers. "I'm an intern for astrophysicist Cora Bradley. Over the course of this summer, I uncovered a century-old tale about a female astronomer, a stolen discovery, and a romance that ended in heartbreak and betrayal."

Rose, the writer triplet, sat at the table over from me. She nodded along as the words she'd crafted came from my mouth on-screen, then turned and gave me two thumbs up.

Thank god the video was so short. I couldn't have taken the agony of me speaking any longer. I focused on the triplets and on the feel of Ethan's hand around mine as we once more watched the video.

"Andrea Darrel was born on this street on Nantucket, to a fisherman and a homemaker," I said on-screen, standing in a quaint, windy street downtown. I explained how she'd been inspired by Maria Mitchell to study astronomy at Vassar; Helen Barbanel, in her polished elegant-lady voice, read excerpts of Andrea's diaries as images from the diaries drifted across the screen.

We laid out what had happened: the astronomy classes, the romance, the engagement, the night when Andrea had written the position of the comet in her diary and woken to find it filed with Harvard under Frederick's name. The recognition Frederick had received, the welcome with open arms into scientific society, the renown to create his own foundation. The legwork we'd done to figure out what happened. Dr. Trowbridge delivered a clip, too.

"My great-grandmother always said she'd discovered the comet. It was an open family secret."

We cut to a shot of Ethan and me in front of the conference hotel, dressed formally: Ethan in a suit and me in my star-studded dress—the same dress I wore right now. "When we brought our research to the Gibson Foundation, they agreed with us and promised to put out a statement about Andrea's discovery," I said, wide-eyed and innocent, before quickly moving on. The less time spent on them, the better.

"Like so many women before her, Andrea Darrel didn't get credit for her discovery in her lifetime. But her family knew, and celebrated with her," I said in a voice-over as a photo filled the screen of Andrea Darrel in the 1940s, laughing with her family, a grandchild on her lap. "And we hope this time, as the comet crosses through the skies, everyone will know."

The video ended with a shot of the last time the comet had passed by Earth. The credits rolled.

Everyone burst into applause. I covered my head with my arms, peeking sideways at Ethan, who grinned at me broadly. "Pretty good," he said.

"I might be dead now. I think I hate public attention."

"Well, everyone loves you," Ethan said. His expression was so bright and gorgeous that though I knew people were looking at us, I didn't care. I scooted closer to him. Hooking my fingers inside his neckline, I tugged him down and kissed him. Long enough that some of the cousins let out hoots. Laughing, I let go.

"Look at you, you're blushing," Ethan said. "You almost never blush."

I cleared my throat. "I'm overwhelmed and happy and I guess you make me blush."

"Yeah?" He grinned at me. "Good. I think making you blush is a decent life goal."

I bit the inside of my cheek so I didn't smile too hard. "Cool, mine's going to be revolutionizing the way people think about space debris."

"I'm happy to be the supportive partner in this relationship."

This relationship. I studied him quickly. Summer was almost at an end, and we were both headed to separate parts of the country in the next two weeks. It was one thing to date on the island, in the bubble of summer and sea, and another to extend it. Which we both clearly knew, given how we hadn't talked about it. "Ethan . . ."

We were interrupted as the triplets bounded up. "It went brilliantly," Iris announced. "Obviously we already knew it was brilliant from our view count and comments, but this is a very different demographic. A donor demographic, if you will. We should start thinking about future content immediately."

"Also, we've compiled the media requests we want to reply to," Rose said, pulling up notes on her phone. "A bunch of the big outlets want to interview you. Especially with the Gibson Foundation putting out their statement."

I froze. "They did? When? What did they say?"

"A few hours ago." Iris frowned at me, as though to say *Where have you been?* I did not respond because a few hours ago, I'd been making out with Ethan. "Same thing you did, basically, but tried to make it more about them. Don't worry. Their public metrics don't look as good as ours, and we're still coming up first on search."

"Um—great?"

"Rose will send you a list of follow-up steps for review," Iris said, then turned and strode into the crowd, Lily and Rose following, to receive their just rewards. Ethan and I glanced at each other and started laughing as quietly and motionlessly as we could.

All night, people kept coming up to us to congratulate us on the video and to ask questions. "Why did you even decide to investigate?" they wanted to know. "Is the comet's name going to be changed?"

"I have no idea," I said, over and over. "I hope so." And I did, but for once, I was too busy being happy in the moment to worry about the future.

And I was happy, really truly happy. Happy and settled and secure. For the first time in a long time, I didn't feel like I had to *prove* I was stable and steady: I felt good. I felt like I had control of what I was doing, like I knew how to take steps to get what I want. Because I'd done that, after all. I'd told my dad about all my anxieties, and I'd gotten a job I loved, and I'd put myself out there with the boy I liked even though it terrified me.

And, it turned out, the more I did things that scared me, the less scary they became. So I turned to Ethan. "Hey. Thought I should tell you. I like you. A lot."

A grin broke across his face. "I like you a lot, too."

"And I want to keep dating. Even after we leave Nantucket. I want to stay together, if you want to, too." I braced myself.

Because while I knew it was the right thing to do, to say what I wanted, this was the part where the heartbreak usually came.

But Ethan Barbanel, he didn't miss a beat. "Cool," he said. "Because I've been thinking. I don't want to bombard you or anything, but it's Rosh Hashanah in a few weeks, and the fam plans to do it in New York. If you and your dad want to come. And then Noah says the regatta weekend in Cambridge in October is kinda fun. I could come to Boston then. And in November I'll have a whole week off for Thanksgiving."

"Well, look at you." A grin broke over my face. "Trying to make plans to date me or something."

"Yeah, you know, I'm organized like that." He leaned forward and kissed me.

A little later, when night had fully fallen and the waning gibbous moon shone bright among the scattered stars, Cora sat down next to me. "Look what I got an email of." She turned her phone toward me.

I leaned in. An article with Cora's name on it filled the screen. I recognized the first paragraph immediately; I'd certainly proofed it enough. "No way! The Harvard Computers article?"

She grinned and nodded. "This is the preview. They're going to run it in the October issue. If you give me your school address, I'll send you a copy."

My school address. "I can't believe I'm going to college after this." I gazed up at the night. "It feels so . . . weird. I can't wait, but also I can't imagine what it'll be like."

"I hope you'll love it," Cora said. "And, selfishly, I hope you'll stay interested in astrophysics."

I smiled a little shyly. "I'm taking Physics 1 and the first-year astronomy seminar."

"Really?" She did a little cheer. "That's great!"

"Yeah." I ducked my head. "I wanted to thank you—it's meant a lot to me, this summer, working for you. I learned a lot."

Cora gave my arm a squeeze. "I loved having you. You contributed a lot, too. You have tons of passion."

For a moment, we sat there in companionable silence, watching the partygoers mingling, drinking their blue and purple cocktails, peering through the telescope to catch a glimpse of the comet making its once-every-four-decades pass through our skies.

"Hey." Cora turned back toward me, her voice suddenly decisive. "How would you feel if I asked your dad out?"

I swear, my eyes bulged out of my head like a cartoon character's. "Oh my god, are you serious? *Thank you.*"

She grinned. "I'm not sure 'thanks' was the response I was going for, but it seems positive."

"Yes. Yes! Definitely!" Oh my god. This was possibly more thrilling than anything else this summer.

"Wow, okay," Cora said, laughing slightly. "A yes, then."

"*Such* a yes. The strongest yes."

When she left, I made a beeline for Ethan, pulling him away from a circle of family friends. "Guess. What."

"Uh . . . The people who control comets' names have acknowledged you're right and brilliant and formally changed the name?"

"Cora wants to ask out my dad!"

His eyes widened. "Really?"

"Yes. She just told me." Holding Ethan's arm, I swiveled both of us, searching the crowd until I found Cora. "Watch."

"She's probably not going to do it right now."

"Maybe she is," I said. "Cora's a go-getter."

Sure enough, Cora made her way to my dad. For a minute, they chatted and laughed, looking impossibly more at ease than they'd looked several weeks ago. Then, for a moment, neither of them said anything. Cora looked away, hands twisting behind her back, before stilling completely. Then she faced Dad and spoke.

His head whipped up, a look of astonishment on his face, which slowly suffused with color. He pointed a finger at himself, and I clutched Ethan's shoulder.

Cora laughed and nodded, but she held a little tension in her shoulders, her expression uncertain, her smile not as full as usual.

Dad stared at her. I willed him to say something.

"Ow," Ethan said.

Oops. I unclenched my fingers, which had slowly been driving into Ethan's flesh. "Sorry."

And then, across the party, Dad nodded once. A smile broke over his face, and he nodded twice more in rapid succession. We didn't need to be close to read the one word he said to Cora.

I let out a little shriek of excitement and threw myself into Ethan's arms. "I did it! Did you see that! They have a date! Or they're going to have a date. I'm a matchmaker!"

"You're a menace, is what you are," Ethan said, a murmur of laugher in his voice. "I think you left bruises."

"Sorry," I said again, unrepentant, and pressed my lips to his shoulder. "I'll kiss them better."

"And I want some matchmaking credit, too. Who suggested the boat trip?"

"You're brilliant." I looped my arms around his neck, reveling in the comfort between us, the spark, how easy it was to be with him and how happy he made me. "We're both brilliant."

He laughed. "I'm going to miss you so much. I'm going to miss being able to see you every single day. Going swimming and stargazing with you. And I'm really gonna miss having you right across the hall from me."

I grinned. "Honestly, I'm kinda surprised we've gotten away with being roommates for the last week. Now that all the parentals know we're dating."

"True." He pulled me a little closer. "We should probably take advantage of it as long as we can."

"I'm down." I glanced across the lawn, at where the telescope had been set up so party guests could look through it. At the moment, it happened to be free. "But first—you wanna go see a comet?"

"Hell yeah I do."

Hand in hand, we made our way to the telescope. I focused my gaze through the eyepiece, looking up.

And Andrea Darrel's comet blazed its way across the night sky.

AUTHOR'S NOTE

While Andrea Darrel is a figment of my imagination, she fits into a long lineage of American female astronomers, beginning with Maria Mitchell. Born in 1818 on Nantucket, Mitchell discovered a comet in 1847, worked for the US Coast Survey, and became a professor at Vassar. The Maria Mitchell Association on Nantucket is a real organization, as are their observatories. Any mistakes about them are entirely my own, and I encourage any visitors to Nantucket to check out the Loines Observatory's Open Nights for stargazing.

To learn more about Maria Mitchell and about the role of nineteenth-century women in the sciences, I read *Maria Mitchell and the Sexing of Science* by Renée Bergland, which is an excellent explanation about the social climate during her lifetime. To accurately capture fictional Andrea Darrel's university days, I visited the Vassar College Student Diaries collection, a digital resource of scanned journals; I particularly relied on Mary Earl's diary from 1891 to 1895 and Ida Guttman's diary from 1883, which described their classes and hobbies.

Some of Maria Mitchell's Vassar students became astronomers themselves, including Antonia Maury, one of the Harvard Computers. I recommend *The Glass Universe: How the Ladies of the Harvard Observatory Took the Measure of the Stars* by Dava Sobel as an instrumental text for entering the world of this fascinating group.

The Harvard Computer and astronomer Annie Jump Cannon is famous for her stellar classification work. I was surprised to learn she'd often visited Nantucket and taught classes there during the summers of 1906 and 1907, which I incorporated into this story. I'm indebted to the Nantucket Atheneum's online archives of *The Inquirer and Mirror*; the newspaper contains detailed descriptions of Cannon's visits, though of course there's no mention of her fictional assistant. Today, the American Astronomical Society annually awards the Annie Jump Cannon Award in Astronomy to a female astronomer.

Andrea Darrel's counterpart, Frederick Gibson, is also imaginary, though Captain Nicholas Heck was a real geophysicist whose wire-dragging technique advanced hydrographic surveying. I apologize to any assistants he may have had, who I'm sure were not as bad as Gibson.

Lastly, my modern astrophysicist, Dr. Cora Bradley, is also invented. For those interested in learning more about the experience of Black woman astrophysicists, I recommend *The Disordered Cosmos: A Journey into Dark Matter, Spacetime, and Dreams Deferred* by Dr. Chanda Prescod-Weinstein. Cora's field—what to do about space debris—is a growing issue. NASA's Office of

Technology, Policy, and Strategy supports studies on the topic and releases the reports online, and the European Space Agency also produces an annual Space Environment Report. I've tried to accurately capture many of the current issues—though given the fast-moving nature of the subject, I'm sure some of my numbers are already outdated!

ACKNOWLEDGMENTS

Every time I write a book, I feel like I've never written a book before. How do you write a book? Who knows? All I know is that this book was largely written in the cafés of Camberville, in the company of Monica Jimenez and Cassandra de Alba (miss you, Emily!). Thank you, guys, for always running late, just like me.

To my agent, Tamar Rydzinski, my very deep thanks for endlessly championing me in the book world and being a sounding board whenever I need one, and to Monica Rodriguez for her stellar marketing advice. Thanks to my editor, Gretchen Durning, both for being incredibly kind and insightful and for making this story tighter and stronger than when I first turned the manuscript in. I'm also grateful to the whole Penguin Teen team for their hard work and sharp eyes. This gorgeous cover was designed by Danielle Ceccolini and illustrated by Nhung Le, and I couldn't be happier with it—it brings me a deep and unique joy to see my characters brought to life here.

Anything vaguely accurate or interesting about the ocean must be credited to Dr. Ann G. Dunlea of Woods Hole Oceanographic

Institution, who let me badger her with far too many questions (and who has been hosting sleepovers since we were in middle school).

Lots of love to all my local writer girls—Diana Urban, Janella Angeles, Mara Fitzgerald, Julie Dao—for feeding that creative well or sympathizing when it's been drained dry. Also much love to my friends for helping me brainstorm title ideas, voting on covers, and celebrating big joys along with the little ones.

And of course, I must express my gratitude to my parents (sorry I killed you off, Mom! It's not you!!). When I was a child, my father instilled a deep appreciation of the night sky in me. He took me to see meteor showers long past my bedtime and fostered a love and curiosity around the planets and space. When I was growing up, he told me stories about woman scientists, including the Harvard Computers. Throughout the writing of this book, he sent me an endless amount of information on space debris, some of which even made it in. He gave me book and article recommendations, explained subjects I knew nothing about, and was, as always, unconditionally supportive. Thanks, Dad.

And I want to thank my readers, who are the reason I do this, whose words and letters make me happier than anything else. Thank you for picking this up. I hope I made you smile.